Eva Gly... ...ired by
beautiful pla... ...he loves to
travel, but fi... ...well at home
o... ...road.

She cut her teeth on just about every kind of writing (radio journalism, advertising copy, PR, and even freelance cricket reporting) before finally completing a full-length novel in her forties. Four lengthy and completely unpublishable tomes later she found herself sitting on an enormous polystyrene book under the TV lights of the Alan Titchmarsh Show as a finalist in the People's Novelist competition sponsored by HarperCollins. Although losing out to a far better writer, the positive feedback from the judges gave her the confidence to pursue her dreams.

Eva lives in Cornwall, although she considers herself Welsh, and has been lucky enough to have been married to the love of her life for twenty-five years. She also writes as Jane Cable.

www.janecable.com

twitter.com/janecable
facebook.com/EvaGlynAuthor
instagram.com/evaglynauthor
bookbub.com/authors/eva-glyn

Also by Eva Glyn

The Olive Grove

THE MISSING PIECES OF US

EVA GLYN

One More Chapter
a division of HarperCollins*Publishers*
1 London Bridge Street
London SE1 9GF
www.harpercollins.co.uk

HarperCollins*Publishers*
1st Floor, Watermarque Building, Ringsend Road
Dublin 4, Ireland

This paperback edition 2021
First published in Great Britain in ebook format
by HarperCollins*Publishers* 2021

A catalogue record of this book is available from the British Library

ISBN: 978-0-00-845329-9

This novel is entirely a work of fiction. The names, characters and
incidents portrayed in it are the work of the author's imagination. Any
resemblance to actual persons, living or dead, events or localities is
entirely coincidental.

Printed and bound in the UK using 100% Renewable Electricity
by CPI Group (UK) Ltd

In memory of my father, who introduced me to folklore and never lost his belief in fairies.

Chapter One

Izzie

The icy air is a slap in the face after the fug of the probate office. And a slap in the face is what I damn well need, but it doesn't help and I am left feeling disoriented. I have to pull myself together. For Claire's sake, as much as anything. A father is irreplaceable, after all – a husband is, well… I don't know… I just don't know… I can't even bear to think about the empty space right now.

She touches my arm. "Come on, Mum, let's go for a coffee now that's over."

"I thought you had to be in college?"

"It's fine – I've got time. No class 'til 11:30."

The closer we get to Winchester city centre the more crowded the pavements become. The early morning shift of Christmas shoppers battles back to Tower Street car park, carrier bags thudding against their legs. Coats, handbags, reddened faces rush towards me and I sidestep into the gutter. A cyclist curses. Claire grabs my arm.

"Watch out, Mum."

"Sorry… sorry."

It is little better when we reach the pedestrian section of the High Street. Crowds ooze around a handcart laden with gloves and scarves. Claire fingers an emerald-green one with orange tassels but I can't stop now; I can see Caffè Nero ahead and I want to be inside, away from all this. I keep walking.

My face meets the softness of an anorak. It is the smell of it that makes me recoil. I look up to see a bearded face framed by straggly hair.

"Sorry," the man mumbles.

"No, no, it's my fault – I wasn't looking."

He melts into the crowd and Claire is tugging at my arm. But I know him; I'm sure I do. Then I'm sure I don't. How could I?

Inside the café, Claire sits me down at the nearest table while she queues for our drinks. She'll be gone a while. I unbutton my coat and spread it over the back and arms of the low leather chair, sliding into its silky lining. I close my eyes but I can still hear Christmas: instrumental carols through the chatter. A face drifts across my memory… a pair of intense hazel eyes. No. It was twenty years ago.

Claire has two mugs of latte in one hand and a plate of banoffee pie in the other.

"They've run out of trays."

"I don't think I've ever seen it so busy in here."

She hands me a fork and plunges the other one into the

pie. "Sugar. We need it." She savours a mouthful. "Mmmm. It's delish. Dig in."

"I'm OK, Claire. Really."

She nods but she doesn't believe me. *Come on, Isobel, get a grip.* I clear my throat. "I'm fine, honestly. I was just... wondering... I think I know that tramp I bumped into."

Claire frowns. "How do you know a tramp?"

"He wasn't a tramp then. It was a very long time ago. I'd only just finished college – if I'm right, of course."

"So what makes you think it was him?" She sounds cautiously curious.

"Two things really – his height and his eyes. You have to admit he was exceptionally tall."

"You only came up to his chin."

Her words stir a warm memory and I pick up my fork.

"So who do you think he is, Mum?"

"Someone I knew before I started my teacher training. I was filling in time selling stationery and he was the office manager at one of the big firms of solicitors."

"Office manager? Wow. I wonder what happened?"

I shrug. "People's lives change. The last time I saw him he was wearing a suit." But that's a lie and I know it; Robin was naked, his face buried in a pillow, our duvet twisted around his legs. I ask Claire what classes she has today.

The clock ticks past eleven and Claire has to go. The crowds outside are even thicker, but through the shifting shapes of bags and coats I spy a bearded man in a grubby blue anorak sitting on the bottom step of the Buttercross monument – right opposite the café door. Claire's eagle eyes don't miss him either.

She nudges me. "Mum, it's your tramp."

I nod. "I know. I think I'll get another coffee."

"You'll be all right?"

"Of course I will. Now run along and I'll pick you up from the station later."

I do buy another coffee, but it isn't for me. I ask for a takeaway and balance some sugar and a stirrer on the lid before fighting the short distance across the street. I put the cup on the step next to the man but he doesn't look up. I am unsure now, unsure of everything, and I don't know what to say, but as I turn away I hear him mumble, "Thanks, Izzie."

I have only moved a few feet but I keep on walking.

Chapter Two

The determination to wrap Claire's Christmas presents gets me home. There are only a few days left before term breaks up and I need to have them hidden before she starts turning the house upside down looking for them. I wonder if she will this year, without Connor to egg her on. He never grew out of it either – they used to drive me nuts.

I stop in the hall, one arm out of my coat, as the memory assails me. There is no leather jacket on the hook, no violin case propped at the bottom of the stairs. I want to curl up and cry – die, even – as the gap left by Connor rises up to engulf me. I fight it with everything I've got and scramble out of the house and into the car. As my breath slows an idea begins to take shape – a distraction – so I let myself follow it.

It is literally years since I've been to the fairy tree and I wonder if it's still there. I know it was when Claire was a child – Connor used to take her because she loved it. I used to pretend it was a load of mumbo-jumbo and he shouldn't encourage her, but he knew at least some of the reason I didn't go with them. In fact he'd forbidden it, and I was glad.

Today is a far cry from the late-summer afternoon when Robin brought me here; the stripped trees give little shelter from the wind and the sky is slate grey. No dappled sunlight now to lure me into mysterious dells; how could I have almost believed the magic was real? My laugh sends a pair of pigeons flapping from the highest branches. I sound like a bloody mad woman. Thank God there's no one around to hear me.

I suppose I almost believed in the magic because I was almost in love. When Robin showed me the notes from the children in the letterbox tacked to the tree, I cried and he kissed me. The guilt I'd been feeling about my boyfriend was swept away and I couldn't help but want him. And later, after everything that happened, we held hands around the tree to wish, and I begged and begged the fairies to take all the obstacles away so Robin and I could be together from that moment. Begging? The fairies? What frigging planet was I on?

It's much too cold to hang around wondering. I march along the path and suddenly the tree is in front of me: taller, broader, but still festooned with ribbons, necklaces, and small toys. All around it little plastic folk are perched in shrubs and on tree stumps, Tinkerbells and Wonder Women jostling for position to guard the approach.

The tips of my fingers scrape over the bark. On closer inspection I see it's studded with coins and I wonder why, but then I spot a note, supposedly from the fairies, thanking the children for the money for Barnardo's. It looks as though it's been there a long time. The letterbox is overflowing and the plastic folder pinned to the back of the trunk is almost devoid of replies. Maybe whoever has been perpetrating this elaborate hoax has finally come to their senses.

I turn away. This isn't really the tree that's drawn me back here. There is another one, a willow close to the river that Connor knew nothing about, where Robin and I ran to escape the storm. Where we made love for the very first time, with thunder rolling around the valley and raindrops skating down the leaves above us. I remember afterwards he sat against the trunk and I nestled into the crook of his arm, full of hope for a new beginning.

But first I had an ending to deal with: my boyfriend Paul. I told Robin I would do it straight away but he was hesitant. "Don't burn your boats, Izzie," is what he said.

I sat up straight and pulled away to look him in the eye. "Do you think you've made a mistake?"

He shook his head. "Not in the way you mean. But you've always been open about Paul and I haven't been the same with you."

I felt my shiny, new world slipping from under me. "You're... you're not married, are you?"

"No, nothing like that. I live with my mother. I care for her – she's in a wheelchair."

I relaxed back against his shoulder. "Well that's OK, it's not a problem."

His fingers dug into the top of my arm. "Izzie, it is. It's a major, major thing. I have to be there every morning to get her dressed, every night to put her to bed."

"But you go to work… and come out…"

"Thanks to the neighbours, my Auntie Jean especially. Mum will have been with her most of this afternoon."

"So your mum doesn't want you to have a girlfriend?"

I heard the smile in his voice. "Far from it – she'd love me to. She says she doesn't want to ruin my life as well. In fact, she knows there's someone I care for at the moment. I've had to promise she'll meet you if, well, if anything comes of it."

"Something has come of it." I stood and brushed myself down. "Come on, it's almost stopped raining. I'll drive you home and I can meet her now."

"Izzie, no. Not yet…"

"Yes, Robin. If it's as big a thing as you're making out then I need to meet her before I burn my boats. But I warn you, they're in flames already."

He stood up and took me in his arms. "You're wonderful, Izzie," he murmured, "a dream come true."

Only, it was actually a nightmare that was about to begin.

Chapter Three

Robin

The tide of Christmas washed me down the High Street. The Salvation Army band was gathered near the Buttercross, the trumpet player's scales rising into the air and mingling with the scent of roasting chestnuts. Further on, the traffic lights glowed into the leaden morning – red, yellow, green. The colours were coming back.

Towards King Alfred's statue the pavements narrowed. Opposite the bus station tourists streamed from a coach, Welsh accents filling the air. I pressed myself against the railings of the park but in truth I need not have bothered. I seemed to have perfected the art of creating an empty space of at least a yard around me. Despite being invisible. One day I'd laugh about it – I hoped.

It was ice cold next to the river. The wind had torn down the High Street after me, ripping away any hope of shelter by the water. It was no surprise most of the benches were free. I put the carrier bag containing my belongings on the first one I came to and crouched beside it in a fruitless bid to escape the worst of the gale.

The Itchen was in full spate. A drake huddled on a flat rock, hunkering down to avoid the wind but finding himself splashed by the freezing waters instead. The gardens rising up on the other side of the river were stripped for winter, naked branches shivering. A single holly bush stood out, glossy green, a miserly few berries left by the birds. Red and green... Colours again. They pierced the fog in my mind, even as my body battled the cold.

I knew when the colours had started. I was on the steps of the Buttercross, nursing the empty paper cup. I turned it in my hand, royal blue with a firmament of Christmas stars. Izzie. A heart-stopping moment of joy, confusion, then shame. But all the same I couldn't tear myself away. I waited for her there every morning, just in case. I could still taste the coffee – bitter, hot, and strong.

The faintness of my memory of meeting Izzie for the first time was frustrating me. It was as if she had faded into view: a navy trouser-suit at a business breakfast, a shock of blonde hair across a bar, manicured nails clutching a leather Filofax, and laughter, always laughter. Sitting opposite me, trying to sell me stationery. And succeeding.

In the mid-80s, graduates in dead-end jobs were not uncommon and Izzie and I were in the same boat. The mathematician and the botanist discussing the relative merits of Tipp-Ex and Snopake, Biros and Bics across a pine boardroom table, our filter coffee (brought in and served by a secretary, naturally) in chunky Denby cups and saucers. I had a habit of spinning the sugar bowl under my hand; it drove Izzie to distraction. The first time she touched me was to give me a slap to make me stop.

I was the office manager for one of the biggest firms of solicitors in Southampton. My mum was so proud – watching me go off to work in a suit and tie. It was what graduates did in her book, but it wasn't what botany graduates who'd dreamt of travelling the world did in mine. But it just wasn't possible – the moment one of her more violent boyfriends had pushed her down the stairs and left her in a wheelchair, my horizons had narrowed too.

My situation had led me into a duplicity that was not in my nature: it was Thatcher's Britain, remember, a dog-eat-dog sort of place where I knew you wouldn't succeed if you were encumbered by a disabled dependant. So I told no one. But deception takes emotional energy – although I was too young to know it at the time – and that is the only reason I can think of why I didn't see the tidal wave that was Izzie until it sent me cartwheeling up the beach.

Solicitors use truckloads of stationery and our regular meetings gravitated first to Friday afternoons and then to the wine bar. And the second time this happened I found myself raising a glass to a beautiful young woman and...

I ran my finger around the damp collar of my shirt. "So what are you up to this weekend?" I asked. "The weather forecast's looking good."

"I hope so. I'll be on the water."

"Sailing?"

"No, rowing. It's our big regatta in two weeks' time so it's non-stop practise."

I gaped at her minuscule frame. "You row?"

"Of course I do."

I must have looked embarrassed because she put her hand on my arm and continued, "I did get into it by being a cox at uni, but when I joined the club at Hamble they persuaded me to have a go myself and I love it. Lesley and I are hot favourites for the ladies' double scull sprint, I'll have you know."

I managed to recover myself enough to say, "I don't doubt it, but you don't look as though you have the build – unless you're hiding your muscles under that dress."

Izzie almost blushed, I'm sure, but still laughing, she rolled up her sleeve. "Tiny muscles, but they're strong, so that's enough."

"It's funny," I mused, trying to drag my eyes away from the delicate skin of her upper arm, "I love the water myself, but I know nothing about rowing."

"So do you sail?"

I shook my head. "I like to get closer to the sea than that: surfing, swimming, snorkelling – even scuba diving when I get the chance."

"Lots of exotic holidays, then."

"No, I've lived around here all my life and there's plenty of coastline to explore."

"But diving? And snorkelling?" Her perfectly shaped eyebrows arched.

"I don't dive so much now because of all the kit, but you'd be amazed what you can see with a snorkel and mask, just within half an hour's drive." I plunged in. "If you want, I'll show you."

I felt a moment of triumph as the grin spread across her face. "I'd love that."

"Well, if you're busy this weekend, how about next Sunday?"

"That sounds perfect. My boyfriend will be working so I won't have to hang around waiting for him to want to do something interesting."

And my bubble burst. Of course she had a boyfriend – all the nice girls did. But the way she spoke about him made me think that perhaps all hope was not lost.

I had eight days to wait. Eight days to plan. The fact it was a Sunday made it easy because Mum always insisted that was my day off. Once I'd got her up in the morning she'd either kick me out of the house or have me wheel her to Auntie Jean's so I could go back to bed. She knew, far better than I did, what you needed to survive as a carer.

So Mum wasn't the problem; it was the car. There was no hiding the fact that it was adapted to take a wheelchair. And the problem wasn't even the car – it was inside my own head. What I should have done was taken it along and used it as a way to let Izzie know about my situation. But by then I wanted her far too much to be thinking rationally.

If only I'd known then what I know now. I'm sounding like an old man but I'm only forty-three. It's just that you can learn a lot in twenty years if you have the right teacher.

Back in 1986 I lied. I phoned Izzie a few days before our date and told her my car was off the road, but it would be fun to get the train to Bournemouth instead. Of course she offered to drive and I wavered, because all along I'd wanted to take her somewhere better than Bournemouth. And going in her car would have been OK – except she wanted my address to pick me up.

That was a real no-no. If I didn't want anyone to know I cared for my mother, there was no way I'd admit to living on a council estate. Even work had the address of my old student digs. But I managed to dream up some story about going out with friends the night before so it would be easier for Izzie to meet me in town.

There was only one place I wanted to take her for her first taste of snorkelling and that was Kimmeridge. I knew the traffic would be rubbish on a sunny weekend so I asked her to pick me up outside Southampton railway station at eight o'clock. Leaving the city behind us, we drove towards the New Forest, a Beach Boys cassette playing in the background and the breeze from the open window wafting Izzie's perfume past my nose.

"If I'd known you wanted to go surfing I'd have brought my board," I teased.

She smiled, looking gorgeous in a red and white strappy top. "Maybe another time," she said and I wanted to punch the air. Maybe there's a way to make this work, I kidded myself.

When we arrived at Kimmeridge the car park was already half full; children and dogs were running around on the grass and groups of youngsters were heaving ghetto blasters out of beaten-up Fiestas and lugging them onto the beach below.

I looked at Izzie. "You up for a bit of a walk?"

"Of course I am."

I pointed to a rock ledge way to the left of the bay,

beyond the fishing boats on the slipway. "It's a bit more peaceful around there and a better jumping-off point to get into the water."

She picked up her beach bag. "Come on then. I can't wait to get in."

To say Izzie in a bikini was a distraction is the understatement of the century. As I said, she was small, but she had a few curves and they were definitely in the right places. Up until then I'd always gone for the more buxom type, but watching Izzie pull off her top and jeans certainly re-educated me to the attractions of a taut stomach and small, firm breasts. My fingers fumbled as I tightened the mask I'd lent her, trying not to touch her skin; somehow I managed it and then we were clambering across the boulders and into the bracing waves.

Kimmeridge is special because the fish hide between floating towers of sea-green vegetation and hunting them down is part of its charm. I had a moment of worry that Izzie would expect a clear blue tropical fish tank but she was transfixed and we stayed in the water for almost an hour, faces in the greenery for a while, then kicking onto our backs and gazing at the sky. Our outstretched hands touched as we floated, just for a moment, until the current drew us apart.

Afterwards we sat on our towels on a rock ledge and let the sun dry us while we munched the sandwiches I'd made and drank Pepsi. Izzie'd brought a packet of Jaffa Cakes and we made serious inroads into those as well, and all the time we talked and talked and talked – kind of 'getting to know you' first-date stuff. During our trips to the wine bar we hadn't gone into histories, but that day felt different somehow, like it was a beginning.

I learnt that Izzie had grown up in Watford then gone to Bristol University. When she'd graduated she'd come to Southampton because her boyfriend had found a job in the dockyard. The relationship was obviously more serious than I'd thought.

"So you've been together a while," I ventured.

She nodded, but she was looking away from me, tracing neat figures of eight onto the rock with her index finger. There was a silence.

"Look, I didn't mean to pry, I was only—"

"No, it's OK. It's just, well... not that great at the moment. Paul's started to talk about marriage and it's made me realise it's not what I want. Well, not with him anyway." She blushed.

"Is there someone else?" More than one rival would be disastrous.

"Robin, I shouldn't be talking to you about this, I..." She glanced up and I caught something in her eyes that made my heart beat ten times faster. But did I imagine it? Did I imagine there was someone and it was me? It didn't seem possible – and I didn't find out because she leapt up and raced across the boulders, calling over her shoulder that the last one in had to do a handstand in the sea.

I didn't mind. I could do those quite easily.

Chapter Four

I said nothing to my mother about Izzie but it took her less than a week to guess. Me coming downstairs freshly showered and changed into a brand new shirt at three o'clock on Saturday afternoon probably clinched it, but I suspect she had already realised something was up due to my unusual state of barely suppressed excitement.

She smiled at me, her eyes sparkling. "Robin, are you seeing someone?"

I fiddled with the car keys. "I'm not sure really, Mum. It's early days and—"

"Well I'd be pleased if you were," she cut across me. "I don't want this"—she thumped her wheelchair—"to stop you having a life, so don't you dare think it."

I leant down to hug her. "Thanks Mum," I murmured. "If... if it does work out I'll bring Izzie to meet you just as soon as I can."

"I'd like that. Now bugger off. And good luck."

It was all very well Mum saying her disability shouldn't

stop me having a life, but I couldn't see how it would work in practice. But then I thought of Izzie on the beach at Kimmeridge and my mood was already lifting as I put the car into gear and eased away from the pavement.

Hamble Rowing Club was based at the Jolly Sailor pub near the railway, so I was able to leave the car anonymously in the station car park. The Jolly Sailor – and Hamble as a whole – achieved a fair amount of notoriety in the 1980s as the setting for *Howard's Way*, the British version of *Dallas*. As a result it was normally packed at weekends and I avoided it like the plague.

Today the pub was even busier with the regatta being run from its jetty. Large groups of rowers in their various club polo shirts stood around with glasses in their hands but I couldn't spot Izzie so I got myself a beer and edged closer to the water. The fact I couldn't get near the front didn't matter – I could easily see over the tops of people's heads.

It also meant that when Izzie and another girl emerged from a skiff she spotted me almost immediately. As soon as she could extract herself from the cheers and back-slapping she dodged through the crowd and hugged me. If there'd been room I'd have picked her up and swung her around.

"Robin, you came." Her cheeks were pink from exertion and she seemed to glow.

I must have been grinning like an idiot, looking down at her. "I only just arrived. Did you win?"

"No, we came second, but that's good enough. Most of these clubs take it far more seriously than we do." She grabbed my hand. "Come on, I want you to meet everybody."

It seemed she really did mean everybody as she hurled me from one group to another, absorbing me into the heart of all her friends. Almost inevitably they asked me if I'd like to row, but I joked I'd never fold myself into a boat.

"Robin prefers being in the water," Izzie explained. "Snorkelling, diving, surfing – that's his kind of thing."

"So is this who you went to Kimmeridge with?" Lesley, her rowing partner, asked and when Izzie said yes I felt myself the subject of her warm but thorough appraisal.

After a couple of hours I had to go and Izzie walked with me as far as the pub door.

"I'm sorry I can't stay longer, Izzie, but, well, there's a few things I need to do this evening."

"I'm sorry you can't too. It's been lovely, I mean, you fit in so well…"

"Who wouldn't? They're a very welcoming bunch."

She dropped her eyes. "Paul doesn't like them."

Before I'd even thought about it the words were out of my mouth. "Paul's a fool." I grasped her hand. "Sorry, Izzie. That wasn't for me to say."

She didn't look up but she said it was OK. "Look, Robin, you know things aren't great between Paul and me. But we're going on holiday in about ten days' time and I can't upset the apple cart beforehand."

"Will I see you again before you go?"

Now she did look at me, her blue eyes huge. "I'd like that very much."

Chapter Five

I used to ask myself why I decided to take Izzie to the fairy tree but over the years I've grown to understand. Back then it was mainly a case of finding somewhere we'd be unlikely to meet anyone we knew – with the bonus of being close to the River Hamble, which Izzie loved.

It took me two buses to get there and I arrived early enough to treat myself to a pint in the garden of the Horse & Jockey. I found myself a shady spot and allowed myself to dream of what the afternoon might bring – what it might be the beginning of.

Just after two o'clock, Izzie pulled into the car park. I disentangled my legs from the picnic table and wiped the sweat off my hands onto my jeans. But I could feel my face crease into a smile as I walked towards her car and, pretending a little bow, opened the driver's door for her. Her yellow sundress and tatty plimsolls were a mixture of sex and good sense which reduced me to stammering out what I'd planned to be a confident hello.

We set off beside the narrow creek towards the Hamble itself. The path was framed by arches of green, and to our left the bank rose steeply towards the fences of the handful of houses with gardens long enough to stretch from the road. The buzz of a lawnmower faded until all we could hear was birdsong above us in the branches.

The track snaked away from the water and halfway up a dusty incline I stopped. "Do you believe in fairies?" I asked.

"Fairies?"

"Fairies, elves, pixies... the wee, small folk of the woods."

Izzie was laughing as she replied. "I try to keep an open mind, but you're a scientist. Don't tell me you do."

"These ones convinced me. They write letters."

"What on earth do you mean?"

"Come on, I'll show you." I took her hand. "Now, close your eyes and don't open them until I say."

I led her forwards, savouring the coolness of her skin as I helped her navigate the tree roots crossing the path. The Hamble, less than fifty yards away down a steep bank to our right, was completely invisible.

When we were in front of the fairy tree I stopped. "You can open your eyes now," I told her and prepared to drop her hand, but much to my delight her fingers stayed wrapped in mine.

"Oh Robin," she breathed. "It's magical."

I tried to remember the first time I'd been here and to see the tree through Izzie's eyes. The oak stood on a rise just above the path, not too tall or wide but graceful and straight, its trunk covered in what I can only describe as offerings – pieces of ribbon, daisy chains, a shell necklace, a tiny doll or two, and even an old cuckoo clock.

"Why do people do this?" Izzie asked.

I winked at her. "To say thank you to the fairies."

"For what?"

"For making their wishes come true, I guess. Look, I'll show you."

On the right hand side of the tree trunk was an old wooden box in the shape of a Swiss chalet, filled with folded pieces of paper. I took out the top one and handed it to Izzie. She read it aloud.

Dear fairies, thank you very much for looking after the woods because the trees are all things bright and beautiful like we sing at assembly. If I can have a wish please can it be to have a proper family? Lots of love, Amelia.

"Oh, Robin, that's so lovely but so sad." There were tears in her eyes and I wished whole-heartedly that the child had had a less distressing request. To distract Izzie, I led her around the back of the tree.

"The amazing thing is, the fairies reply." I showed her a plastic folder tacked to the trunk, full of letters from the fairies to the children.

Her chest heaved as she tried to stifle a sob.

"Izzie, Izzie, what is it?" I hugged her to me and after a few moments she sniffed and looked up.

"I'm sorry, Robin. I don't want to spoil today. I'll be fine in a moment." But her voice was cracking again and I couldn't help but touch her cheek. She tilted her face towards me and then we were kissing and I could taste salt and the inside of her mouth at the same time.

After a little while she pulled away. "That shouldn't have happened – not now in any case."

"Paul?"

She looked down at her right plimsoll, which seemed to be making circles in the dust of its own accord.

"He thinks I'm at the rowing club. I never lied to him before I met you, but... but I just wanted to see you. Robin, I'm in such a mess."

The roof of my mouth went dry. "It's OK, Izzie. Take your time to decide what's right for you to do about Paul. I'll wait."

She grabbed my hands again. "It won't be long, I promise. I'll use the holiday to—" But her voice was cut off by a yell for help from the river. We stood for a moment, listening. It was a child's voice – just kids larking about? But no, it came again and sounded like genuine distress.

"Follow me," I called to Izzie and started to run along the path.

It wasn't a quick descent to the water. I knew a deep gully cut through the woods and I could tell the voice came from beyond it – or rather voices, because the next time there were two yells, increasingly loud and desperate. I stopped and cupped my hands.

"Don't panic! We're coming," I called. "Where are you?"

"In the river."

"Where?"

"By... by the big bend."

Izzie had caught up and we were off again to the edge of

the woods and down a path that ran alongside a field. At the bottom was a wide strip of land where the Hamble had been dumping silt for generations as it curved towards the sea. And sure enough, about a third of the way across the river were two children – one of them little more than a toddler – clinging to each other as the water swirled around the taller one's knees.

"Don't try to move. I'm on my way," I called and started peeling off my shoes and clothes. Izzie bent to take off her plimsolls but I stopped her. "Stay here. You don't know the river this far up."

"I want to help."

"Then stay on the bank and if I get into trouble run for your life up that field. There's a farm at the top. But I should be OK. I can probably pick my way to them across the sandbanks; they can't have crossed the main channel."

I walked to where the end of the spit was being submerged by the rising tide and started into the water, following the ridge of silt as far as I could. The river wasn't wide – only about ten yards – but it was freezing cold and I had to make my way upstream to reach the children. I could tell now the older one was a boy of about seven or eight but the smaller child was clinging to him so hard all I could see was a red T-shirt and a tangle of fair hair.

I was near enough to talk to the boy and tell him to stand firm and stay calm.

"But it's getting deeper," he whimpered.

"It's OK. It's only the tide coming up and it's not happening that fast. I'll take the little one first then come back for you." That was moments before I realised that they were the other side of the deep channel and I cursed inwardly.

I edged as close to them as I could. I could swim to reach them, but then what? They were entirely surrounded by water and I couldn't hold two children out of it for very long. But I was almost within touching distance and it gave me an idea.

I looked back at Izzie on the bank. "Can you manage to follow the way I came?" I called. She'd tucked up her dress and was in the water almost before I'd finished speaking.

"OK," I told the boy. "You hand the little one to me, I'll hand him to Izzie, and then I'll come back for you. I won't get out of this river without you, I promise."

The boy was shivering but he nodded. "G-go with the man, Toby," he said, but Toby wouldn't relax his grip.

"Toby," he tried again. "You have to. Gran will be really cross. He's going to carry you to that nice lady then come back for me." His voice shook despite his attempt to sound brave.

"Come on, Toby," I said. "It'll be an adventure."

Finally the toddler looked at me and I held out both hands. "Can you edge a bit closer and still be safe?" I asked the older lad.

He nodded and shuffled near enough for me to grab Toby's arms, then gave the child a little shove and the force was enough for me to swing him up towards me and he clasped his hands around my neck in desperation. I wobbled for a moment but held my ground and turned to take him towards the shore. Izzie was only a few feet away and I handed him over, returning for the older boy.

I took both his hands across the deep channel of water. "Now jump," I told him, "and try to swing out past me. I won't let go of you, whatever happens." He launched himself towards me and I used his momentum to pull him across. We both stumbled and I almost slid over, but we fought to remain upright as the river swirled around our legs, the lad clinging to my waist.

Izzie was knee-deep with Toby in her arms but at that moment the toddler decided to make a bid for freedom. Struggling to hold onto him she slipped and they both fell headlong into the river. To her credit, she didn't let go of his hand and I was able to push past the older boy and grab Toby before he had spent very long in the water. He promptly threw up an improbably large amount of river and then started wailing as I carried him to the shore. Out of the corner of my eye I saw the other boy help Izzie to her feet and, hand in hand, they picked their way back to dry land.

I had no idea what to do with a screaming toddler so I put Toby down on the grass while holding him firmly by the shoulders. Izzie looked equally helpless but the older boy, who I took to be his brother, was more experienced in these matters.

"Toby, shut up." Nothing happened.

"Tobes, I'm telling you, put a sock in it." Still no response, but he had a final gambit. "If you stop crying right now I'll let you play with my Death Star." It worked a treat and there was silence on the riverbank.

I turned to Izzie. "You're soaked through." It was a statement of the obvious if ever there was one; her sundress clung to her in a way that only accentuated her curves. "Take that off and put my dry clothes on," I told her, as much for my own sake as hers.

Her eyes sparkled. "And what are you going to wear? My dress?" I followed her gaze and suddenly felt very naked in just my damp boxer shorts.

"Don't be so silly," she continued, "put on your trousers and wrap that baby in your shirt."

"Why don't you come back to Gran's?" asked the older boy through chattering teeth. "Then you can tell her how you rescued us and perhaps I won't get such a tongue lashing. Not until you've gone home, anyway."

"And do you deserve a tongue lashing?" I asked.

He nodded. "I'm the oldest. And it was my idea to cross the river." All of a sudden he looked close to tears.

"Where does your gran live?" Izzie asked.

"In the big house next to the farm. She keeps chickens." He sniffed, trying to smile.

The boy led us up the side of the field and behind the woods. We passed the farm buildings some fifty yards away then came to a tall beech hedge which seemed filled with contented clucking. At the corner was a gap and we emerged into a wide, open space with a chicken coop to our right and a patchy lawn to our left. I'd been carrying Toby but he cried out to be let down and raced across the lawn towards the house.

Doubtless due to his yelling, the French windows opened and a tall grey-haired woman stepped out, dressed in brown slacks and a blouse the colour of the mellow

27

bricks that framed her. Toby barrelled into her legs and she picked him up.

"You're soaked through! Stephen, what on earth's been happening?" There was the vaguest hint of a guttural accent in her voice but I couldn't place it.

When Stephen didn't reply I started to explain. "They got stuck halfway across the river when the tide came up. We pulled them out but we all got a bit wet."

"You can say that again, young man. You'd better come in and get dry; it's the least I can do."

Before we knew it, their gran was bustling us through a dining room, seemingly oblivious to the trail of wet footprints across the Chinese carpet. An oak staircase rose in two flights from the hall and once we had reached the top she made the boys wait while she showed Izzie and me into a narrow shower room.

"Take off your wet things and put them out on the landing then have a shower to warm up. I'll get these two into a bath then put your clothes in the tumble drier and find something for you to wear while they dry. There's plenty of clean towels on the airer."

Never, in all my daydreams in the pub garden, had I imagined we'd end up in a strange bathroom with orders to strip off.

"You're wetter than I am," I told Izzie, "so you go first." I handed her a large towel. "I'll look away until you're decent again." Turning around I found myself looking straight into a mirror and I could see her peeling off her dress. "Izzie, stop," I panicked. "I'll have to look at the back of the door or something."

Her touch was gentle on my shoulders but then she hugged me so hard that the damp from her dress seeped through my jeans. "Robin, you're one in a million, do you know that?"

I grunted. "It's just good manners."

She grinned. "I'll be tempted to look when it's your turn to shower."

"Then I hope you won't be disappointed." I twisted around and kissed the tip of her nose. "Now please get on with it, Izzie. You're beginning to shiver again." And I was beginning to get a hard-on that it would take all my reserves of willpower to deal with before it was my turn to wrap myself in nothing but a towel.

Chapter Six

Only my shirt was really wet so once I had showered I was able to go downstairs looking reasonably like myself in my own jeans and a sweatshirt we had found neatly folded on the floor outside the bathroom door. Izzie had fared rather worse in a floral blouse and a navy skirt so long she had to hold it up as we made our way downstairs.

The boys' gran must have heard us and was waiting in the hall. She led us into a bright kitchen at the back of the house, completely dominated by a scrubbed pine table. Our clothes hung limply on a rail over a cream Aga. "They're almost dry," she reassured us, "I'm just airing them off." Next to the hob was a huge jug of roses, their scent filling the air.

Introductions being well overdue I put out my hand. "I'm Robin Vail," I told her, to be greeted by a firm, dry handshake.

"Jennifer Dodd. I'm the boys' grandmother and I can't

begin to thank you for hauling the little buggers out of the river."

I looked around. "Where are they?"

"Tucked up in bed with instructions to stay there, out of trouble, until their clothes dry. Not that they don't have other clothes," she twinkled, "I just like the punishment to fit the crime."

I smiled at her. "Stephen hoped he wouldn't get his tongue lashing until after we'd gone."

"Then Stephen hoped wrong. They had at least ten minutes while they were in the bath. They scared me so much – but that will be the end of it as far as I'm concerned. And in truth, I'm blaming myself for letting them go into the woods on their own. I never dreamt they'd go near the river, let alone cross it. The tongue lashing I've given them will be nothing compared to the one I'm going to get from my daughter when she comes back."

"You were only trying to give them a bit of freedom," Izzie chipped in. "It's too easy to mollycoddle children in this day and age."

Jennifer's sharp eyes looked from one of us to the other. "You two look a bit young to have a family."

"We haven't known each other that long." Izzie was blushing.

"Oh dear, so your quiet, romantic walk in the woods was interrupted by my young hoodlums. I'm so sorry, but on the other hand I am really very glad you were there."

"I brought Izzie to show her the fairy tree."

"And did you make a wish?"

I shook my head. "We'd only been there a few minutes when we heard the boys calling for help."

"Then you must go back and do it as soon as your clothes are dry." She pulled out one of the chairs from the table and gestured to us to sit down.

"Another time. Izzie's probably going to be late as it is."

"It won't take you five minutes – and the hidden folk will look especially kindly on your wishes after your good deed for the day," Jennifer persisted as she started to pour mugs of tea from an earthenware pot.

"There'll be another time." I wanted to sound firm but when Izzie pleaded to go back it wasn't in my heart to refuse.

So once our clothes were dry we retraced our steps through Jennifer's garden and back onto the path between the trees. I don't recall us saying much as we walked along; in fact, the woods seemed eerily silent, the air oppressive in the late afternoon heat.

Then we were in front of the tree.

"What do we do?" asked Izzie. I shrugged my shoulders. "Just close our eyes and wish, I guess."

"No, we have to make it more special than that. Come on, we'll hold hands around the trunk."

So Izzie stood on one side of the fairy tree and I stood on the other and we stretched. The tree was of a size where we could hold hands without having to hug it so closely that the little offerings would snag in our clothes. She gripped my fingers and there was only one wish in my mind: please, please, let it come right for Izzie and me in the end.

A distant rumble of thunder broke the stillness and I let her go.

"What did you wish for?" she asked.

"Oh, nothing much – world peace, that sort of thing."

She tucked her arm into mine. "I like a man with big ideas," she joked and then added as an afterthought, "Should we leave a present for the fairies, do you think?"

"I think they're more in the way of thank yous than bribes," I told her.

"Well then," she replied, "we'll bring them something next time."

Next time? She wanted there to be a next time?

In that single moment I knew what hope was. And love.

Chapter Seven

After my visit to the fairy tree, I distinctly remember whistling all the way from the corner shop – where I'd made Izzie drop me – to my front door. I called to Mum as I opened it but assumed her reply was drowned by Frankie Goes to Hollywood blaring from the kitchen.

It wasn't.

I know I ran across the room but it felt as though I was wading through mud. I lifted her up but there was no resistance, although she felt warm. Still holding her, I groped for the phone and dialled 999. They had an ambulance on the way within minutes, and in the meantime I was to check her pulse. I couldn't find it; the sweat pouring off me made her skin slippery, but I kept trying and yelling at her to wake up. Then the ambulance men were at the door, closely followed by Auntie Jean and a couple of other neighbours.

It was Auntie Jean who led me into the front room once they told me she was dead, Auntie Jean who went straight to the drinks cabinet and poured us both a large scotch, forcing me to gulp mine down through chattering teeth. It was Auntie Jean who kept me away from the kitchen while they came and took her for a post-mortem. It was Auntie Jean who cried with me until neither of us could cry anymore and the whisky bottle was empty. I suspect she might even have put me to bed, but I was so drunk I can't honestly remember.

I sleepwalked through the next few days with Auntie Jean at my elbow. I got compassionate leave from work and she kept me busy sorting through Mum's things and cleaning the house. Then came the second blow: the post-mortem showed Mum had died from an overdose of painkillers. Whether deliberate or accidental, they couldn't say.

The police came to question me. When had I left the house? When did I come back? Had Mum been depressed? Where were the tablets kept? Had I found a note? I struggled to fathom what they were getting at, but Auntie Jean was sharper. She told them that she – and a number of other neighbours – had seen me leave and seen me come back. And that Mum had spent most of the afternoon with her anyway. But she had been in pain, terrible pain... It must have been a mistake; she'd just taken too many tablets.

As soon as the police had gone I confessed to Auntie Jean that Mum had never told me about the pain.

I heard the slams of their car door as she turned away from the window to face me. "Me neither."

"Then why... why did you tell them she had?"

She sat down on the sofa and held my hand. "Robin,

love, they'd never have left you alone. And even if they had, they'd have tried to slur her memory with suicide."

"Is that what you really think she did?"

"I think... she was in pain. She just never told us. Why else would she have had those tablets in the first place? But she'd never have chosen to leave you, Robin – that's one thing I do know."

The inquest recorded an open verdict.

I may have sleepwalked through those days but I wasn't actually sleeping. Every time I went into the hall I heard Mum saying she didn't want to ruin my life as well. I couldn't avoid that hall; even if I used the back door I still had to go up the stairs to bed. I couldn't stand the kitchen, either. Slowly I realised that being in that house would bring me no peace; everywhere I turned were reminders of my guilt.

Leaving was harder. I wandered about, looking at the pictures on the walls, turning Mum's ornaments around and around on the mantelpiece then finally going upstairs to her room. I opened the wardrobe; it was empty, but somehow the musky scent of Opium clung on. I sat on her bed and cried for ages, then I must have fallen asleep and rested, because I woke with enough resolve to see out my plan.

I went up to the attic and found my rucksack, my tent, and the rest of my camping gear. Then I went into my bedroom and stuffed the rucksack full of clothes. Well, not quite full; I left enough space for the photograph of Mum and me that she had kept in a frame on her bedside table. I burrowed it in with my T-shirts then collected my driving licence, my Post Office passbook and bank card. I didn't think I'd need anything else.

When I knocked on Auntie Jean's door there was no reply so I wrote her a note saying I needed a break before I could handle all this and I'd see her soon. I don't know whether I was telling her the truth or not.

I got the bus into town and a train to Bournemouth. I bought myself a burger and chewed through it sitting on the beach, watching the lights on the pier twinkle in the dusk. The resort was buzzing behind me like an angry wasp so I picked up my rucksack and walked along the sand until all I could hear was the sea.

I woke with the draw of the waves on the shingle in my ears then sat in my quilted cocoon, hugging my knees as I watched the sky lighten over the sea. Nothing moved in that great expanse of water. Nothing moved inside me either. But I could cope with that.

I could also manage stiff, cold, and dirty. Once the sun was up I packed my sleeping bag away and found a tap near the beach huts where I gave my face a cursory wash, damped down my hair, and drank handfuls of the icy water. Then I set out along the beach underneath Canford Cliffs and across the spit of land to Sandbanks.

In terms of finding something for breakfast, Sandbanks was limited but adequate. There was no way I could walk up to one of the swanky hotels, but there was a newsagent selling a few groceries and polystyrene cups of instant coffee. I bought one and a KitKat and sat down on a bench next to the harbour while the ferry hauled its cargo of commuters back and forth across the water. I looked at my watch; it was just after eight. I should have been waving Mum goodbye and hurrying to catch the bus into Southampton. My first sip of coffee scalded my throat and brought tears to my eyes.

If I crossed on the ferry I would have two choices: meander along the beach then make the stiff climb to Old Harry Rocks or take the road to Studland then Swanage, about nine miles in total and easily achievable. The coastal path was tempting but the reality was that I wouldn't get very far on a KitKat and I knew there was a good chippie in Swanage. Even a decision like that was hard to make, but I told myself I could always go home past Old Harry instead.

My rucksack was heavy and I was out of condition so my journey took me until early afternoon. Ravenous and thirsty, the first thing I did when I arrived was wolf down a large portion of fish and chips and a bottle of Coke. But again, sitting on the seafront, eating and drinking, my mind slid off to where I didn't want it to go – I had been all right while I was on the move; somehow I had to out-walk my thoughts.

Or perhaps it was just that I was better alone. I realised I was watching everywhere for mothers and sons: a toddler and a woman little more than my own age playing on the beach, a man in his sixties cosseting an even older lady across the road. My best chance of escaping my guilt was to get the hell out of here and onto the cliffs, so I stirred myself, went to the cashpoint and the supermarket, then headed up to Durlston Head.

The first few miles I had walked many times, but had always turned inland to Langton Matravers and the delights of the Square & Compass. It was a very sociable pub, and sociable was the last thing I wanted. So I plodded on past Dancing Ledge and into unknown territory.

I had seen pictures of the Anvil Rock but they hadn't prepared me for the drama of its precipitous position overlooking the sea. It stood proud and strong in the early evening light, so close to the edge it appeared that only the counterbalance of the anvil stone on top of the upright stopped it from toppling onto the rocks below.

There was a stone staircase built into the cliff which led to the ledge where the rock stood. As I climbed down I saw that *ledge* was a misnomer; in front of me was a plateau some thirty metres wide with a cluster of ruined walls where buildings once had stood. It was the perfect place to pitch my tent for the night, hidden away amongst the overgrown masonry, out of sight of the path.

The sun was setting and I was drawn to the rock. I shrugged off my rucksack and went closer. I felt compelled to touch it, but doing so meant either stretching up to the anvil from a relatively safe position close to the path, or leaning into the upright with the cliffs dropping away from me on both sides. But what did it matter if I fell?

I edged forwards. Beneath my feet was crumbled stone and a piece of it slid away, startling a seagull drifting below. I lunged and wrapped my arms around the rock. The sea glistened with the last rays of sunlight and the beauty of it almost took my breath away. The breeze ruffled my hair and I let my weight sink into the coldness of the stone.

The easiest route was down. To let go and slip away, past the wheeling gulls, gathering pace and bouncing off the rocks until I was smashed to pieces. I wouldn't hurt anymore and there would be no one who'd care. I remember wondering at what point I'd lose consciousness. I remember trying to calculate how fast I'd fall. I must have clung to the rock for a long time, until the colours of the sunset leached from the sky and it became quite dark. I was so tired I almost felt myself drift into a dream where I had my arms around the warm bark of the fairy tree, with Izzie's hands in mine.

Rustling branches drowned the smash of the waves, whispering with voices I knew, but couldn't place. The hidden folk... looking kindly on my wishes... not to slur my memory... nor hers... and then, finally, my mother, emerging from the mist of sound...

"I love you, Robin." I was inches away from being with her again, moments perhaps. Inches and moments; that's all it ever takes.

Chapter Eight

Izzie

I swear – I really do swear – this Christmas, everything is going to be different. There's simply no other way to get through it. Claire and I have put the tree in the hall, not the living room; we have decided not to go to midnight mass, and instead of staying at home we are going to the Solent Hotel for Christmas lunch. We won't be watching the re-run of *Morecambe and Wise* either, not without Connor there to fall about laughing. It was the only funny thing about it.

But we do not ignore her father. Early on Christmas Eve we drive up the Test Valley to his favourite pub and drop a paper boat into the river below The Mayfly's garden. It was Claire's idea and she has a little cry as it bobs about then catches on a stone and sinks. That makes it even worse, somehow, and I hug her to me, her fine blonde hair tickling my skin and her own special scent filling my nose. It's just the two of us now.

On the way back, Claire is looking to make conversation and tells me my tramp has vanished.

My tramp?

"What do you mean, vanished?" I ask.

"Well I kind of looked out for him after what you said, and he was at the Buttercross until the end of term and over the weekend, but when Sasha and I went into town yesterday he wasn't there."

"He's probably just moved on." I put the car into gear and turn into the main road.

"Do you really think it was the guy you knew, Mum?"

"It's hard to be sure…" I catch myself lying to her again. "But I think so, yes."

"Don't you want to find out what happened?"

"Oh, I don't know; I didn't go out with him for long…"

She spins around – as much as she can with her seatbelt on, that is. "You went out with him?"

I shrug. "Just for a little while; then I met your father."

That, at least, is the truth. Connor came into my life shortly after Robin left it. I met him in a bar when I was celebrating my teacher-training place. Robin had walked out in March; I cried on and off for a month then my mother gave me a kick up the arse. She was right; it was getting late in the day to apply for college but I squeezed in at the last minute. I suppose it helped that I wanted to teach maths. It's not a popular subject, but it has rights and it has wrongs. And I like that.

Connor was a musician, an Irish free spirit. He said he loved me because opposites attract. The only thing he ever took seriously was his music; all his life he played the violin, and by the time he died he was leader of the Bournemouth Philharmonic Orchestra. That instrument was his work – he would practise for hours, but never, as far as I know, play for his own pleasure. Everything else was for fun.

Physically he was as far apart from Robin as it was possible to be and maybe that was why I agreed to go out with him. He was a true Celt with his compact body, fair skin, and shock of black hair. He always kept himself trim and fit, so why he should have had a massive heart attack at the age of forty-three is beyond me.

It happened when the orchestra was playing in Frankfurt. Claire and I got on the first flight we could but it was still too late. They had resuscitated him so many times they told me if he'd lived he would have been close to a cabbage, and none of us would have wanted that.

Connor died at the very end of the summer holidays but at least Claire and I had memories of a wonderful fortnight in Malta to sustain us through the darkness of the autumn. Obviously Claire crumbled, but I managed to get her back on an even keel. It took a lot out of me though – I'm not sure why – and I suppose I was relieved when Fiona, my head of year, suggested I take an elongated Christmas break. I'm fine now though – well, I was before I saw Robin. No, I am fine, and I'm going to be back for the first day of the new term, ready to give my A-level group hell.

Claire goes to bed when I pour my third gin. It was a mistake to go to The Mayfly this morning; she hasn't been herself since. Sixteen must be a horrible age to lose a parent; you think you know it all, but underneath you kind of realise you don't. And hormones are all over the place.

But is there ever actually a good time?

Maybe. Perhaps there is. When the parent is no longer really part of your life. When Mum died four years ago I suspect her friends in the WRVS missed her more than I did. The truth is that Mum had needed to be needed so we'd grown apart. But, if there's a heaven, I like to think she's up there mending angels' wings right now.

I look at the tinsel-decked clock above the fireplace for the hundredth time; not quite five past nine. Today has been endless. Tomorrow will be worse but it's just thirty-six hours and then the first Christmas without Connor will be over. Box ticked. Move on.

I pick up the remote control from amongst the magazines on the coffee table and Marley's ghost appears. No bloody thank you. Christmas past is something I've been avoiding, but now the tunnel sucks me back: the M&S socks that turned out to be odd, the year we forgot to defrost the turkey, Claire getting drunk on Baileys when she was twelve. And further... Barbie dolls and Thomas the Tank Engine, a snowy white teddy called Mr Jim (why?), the secret bedtime unwrapping of satin and lace.

The glass on the table swims in front of me. Rain beats on the window as I think back to that Christmas before Connor entered my life.

"You promised you'd come with me!" I scream and

stamp my foot on the lino. All he does is shake his head. He must be drunk again. I slam into the bedroom and bark my shin on the dressing table as I reach for our suitcase. My suitcase. I open it. Shirts and socks fly out and a parcel spins onto the floor, reindeer-wrapping splitting open. Then I run down the stairs and into the street. Fuck him, fuck him, fuck him.

The warmth of the gin tingles through me. It is so hard, this first Christmas. And I didn't know – I didn't understand. I thought: it's almost four months – he should be getting over it by now. I see him again at the kitchen table, but this time I notice the shadows beneath his eyes, the downward slope of his shoulders.

Would I look at it differently now? Would I recognise the signs?

Chapter Nine

I would be lying if I said I hadn't wondered what it would be like waking beside Robin, but that first morning was as far from my dreams as it was possible to be. I can't say I slept much; I was terrified he'd be sick and choke. He'd got so drunk on whisky it had taken all the strength Jean and I had to get him up the stairs and now the stench of stale booze filled the room.

Robin was dead to the world and I was glad. I edged off the bed and picked up my sundress from the floor. The morning was overcast and the bright yellow fabric felt singularly inappropriate to the circumstances. But it was all I had.

There were three other doors on the landing. The one at the far end was ajar and I peeped in. A double bed with a deep-pink cover and white fitted wardrobes filling one wall. Some instinct made me want to go in and draw the curtains, but somehow crossing the threshold felt wrong. The twist of pain in my chest for Robin ripped me apart.

I knew the next door along was the bathroom. The one nearest Robin's bedroom housed an airing cupboard and in it I found some towels and a pile of freshly laundered clothes. Near the top was a blue jumper I knew to be Robin's so I took that out as well. It would warm me after my shower and its length would cover the startling brightness of my dress.

It was just gone nine o'clock when I made my way down to the kitchen and I headed straight for the phone to call the office and explain I wouldn't be in. A friend's bereavement. I needed some time. But on the other hand, I wouldn't be taking all my holiday. I stared out of the window over the patch of grass at the back, turning my mind away from the awfulness of the telephone conversation with Paul the night before. Instead, I put on the kettle and dialled Robin's office number.

I had done everything I could think of to do. I crept back upstairs as quietly as I could, but Robin was already sitting on the side of the bed in his boxer shorts, his hair tousled from sleep.

"How are you feeling?"

He moved his head slowly from side to side. "Better than I deserve. But still like I might cry any minute. I'm so sorry, Izzie…"

"It's not your fault."

"I'm not even sure about that."

I sat down next to him and took his hand. He squeezed it tight.

"Last night…" His voice was cracking and he coughed. "Last night, when we were sitting downstairs, I felt… I thought… your little hand was the only thing stopping me from drowning. It was like a lifeline…"

"It is your lifeline, Robin, for as long as you need it. I won't take it away." And I meant it, really I meant it, with all my heart.

Later, Jean told us there was nothing we could do until they'd finished the post-mortem and we had Rene's death certificate, except perhaps to clear out her wardrobe. The look of horror in Robin's eyes told me that was a bad idea, but at the same time Jean's words made me think.

"I need to collect some clothes. I've only got this dress. In fact, I need to collect everything at some point."

Robin looked up. "I'm sorry, Izzie. I didn't even think about Paul. Your holiday…"

I shook my head. "There's no need, Robin. It's over; I told him last night."

"You saw him?"

"No, I phoned him. He had to know where I was."

Robin rested his head in his hands. "I've made it bloody difficult for you, haven't I? I'm so sorry."

Jean appeared at the door and then moved towards Robin, shaking him gently by the shoulder.

"It's not you, Robin, it's Rene going like that. None of us could have seen that happening."

"No… no… you're right." His reply was muffled.

"Why don't you go with Izzie to collect her things? It'll get you out of the house."

I put my hand on his arm. "And it'd help me so much – there'll be a lot to carry and it's a first floor flat."

He nodded and almost smiled. "Sounds like a plan."

"And in the meantime I'll start going through Rene's bedroom to make a bit of space for Izzie's stuff."

"No, I feel I should…"

But Jean held firm. She was that sort of woman.

By the time Robin had carried two or three boxes of books and records down the stairs and packed them in the boot of my car, he seemed two inches taller and there was a glimmer of light in his eyes. I was even pleased when he took the micky out of my collection of Duran Duran singles in their picture sleeves, although of course I pretended to be affronted.

He shook his head, a sardonic grin spreading slowly across his face. "I may have a better haircut, but I'm no Simon Le Bon, Izzie. I hope you realise that."

I looked up from stuffing handfuls of underwear into my overnight bag. "I'm no Yasmin, either."

"I don't want you to be anyone but you."

No one had ever said anything like that to me before.

That night we made love – a slow, sensuous affair, the softness of Robin's fingers trickling over my skin and lodging deep into the corners of my mind. It was a voyage of discovery into each other's nakedness that left me sated, but all the same longing for more.

Is it distance that makes me remember it so vividly? It's strange; once we were over I locked those memories away. Why am I punishing myself with them now? Because there's a chance – a tiny chance – that I can bring them back? Or simply that I might be able to make amends?

The darkness set in quickly, knock after knock leaving Robin punch-drunk and dazed. Next was the result of the post-mortem: an overdose of painkillers. Jean and I told Robin time and again that Rene hadn't meant to do it, that she'd never have left him, but we could see it wasn't sinking in. And when the police came to question him he crumbled onto the sofa, asking them again and again what they wanted. Jean shielded him. I was his alibi. He would never in a million years have harmed his mother; Jean and I knew it and even the police seemed to accept it by the time they left. I'm just not sure Robin did. That's all.

By the day of the funeral he was calm. We went into town early to buy him a black tie. We sat in the park next to the Guildhall, watching the city come to life around us while we waited for the shops to open. One of the partners from his firm walked by, on his way to the office. He spoke kindly to Robin, told him to take his time. Robin told him he'd be back at work the next week.

We were a select band at the crematorium. It was mainly neighbours, but also a man Jean told me had been a boyfriend of Rene's when Robin was in junior school.

"If only she'd stayed with Davey, none of this would have happened," she sighed.

"Why didn't she?"

"He was too nice, too normal. She liked a streak of danger in her life, Rene did."

Robin had chosen 'The Green, Green Grass of Home' to be played as the curtain squeaked and squealed closed in front of the coffin. Robin had chosen the single red rose that graced it. Jean sobbed until I thought she could sob no more but Robin seemed beyond emotion.

That night he fucked me. There is no other word for his empty-eyed thrusting, and I lay awake afterwards, throbbing and raw.

The reading light over the bed cast the veins on his eyelids and the black blue bruises beneath into sharp relief. And I was scared, but only for a moment, until he spoke.

"God, Izzie. I'm sorry."

"It's OK. You didn't mean—"

"I really didn't. It was almost like... you weren't even there. I swear to you, it will never happen again."

So he found his release in other ways, ways that turned his anger and grief back on himself.

But I didn't understand – not then.

Chapter Ten

Robin

I don't think I ever made a conscious decision not to go home. I sent Auntie Jean a postcard from Weymouth and another from Lyme Regis, but by the time I reached Exeter she seemed irrelevant.

Postcards. That's how I see my journey now – black and white postcards. Towering cliffs beyond Dawlish I now know to be red. Rain-lashed palm trees at Torquay. Christmas lights slung across the harbour at Looe. At any other time they would have looked like a stunning array of jewels. But not to me. Not then.

Endless stretches of grey moorland. The forbidding granite of Bodmin and its jail. The coldest wind in the universe cutting through me. And then, from nowhere, a softness in the air. Daffodils edging the track to Constantine Bay. Yellow daffodils. White horses riding a promise of blue. An end to hibernation.

The stretch of coast between Padstow and Newquay is one of the most beautiful in the world. Cliffs dip into sandy bays lapped by the azure grandeur of the ocean. All around me the early Cornish spring was coming to life with a slow sloughing-off of winter that seeped into me too. I positively dawdled and the weather was kind. And now I began to think – just a little bit – about the immediate future.

My funds in the Post Office had run out some time before and a visit to the cashpoint in Padstow had shown me I was dangerously short of money in the bank so I decided Newquay would be a good place to find seasonal work. I'd been there surfing a few times so knew it was crammed with hotels, shops, and cafés, which would all need extra pairs of hands over the summer. It was still a little early to be looking for a job so my first priority would be to find a place to live.

I thought if I saw the right flat in an estate agent's window it would be easier to pluck up the courage to go inside and ask. But the reality was that there were very few places to let and all the little cards bore the terrifying words 'month's rent in advance – deposit required'. I didn't have that sort of money left.

The tiny bit of confidence I'd mustered was trickling away, not helped by the way the woman in the bakery looked at me as she sold me a pasty for my lunch. But it was good and hot and as I ate it, sheltering in the doorway of an empty shop, the sun appeared from behind a bank of cloud. I decided to take a walk while I figured out what to do.

I turned my back on the town but had only gone a few paces when I was drawn to a display of longboards in the window of a surf store. I remembered my own board, wedged, along with my bicycle, into the tiny shed at the back of the house. I steeled myself against the stab of pain that inevitably accompanied these memories but it didn't come. Maybe I was winning; maybe it wasn't just the scent of spring making me feel more positive.

The discovery made me a bit lightheaded so I steadied myself by reading the notices in the window and amongst them was one that simply read, 'rooms to let – enquire within'. The coincidence was enough of a boost to propel me into the shop.

Behind the cash desk was a woman of about forty with long red hair and a healthy outdoor glow about her skin. She looked up and started to say, "Can I help you?" but stopped.

I stopped too, my hand still on the door. On the wall opposite was a mirror and as I caught sight of my reflection I could see why she seemed so horrified. I couldn't look at her. "I'm sorry. I came about the room," I muttered.

She didn't reply.

"I'm sorry. I've been... camping... for a while. But now... I need somewhere to stay." I indicated the rucksack on my back with a jerk of my head.

"Do you then?" was all she said, her voice a Cornish lilt.

Silence.

"Look," I ventured, "I'm not as rough as I seem and I've got the money to pay for it. As long as it's not too expensive," I added as an afterthought.

"It's thirty pounds a week, plus a quarter of the bills.

There's two rooms at the top of the house sharing a kitchen and bathroom."

She was telling me about it. She hadn't thrown me out. I pushed my advantage.

"Sounds good. When can I see it?"

"I'm not sure you can. The rooms are in my house."

I was about to argue when I caught sight of my reflection again: ragged beard, grimy anorak, and hair so filthy it clung to my scalp in great clumps. She was right. Of course.

"Oh, I see. Well, you can't be too careful, I guess. Sorry I troubled you."

I was sorry I'd seen that mirror too.

But before I had quite closed the door she spoke. "Give me time to think about it. If you don't find anything come back just before I close at five o'clock."

I didn't look anywhere else. I'd noticed a launderette while I was wandering around the town so I washed and dried everything except what I was wearing. Then I braved a public toilet near the deserted beach and although the water was ice cold I washed as thoroughly as I could and changed into clean clothes. There was no way I could shave or do anything about my greasy hair but I trimmed my beard with the scissors on my Swiss army knife and spent ages trying to get a wet comb through my rats' tails. The effect was negligible so I bought a cheap bandana, hoping the impression would be more surfer than beggar. By that time it was half past four and I went to the cashpoint to withdraw £60 then made my way back to the surf shop.

I was relieved when the woman smiled. "That's something of a transformation," she said.

I indicated the glass on the wall. "I hadn't looked in a mirror for a while. I was a bit shocked when I did." I reached into my pocket and pulled out the notes. "And I've got two weeks' rent up front – just in case we can come to an arrangement."

"Well I'll cash up then we can go. My name's Megan Tregea, by the way."

I held out my hand. "Robin Vail." She didn't shrink away.

I wandered around the shop as I waited, my footsteps echoing on the wooden floor. Megan had some seriously good kit: boards of all sizes, an impressive array of wetsuits and accessories, as well as a few rails of surf-fashion clothing. The place had a slightly rundown air but the chipped paintwork oozed cool. I knew she'd make a mint in the summer.

Megan's house was in the jumble of roads between the harbour and the golf course. It was halfway along a terrace and had three storeys: a basement and ground floor where Megan lived and the letting rooms upstairs. As she had told me, there were two good sized bedrooms with a windowless bathroom and a kitchen sandwiched between them. I asked about the other tenant.

"There isn't anyone yet. I only put the notice up yesterday. If you like it then you can have the pick of the rooms."

"You're sure I'll do? You feel comfortable?"

"The very fact you're asking means it's OK." She smiled

properly this time and I realised that although she was much older than me she was really quite pretty.

I paid my rent, chose the room at the back and set about unpacking my few belongings. Megan had told me there was an open-all-hours a few streets away so I was able to buy some basic supplies – bread, milk, cereal, and some battered fish portions that would do for supper. It was a long time since I'd had a kitchen and I vowed to cook properly tomorrow, but for the moment I wolfed them down then had a long, lazy bath and washed my hair.

In the bedroom I didn't bother to turn on the light. I sank onto the duvet and ran the flat of my hand over the coolness of the pillows. Music drifted up from Megan's part of the house. I hesitated, savouring the moment. I knew as soon as I put my head down I would be asleep.

Chapter Eleven

The thin Cornish wind was finding its way through both my jumpers, so reluctantly I turned inland towards the town. The beach was dotted with dog walkers making the most of the sunshine and I had enjoyed leaning on the rail watching them roam the ever-lengthening expanse of sand as the tide dropped.

The road was lined with Victorian villas, most of them boasting B&B signs in their small front gardens. Halfway along, on the sunny side of the street, a man was cleaning windows. I thought to myself, *I could do that*. I'd just need a ladder, and a bucket, and maybe a bicycle. And, of course, the courage to knock on people's doors.

I paused to look in the window of the baker's shop. I was hungry, but there was perfectly good bread and cheese in the fridge at home… I wavered. The woman behind the counter looked at me and I wanted to shrink away, but to my amazement she smiled. The only difference today was that I was clean. She probably didn't even recognise me.

A few paces on at the top of the hill I turned left towards Megan's shop. I wavered again. On the one hand, it would be nice to pop in and say hello, but on the other I didn't want to seem needy. In the end I decided to ask her if she minded me putting up a picture or two in my bedroom – it was a good excuse, anyway.

As it happened, the shop was busy so I slunk away to where the surfboards were lined up along the back wall. A boy of about nine or ten was trying to persuade his mother to buy a full-size adult longboard; it could be a costly mistake and I found myself asking the lad how much surfing he'd done.

"None, as yet," his mother answered. "I've booked some lessons for the Easter holidays but he's adamant he wants his own board."

I looked at the boy. "Wow, you sure, dude? Never surfed and you pick the toughest board going? You'll still be dragging it down the beach when the other guys are catching their first waves."

His mouth set into a hard line. "I don't want a baby's board."

"I'm not saying that, but a longboard? Jeez. I'd think twice before handling one of those; they're just too much hard work to be fun."

His mother pounced. "What board do you have?"

My eyes flicked over Megan's stock. "A really light one. Much more manoeuvrable. I mean, mine's a bit old now but… something like this?"

It was lucky I'd been a bit of a gear freak when I was a student surfer. We went through a few boards and the lad finally chose one and I also managed to persuade him into some neoprene gloves – his hands would have frozen otherwise. I felt a bit sheepish taking them to the till and offloading them to Megan to take the money, but she played along with the idea that I worked for her and I drifted off to tidy a pile of sweatshirts.

There was one more customer and then the shop was empty. I turned to Megan. "Sorry if I interfered…"

"It's fine. I had half an eye on you and you seemed to know what you were doing. It's been manic this morning – any chance you can help me out for the rest of the day? I'll pay you a tenner."

I had nothing else to do so I agreed, which was how I ended up with a part-time job in Megan's shop. She asked me while she drove us home if I'd work Fridays and Saturdays, just until I found something else, and then she asked me to supper the next night. She was nice, I was lonely, and I ended up saying yes to both.

It never entered my head that she was being anything other than kind. I spent some of my ten pound note on a bottle of wine and we drank more than half of it before she got around to serving up the fish pie she'd cooked. She told me she'd not long inherited the house and was letting the rooms because it was too big for one person. We talked about Newquay in the summer. We talked about surfing and about the sea. We opened a second bottle of wine but didn't finish it because one thing led to another and we ended up in bed.

I'd got out of the habit of drinking so I don't remember much about our first night together, but I will never forget waking the next morning: the sound of a milk float and a car door slamming in the street; opening my eyes and for a moment or two not knowing where I was; looking across at Megan's hair spread across the pillow and wanting Izzie with a pain so intense that bile filled my throat.

I rolled over with my back to Megan and curled into a ball. What the hell had I done?

I didn't have too long to think about it before the room was filled with Madonna mingling with the seven o'clock pips. Megan reached over me to turn the volume down.

"Good morning, Robin."

"I'm so sorry, I..."

Her eyes were above mine, deep-lined and almost black. "Regrets, then?" Her voice was light, but underpinned by a slight shake.

"Not at all," I lied. "Just a blinding hangover."

And then she was smiling. "I have to say, I've felt better myself. I'll make us some coffee."

Thankfully she disappeared and a while later I heard the shower. I should have got up and dressed but I felt too leaden to move so I rolled over and closed my eyes. She put my coffee on the bedside table then rustled quietly around the room, getting ready for work. Finally she touched my shoulder.

"Stay here to sleep it off. Just pull the door behind you when you go."

"Thanks, Megan," I mumbled. But once I was sure she had driven away I grabbed my clothes and raced for my own room just as fast as I could. I pulled the duvet over my head. My own stupid, drunken, testosterone-fuelled nightmare had punched a hole so large in my defences it was impossible to stem the raging tide of Izzie, engulfing me from all sides.

It was late afternoon before I was able to crawl out of bed. Even then my hands were shaking as I filled the kettle to make a cup of tea. No sugar, so I helped myself to a chocolate digestive instead. A crumb lodged in the back of my throat and I coughed so much it was all I could do to stop myself retching.

I took my mug back to bed and sat, propped on the pillows, gazing out over the grey-tiled roof of the terrace behind. Where was Izzie now? A Monday afternoon, in early spring. I pictured her, clipping down the pavement in her kitten heels, navy mac billowing in the breeze, right shoulder dragged down by the weight of her briefcase. Going home later to what? To Paul? I sincerely hoped she hadn't burned her boats on my account.

For the very first time I thought about what had happened from her point of view. When she came back from her holiday, I would have simply disappeared, leaving no trace. And I'd promised her, promised her I'd wait. She'd probably decided to stay with Paul anyway and I'd let her off the hook. The idea salved my conscience, but not my heartache. All through the hours of darkness, an Izzie-less emptiness stretched before me. If this was how sex with another woman made me feel, I was determined to become a monk.

Of course daylight brought a sense of proportion and even with the dull ache behind my eyes and lodged in my chest I knew I had to make the best of the bed I had made for myself. I went for a walk, out to Towan Head and the length of Fistral Beach. Meandering back along the edge of the golf course I found a bank covered in early primroses. On impulse I picked some for Megan and left them in a milk bottle by the door to her flat with a note thanking her for dinner on Sunday.

And that's how we slid into a relationship. She came upstairs for a chat that evening and we sat in the little kitchen drinking tea. We woke up together the next morning and I went into the shop with her to tidy the stockroom. I started going into the shop most days, and she stopped taking rent from me and bunged me the odd tenner so I could buy a round when we went out with her friends. After a few weeks, Ed, who ran the surf school, offered to rent both rooms for his summer staff so I moved downstairs.

It was when we were turning out a cupboard to make room for my stuff that I found out just exactly how old Megan was. It was a passport application and it had her date of birth on it: 7th of June 1945. A year to the day younger than my mother and eighteen years older than me. I piled the papers together and shoved them into a box ready to carry up to the attic.

Chapter Twelve

It was surprisingly easy to forget the age difference. Almost every evening Megan and I would surf on Towan Beach with her friends, the low sunshine silhouetting her slim figure against the waves. There was beer, and laughter, and seagulls, and Wet Wet Wet on the radio. And what's more, Megan was a superb surfer – a real natural. Her body was built for it and seeing her in a wetsuit it was easy to want her.

So it was fine – until her birthday. My mother's birthday. I never realised – it never even occurred to me – the pain an anniversary can bring. It suffocated every spark of life out of me and the closer we got to the day itself the feebler my attempts to conquer it became.

Even pretending became too much so I told Megan I was coming down with something so I'd be better sleeping in the spare room. She wouldn't let me. That night I heard every car door slam in the street, every dog bark. In the smallest of hours Megan woke and tried to hold me – an ungrateful, rigid, lump in her arms. I wanted to say sorry, but no words came.

I watched the greyness of dawn creep around the colourless curtains. Then there was the alarm and Megan speaking from a distance. I pointed to my throat and she nodded and kissed my forehead. I stared at the ceiling, tracing the crack from one end of the bay window to the other. And after she'd gone to work I cried, like the baby I'd damned myself to be, for hours and hours.

Something, though, released, and when I felt strong enough I went to have a shower. Mum, Izzie, Megan all crowded in on me as the water thrummed onto my skull. I needed to push myself into the practicalities of the day.

Megan was serving a customer when I arrived at the shop and there was someone else waiting so I dived straight in, taking their money and popping their sweatshirt into a bag with the best smile I could manage. Megan was having a tough time of it with a lippy teenager who wanted to return something and when the shop was finally empty she turned on me.

"You look a right prick wearing those shades in here. Take them off."

"I look worse without them," I muttered.

"I'll be the judge of that. Take them off."

I did as I was told.

There was a sharp intake of breath. "What the fuck have you been doing to your eyes?"

"Nothing. It must be an allergy of some sort – probably why I was feeling so rough."

She swore again and pulled a fiver out of the till. "Well,

do what any sensible person would do and get yourself off to Boots and take something for it. Or were you waiting for me to give you the money?"

I put the note back on the counter. "There's no need for you to give me anything I haven't earned," I said with as much pride as I could muster, and, putting my sunglasses back on, made for the door.

I didn't go to Boots; I went to Towan Beach. Ed was outside his surf shack hosing down wetsuits, the spray darkening his hair almost to the colour of his bronzed skin. He turned the water off when he saw me.

"Quiet in the shop?"

"So-so."

He raised his eyebrows.

"To be honest, Ed, it isn't that great me working for Megan as well as... You don't know anyone who needs part-time help? I mean, I can't leave her in the lurch and I wouldn't want to, but a bit of independence..."

He laughed. "I know what you're saying. Not nice being a kept man, I'd guess."

I sat down on the low wall. "I've only just realised that's what I am."

"You're young yet, Rob. Strikes me you've got a lot to learn about women. But that's by the by. Have you got a driving licence?"

"Yes."

He sat next to me, stretching his legs towards the sand. "Then how would you like to take the trailer over to Watergate for me when the season gets going? Two runs, morning and evening, then I've got the van back here in case I need it during the day – and you could still work in the shop between times."

"It sounds too good to be true."

"Yeah, well, you're making Meg happy and that's important to me. Couldn't do it myself – she's not an easy woman – but the spring's certainly back in her step since you've come on the scene."

I'd never thought of Megan as difficult although I had to admit she was a bit mercurial. When she came home that night she was nice as pie, but on Sunday – her birthday itself – we had another almighty row.

It was my fault, I know, but I was so haunted by thoughts of my mother that I couldn't betray her by staying on the beach, laughing and joking with everyone else. Claiming I was feeling rough again I walked home and curled up on the sofa and wept. I must have cried myself to sleep, because the next thing I knew Megan was shaking my shoulder and demanding to know why I hadn't told her I was going to work for Ed.

I struggled to sit up, my eyes too full of grit to focus. I started to apologise but she was ranting and raving about how I'd made her look a fool and she didn't believe this allergy thing for one minute, that if I wanted to leave her I just had to say, and that everyone was laughing at her anyway, because I was so young.

"That's not true," I yelled. "Ed says he's pleased I'm making you happy. He—"

"Well you're not making me happy, are you?" she stormed.

"I thought I was. I..." And despite myself, I started to cry again.

She threw me a look of total disdain. "You fucking baby."

I put my head in my hands and stayed that way until she slammed the living room door behind her.

I did sleep in the spare room that night and in the early hours I felt Megan slide in behind me. I turned to face her and held her in my arms.

It was either that or walk away and I had nowhere to walk to.

Chapter Thirteen

Week by week the days lengthened and the sky became bluer. Newquay's beaches thronged from early morning to dusk, people spilled out of the pubs onto the pavements, and families wandered along eating ice creams or fish and chips. For those of us who worked in the tourist industry there was no let-up; at least Megan and I had Sundays when the shop couldn't open, but Ed's surf school was a seven-day-a-week operation and I still had to get up to drive the trailer.

Megan would be grumpy for hours if I woke her, so I'd slide out of bed, pull on my shorts and a sweatshirt and walk down to the beach to unlock the shack, attach the trailer, and load up the van with gear. Then I'd make myself a coffee and sit on the wall, watching the dog walkers and waiting for the instructors to turn up from whichever bed they'd found themselves in the night before.

That half hour every morning became the most precious part of my day – the part I let Izzie creep into. The memory

69

of her was a warm secret held to the very centre of myself. A longing for the past, imagining what could have been, and even – when I was feeling particularly strong – fantasies of how I might find her again.

The secret pleasure and despair in these moments imbued my relationship with Megan with guilt. I was using her, and that knowledge made me feel even worse when I did something to make her cross, like giving the wrong change in the shop, or buying the wrong sort of beer at the off-licence on the way home.

The previous day had been crap in that respect and I was determined to make it up to her. As soon as I'd done the morning run I was going to make her a slap-up breakfast in bed then spoil her for the rest of the day. I knew how tired she was – the depth of the lines under her eyes gave her away.

When I got home she was still asleep, even though it was close to eleven o'clock. I crept into the kitchen and started frying sausages and mushrooms, and very soon she appeared behind me. She looked annoyed but I wrapped my arms around her and told her to go back to bed, which thankfully defused the moment, and after that the day was a really happy one. I'd begged Ed to do the afternoon run so Megan and I lazed in the garden drinking wine and reading the Sunday papers, and she said she wished every day could be like this. And I felt better, because I'd made her happy.

But many times I didn't. Like when I talked for too long to a pretty girl in the shop. Or when I was late back from an evening trailer run and she thought she could smell beer on my breath. The rollercoaster wasn't only inside my head and I had absolutely no way of controlling it. On top of that, the anniversary of Mum's death was looming and I was beginning to live in terror of it.

It was only a matter of time before things really kicked off between Megan and me.

It was after supper and I was meant to be washing up while she changed the sheets on our bed, but instead I stayed at the table, lost in my own thoughts, and when she came back she was furious.

"You lazy little shit! The flat's a pigsty. I just tripped over your fucking trainers in the hall."

I started to apologise but she wasn't having any of it.

"I bet you were spoiled rotten by your mum – bet she never let her precious boy do anything. Do you know what an iron is, Robin? A hoover? Do you know toilets don't clean themselves?"

Of course I knew all those things. But I wasn't prepared to tell Megan that or the reason for it. I stood up and towered over her.

"Don't you dare talk about my mother! You're not fit to — About the only thing you've got in common with her is your age."

I didn't stay to listen to the abuse she was hurling after me. I grabbed the offending trainers and my jacket and stormed out of the flat.

It was dusk and I stomped along the streets towards Fistral Beach. A solitary surfer was still in the water but most were in groups on the beach, with courting couples dotting the sand between them. I wanted no company so I walked the track along the golf course until I found an isolated bench tucked into the folds of the dunes, but still their bursts of laughter drifted towards me.

I'd burned my boats with Megan and I had nowhere else to go. But maybe it was time I stopped using her anyway. I still loved Izzie and I spent the night convincing myself I should find a shred of courage from somewhere and do something about it. Again and again I pictured the look on her face as we held hands around the fairy tree and it planted a tiny seed of hope to cling on to.

I must have slept a little because I remember waking to a pale-grey light in the sky. And it was cold – my fingers were completely numb. As I flexed them I looked at my watch. Coming up to five o'clock. I got up, stretched my aching limbs, and headed off in the direction of Ed's surf shack where at least I could make myself a hot drink and have some sort of wash.

When Ed arrived he had only to glance at my face. "What gives, young Rob?"

"I was a shit to Megan last night," I told him. "I can't go on using her like this. It's not right."

He sat down on the wall next to me. "Has it occurred to you that she's using you as well?"

"In what way? She's given me a home, a job…"

"And you've given her a source of cheap labour and a massive one in the eye for that bastard ex-boyfriend of hers up at the hotel every time he sees her with a guy twenty years younger than him."

"I didn't know anything about that," I murmured, spinning my empty mug around on the wall by its handle.

"Well maybe you don't need to, but all I'm saying is if there's using going on then it's cutting both ways."

"But it's still not right…" The mug started to topple but I managed to catch it.

"Like I've always said, Rob, you've got a lot to learn about women. What else is a relationship, anyway? It's just a transaction where you've got something she wants and she's got something you want – everything from a twenty-five year marriage to a one-night stand is based on that so you'd better get used to it."

As I drove to Watergate I thought about what he'd said. Was it true? Looking back at my mother's various partners I could see he had a point, but I couldn't imagine life being like that with Izzie. Ed made it sound as though love didn't exist. Perhaps it was rare, and in which case it shouldn't be wasted. By the time I was driving back to Newquay I'd made up my mind: even then I knew Izzie's work phone number by heart and I was going to call it. If she'd married Paul then I'd forget all about her, but if not…

Except, when I got back to the surf shack Megan was waiting for me and she looked as though she hadn't slept either.

She didn't beat around the bush. "Robin, we've got to talk. Ed's minding the shop for an hour or so. Shall we get some breakfast?"

We made our way to a table in the back corner of the beach café. As soon as we sat down I started to apologise but she held up her hand to stop me.

"OK, you said some horrid things – well, one in particular stung – but it was the truth. I thought about it all

73

night, while I was worrying where you were. I touched a really raw nerve, didn't I?"

The lump rising in my throat made it hard to tell her what she wanted to know. "My mum's dead. Coming up for a year ago."

"Oh, Robin, I'm so sorry. I've lost both my parents and the first anniversary's the worst, I promise. It hits you for six but it does get better. Tell me when it is, so I can look out for you."

"Seventh of September." I just managed to say it before I broke down and buried my head on my arms on the plastic tablecloth. I heard the scrape of Megan's chair as she moved next to me to put her arm around my shoulders.

Chapter Fourteen

It was the sixth of September when I finally plucked up the courage to call Izzie. I knew if I let it drift more than a year then I would be the other side of a significant watershed and it would never happen.

There was a telephone box in Porth, on my way back from Watergate, and I had been eyeing it up for a while. I generally came back that way at about quarter to ten in the morning and I knew it was a time Izzie would be in the office, taking telephone orders and preparing for her day.

I pulled the van off the road into the lay-by next to the beach. I listened to the waves crash on the rocks for a long time before I locked the door and crossed the road. The phone box was occupied by an elderly lady with a small poodle and I almost turned away, but she finished her call and my last excuse had gone.

The receiver slipped in my hands and I dropped my ten pence piece. As I scrabbled to pick it up I noticed there was a child's bracelet on the floor and it made me remember the fairy tree. It was the kick I needed and I pressed the buttons quickly before I could change my mind again. The phone rang three times and then I heard the familiar voice of the receptionist. There was no chance she would remember me.

"Can I speak to Izzie, please?" I asked, my heart thudding so loudly it threatened to drown out her answer. I wish it had.

"I'm sorry, she doesn't work here anymore. Can anyone else help you?"

I placed the phone back on its cradle. I stood for a few moments, my forehead on the glass, inhaling the pissy metallic smell. That, more than anything, drove me to open the door, stumble across the road to the van, drive to Newquay, and get on with my day.

Chapter Fifteen

T he holiday season was effectively over by the middle of September. The shop became quieter and Ed only needed my services over long weekends. It would stay that way for another month and then my sole source of independent income would dry up. Megan wouldn't really need me in the shop either and when I spoke to her about it she had a go at me for not trying to find non-seasonal work sooner. Given I'd been working more than full time over the summer I thought that was a bit much and I told her so.

By now our arguments ran a familiar course: I would do something wrong, she would tell me how useless I was, I would bite back then sulk for a while, and then we would make it up, normally in bed or over a bottle of wine. But each time it happened I sank lower into an endless mist of grey, made more mistakes, became less willing to open my mouth, and so things went from bad to worse.

It was Ed who eventually spoke to me about it, poor bugger; Megan probably put him up to it. He had become a bit of a father figure to me – probably the only one I've ever had – but it wasn't his way to talk about emotional stuff and, as I didn't want to either, it was a bit of an awkward conversation.

We were putting the trailer away on a Sunday night in early October when Ed suggested we crack open a few beers. I was hesitant, fearing getting back to Megan late with alcohol on my breath, but Ed wasn't put off by the feeble excuse I gave him and had already opened the cans.

"D'you want to tell me what's up, young Rob?" he asked as he handed mine over.

I shrugged my shoulders. "Nothing, really."

"Oh come on, you've been miserable as sin for weeks now. Everyone's noticed and we're worried about you."

It was nice of them, but I really had brought this on myself. But how to explain it all to Ed? Did I even want to? He'd probably tell Megan and then… And then, what? And did I care, anyway? It seemed too much trouble to care about anything. But Ed was looking at me, waiting for an answer.

"It's nothing really. It's just, you know, the future looks so uncertain." The metallic taste of the beer can reminded me of the phone box at Porth.

"The future is uncertain – not just for you, now, but for all of us, all the time. We're still caught up in this bloody recession for a start. It's not great for old hands like me but it's bloody unfair on bright kids like you, scraping by doing dead-end jobs."

"I'm not that bright. Lots of people have degrees nowadays and I've never even used mine."

"Because you can't or because you won't?"

It was a good question. When I'd first graduated my choice had been limited because of Mum. I'd wanted to travel, work overseas even, but that avenue had been closed to me. Now I was a free agent and Ed was right. Instead of doing something about it I was bumming around. Only, I didn't feel free; I felt more as though I was serving a life sentence.

I shook my head. "I don't know." I stood up and gazed out of the window onto the beach, waiting for my vision to clear and to be able to speak again.

But Ed spoke first. "Megan's especially worried."

"She hasn't said anything."

"She says she can't reach you. It's like you've shut yourself off from her."

It wasn't deliberate. "Can't do a thing right, that's all," I muttered.

I heard the smile in Ed's voice. "That's Meg for you."

"I can't handle it." I was close to tears again.

"You won't change her."

"I don't want to. I... I want to stop using her." I burst out. "It's not doing either of us any good and I'm too much of a wimp to walk away. And anyway, I've got nowhere to walk to."

"You can have my sofa for a few weeks if that'd help?"

"No, Ed. It's time I was a man about this." Which was a really immature thing to say, although I meant it at the time; I really did.

It quite literally took a hurricane to make me act. To be honest, the infamous hurricane of 1987 didn't hit our part of

Cornwall that hard, but waking up to the radio news about what had happened in the south of England turned my thoughts firmly to home.

The last group of surfers of Ed's season was a stag party from London and their tale of travelling through increasingly windy conditions the night before was regaled long and loudly while they put on their wetsuits. One had called his girlfriend in Wimbledon and was amazed to find she had no power, not a tube running, nor indeed much in the way of buses because so many trees were blocking the roads.

Driving the van back on my own I was trying to picture tree after tree, crashing down in the wind, like so many dominoes. The devastating impact of nature on nature made me feel strangely agitated: for the first time, something was hauling my mind kicking and screaming out of the grey. It was awful, exciting, and stimulating all at the same time. Back in the shop I talked to Megan about it like a man possessed. I remember her smiling and nodding; she was probably just pleased I was communicating again.

But then it started to get personal. That evening, on the TV, there were pictures from all over the south of England. Mainly London, but also some of Southampton and a vague unease crept into the edges of my mind. I watched the *Nine O'Clock News* then turned over for *News at Ten*. Megan said I was becoming obsessive and rather than argue with her I switched off the television and we went to bed.

I woke in the deepest blackness of the night with an image of the fairy tree implanted into my brain. Not the fairy tree as I had last seen it, but lying skewed and broken in the middle of a tangled heap of twisted vegetation, the offerings pinned to its bark shredded and smashed under the fallen branches.

I tried to focus on Megan's easy breathing beside me but the image was so strong I knew it was real. With such devastation, how could the tree have survived, so close to the top of the steep bank up from the Hamble? It had never felt exposed with the woods all around it, but with a great wind ripping and roaring up the river, it would surely have had no chance. But I had to find out for sure.

I said nothing to Megan as I worked my last weekend taking the trailer back and forth to Watergate and my last Saturday in the shop. It was very quiet – I guess a lot of weekenders' plans had been put off by the weather. On Monday I helped Megan sort out and mark-up stock for the end-of-season sale in virtual silence.

Megan never knew how close she came to the truth when she accused me of being away with the fairies but she gave me the opening I was looking for.

I put down the pile of shirts I was carrying and took hold of her hands. "I sorry. I'm so worried about what's happened back home. I'm going to have to see for myself."

She nodded. "That's understandable. When are you thinking of leaving?"

"Tomorrow."

She never asked if I would be coming back, and I never told her I wouldn't. The weather was awful so she lent me some waterproofs from the shop. I felt bad about those for a long while, until someone made me understand that perhaps Megan knew, after all, that they were a parting gift.

Chapter Sixteen

Izzie

On Boxing Day morning, Claire and her friend Sasha want to go to Winchester for the sales. Early. Very early. I buy them breakfast at Caffè Nero then leave them to shiver in the queue outside Next. Thick tights or not, their skirts seem impossibly tiny for this time of year. What are they thinking?

Perhaps I'd rather not know. I escape down a side street towards the cathedral.

Inside, the world is muffled. A few worshippers thread their way through the unmanned pay stations to morning prayer, but I'm not here to join them. Instead, I study the parish notice board and amongst the posters for carol services and Christmas appeals I strike gold: the Winchester Churches Nightshelter is not far away in Jewry Street. I fight my way back through the bargain-hunters but once I am outside the red brick building I hesitate. What will I say if I find him?

I need not have worried. There is hardly anyone around but the volunteer who answers the door tells me she worked a fair bit in the run-up to Christmas and has never seen Robin, or anyone vaguely fitting his description. She suggests I try Hyde Street Hostel instead.

Hyde Street has an air of being a little more open. A man in overalls is painting the inside porch and just beyond him is a window with *Reception* etched onto the glass. The woman sitting on the other side slides it across when she sees me.

"Can I help you?" she asks, in a surprisingly posh accent.

"I'm looking for someone who might be staying here. He's called Robin Vail. Very tall man, straggly hair and a beard."

"I'm sorry, we can't divulge details of our residents." She folds her arms over her cashmere jumper.

"Whyever not?"

"They have a right to privacy," the woman snaps.

"But he is one of your residents then?"

"I didn't say that."

"You implied it."

She draws in a sharp breath. "I was speaking hypothetically."

But I know she wasn't. "Can you at least pass on a message?"

"I told you, I was speaking hypothetically." She

enunciates each syllable as though I am too stupid to understand it.

"Oh for God's sake. I'm his oldest friend and I want to help him."

The woman slams the glass shut in my face and I explode. "You miserable old cow! Get off your high horse and think about people's feelings for a change."

I turn on my heel and march towards the door. The man in overalls leaps up to open it and I thank him.

"Try the hospital," he whispers. "I heard he was taken there."

Outside, I watch the exhaust plume behind a Mini waiting at the lights. Robin is ill. What sort of ill? I waver, but perhaps now he needs someone even more. I don't walk straight to the Royal Hampshire; I go back to Caffè Nero, treat myself to a caramel latte, and phone them on my mobile to ask which ward Robin is on. Shawford; visiting three to eight. Easy.

Claire casts the die when she texts. She and Sasha have bumped into a friend from college and they want to go to her house for the afternoon. I offer to pick them up at five so I'll have to come back to Winchester anyway. I go home. I have lunch. I wonder what to wear. In the end I decide not to change in case Claire notices. I don't want to tell her about my search for Robin in case it all goes pear-shaped. I have a horrible feeling it will, but the last few days have made me realise that perhaps the way I behaved years ago is at least in part responsible for Robin's predicament. I have to see if there's anything I can do to put that right.

The thought keeps me going all the way to the hospital

and then to the ward. The Christmas tree on the reception desk winks at me as I wait for a nurse to pass. I ask her where I can find Robin. If she is surprised that he has a visitor she doesn't show it and I traipse after her almost to the end of the largest room on the ward.

There are green curtains with a horrible zigzag pattern around the bed and she peeps inside before pulling them part way back.

"Someone to see you, Robin, love," she says.

He is propped on a mound of pillows, holding an oxygen mask over his face. His eyes flicker with surprise. He closes them.

"Would you rather I came another time?"

He pulls the mask away to speak and there is a ghost of a smile. "I thought I was hallucinating – I'm pumped so full of drugs I might be."

"And we're going to keep pumping them into you until you can breathe properly again, so you might as well lump it." The nurse laughs as she pulls the curtain back around us and it makes me feel more comfortable.

I perch on the chair next to the bed.

"So, how are you?"

"Better than I was. Chest infection coupled with hypothermia. They've only just stopped checking to see if any of my toes have dropped off."

He's making a joke of it but my eyes fill with tears. This is so rubbish. I have to be strong.

"Thank you for coming, Izzie," he wheezes. "I meant what I said about hallucinating. I really thought I was."

"I wasn't sure you recognised me at the Buttercross."

The plastic digs into my fingers as I grip the edge of my seat.

"Soon as you walked into me; you haven't changed that much."

"It's twenty years…" I venture.

"I know. What have you been doing all that time? You have a daughter? A husband?"

"I have a wonderful daughter, Claire, but her father died at the end of August."

"Oh, Izzie, that must be so tough."

"Well we're through the worst of it now… first Christmas and all that. You'd know." I bite my lip; should I have said it?

"First Christmas, first birthday, first anniversary – but you move beyond it, Izzie, really you do."

Robin's speech is becoming more laboured and he reaches for the oxygen mask.

"Am I tiring you?" I ask.

"A bit – but I haven't had a visitor before. Makes me reluctant to let you go."

He is speaking between gulps of oxygen. I want to touch his hand but the drip is in the way. "I'll come back tomorrow."

"Really?"

"Yes."

He nods, and with the mask over his face, closes his eyes. I slip through the curtain and almost collide with a metal trolley stacked with cups. Apologising to the woman pushing it, I hurry away.

Chapter Seventeen

Claire is so full of her day that she doesn't ask about mine and I'm glad. It's not that I want to hide Robin from her, exactly; it's just hard to come to terms with them colliding on the same page of my life.

I need to see Robin again before I come clean with Claire but I don't know how to lie to her. I toss and turn most of the night but I'm saved when over breakfast she asks, somewhat tentatively, if I'd mind her going over to Sasha's for tea and maybe even to sleep over if I won't get too lonely. I don't know why she worries but I assure her I'll be fine and as it's a nice, crisp day, suggest we go for a walk in the New Forest and have a pub lunch together first. It'll be time away from this memory-ridden house – I can't quite square the Robin thing with Connor's ghost either.

If anything I'm even more nervous about my second visit to the hospital. After dropping Claire at Sasha's I go home and this time I do get changed and put on a bit of makeup. Nothing dramatic: a nice embroidered T-shirt and cardigan over my jeans, with just a touch of mascara and lip gloss. I feel I should take Robin something but I don't know what. I don't know what he likes to eat these days, whether he reads, if there's anything he needs. In the end I opt for a chocolate orange – pretty safe ground at Christmas.

It's past seven o'clock when I reach the hospital. This time I find Robin's bed without assistance but he doesn't raise his head from the local free-sheet folded on his lap until I speak.

"Hello Robin. How are you today?"

In truth he seems better, but mainly because his beard is tidier and now his hair has been washed I can see it hasn't lost its chestnut sheen.

"Izzie, it's you. I didn't look because every time I have, it's been someone else."

Something catches in my throat. Has he really been waiting for me to come since three?

"I had to drop Claire off at one of her friends' first," I explain. He smiles.

"Oh, no, I'm not saying you're late – I just thought you'd changed your mind."

"Not at all."

I move the plastic chair closer to him and sit down.

"Well a lot of people would have. It's not everyone who spends Christmas visiting a tramp in hospital."

"I'm not visiting a tramp. I'm visiting a…" I pause, groping for the right words. "An old friend."

He shakes his head. "It's been such a long time."

"Too long?"

"Well we can find out, can't we? Or we can start again from scratch." A pillow slides towards me as he eases himself up the bed.

"What, like we know nothing at all about each other? Like nothing ever… happened?" As I wait for his reply, to my shame I know which option I'd prefer. And Robin chooses it.

"It's very nice of you to visit me, strange lady, but who are you?"

"Who…?"

"Name, rank, number… life story…" He says it as though he's playing a game, but at the same time he is pulling his mask towards him.

"OK," I say, "I'll talk, you listen. And try to stay awake."

As he takes a draught of the oxygen he raises his eyebrows. Whoever he is, I like this man.

"My name is Isobel O'Briain and I'm forty-four years old. I live in Bishop's Waltham with my wonderful daughter, Claire. She's almost seventeen and she's studying for her A-levels at Peter Symonds. I'm a teacher myself – I work at Fareham College – everything from adult numeracy to A-level maths.

"I did a degree in pure mathematics at Bristol University then I moved to Southampton and worked selling office supplies for a while. Then I got on a teacher training course but I'd only been working for a year when I had Claire. We didn't have much money so I went back to work as soon as I could but Connor – her father – was a musician so he worked irregular hours and between us and the crèche at the school it worked out fine.

"We moved to Bishop's Waltham when she was eight and we've been in the house ever since. It's a nice house, and we had a nice car and nice holidays..." I find my voice cracking. Oh God, why do I have to be so frigging weak?

Robin takes the oxygen mask away from his face. "I'm sorry, Izzie. I didn't mean it to hurt. It was thoughtless of me; it must all be so raw."

I try to stop my voice from shaking as I say, "Well, you'd know."

"Yes, and I also know the pain doesn't go on forever. You have to believe that – hold onto it. It took me too long to find out for myself."

I bow my head. If only I'd understood back then.

"Come on," Robin wheezes, "let's think about something else. I couldn't finish the crossword in the paper. Can you help me?"

The rest of the hour passes quickly. I leave Robin with his chocolate orange and promise I'll be back the next day.

Chapter Eighteen

It's more by luck than judgement that I find the right opportunity to tell Claire about Robin. Sasha's mother drops her home just as I'm finishing my second cup of coffee and trying to come to terms with the thought of breakfast. She breezes into the kitchen and gives me a big kiss before her eyes lock onto the wine bottle on the table. It is three-quarters empty.

"Oh, Mum," she says, "I hate thinking of you sitting here on your own all evening."

"Don't be silly. I had a couple of glasses on Boxing Day and there's a couple left for tonight. And anyway, I wasn't here all evening; I went out."

She gapes at me. "Where?"

"Remember that tramp we saw before Christmas, the one I knew from years back? Well you were right, Claire. I did want to know what happened to him. And he's in hospital."

She leans against the work surface, biting her bottom lip as she processes the information.

"How did you find out?" she asks after a few moments.

"It wasn't that hard. I just contacted a few of the hostels in Winchester and someone told me he'd been taken ill."

"What's wrong with him?"

"Pneumonia and hypothermia. He told me they've only just stopped checking none of his toes have fallen off." I laugh, encouraging her to do the same.

"He's got a sense of humour, then?"

"Claire, Robin is an articulate, intelligent man." I stand up and open the bread bin. Time for some toast.

"Then why is he on the streets?"

"I don't know."

"Didn't you ask him?"

I look up from cutting a thin, thin slice. "He's on oxygen most of the time; it's hard for him to talk. I didn't stay long. But I'm going again; there's no one else to visit him."

"Oh, Mum, you are lovely. There aren't many people who'd spend their Christmas break visiting a tramp." It's more or less exactly what Robin said.

Visiting is one thing but the next time I go in they're thinking about discharging Robin and it's hard for them to find somewhere for him to go. He doesn't actually tell me this. There's a nurse talking to him about it when I arrive and it's clearly a problem; he can't go back on the streets. Night hostels are apparently exactly that and with council departments more or less closed it's difficult to see where the funding for anything else would come from.

After the nurse leaves, Robin and I talk about other things, but the ugly grey elephant looms large between us. I've bought him *The Times* and we struggle with the crossword together, failing miserably. I stop in a lay-by on the way home, and as I watch the dusk fall I wonder if I'm going to fail him miserably again.

If I was on my own I would have no hesitation in asking Robin to convalesce in my home, but it isn't fair on Claire to expect her to live with a stranger, however temporarily. And I hardly know Robin now. What sort of man would I be bringing into close contact with my teenage daughter? It's really too stupid to contemplate – and yet I am. A sunny, freckly Robin on the beach at Kimmeridge flashes through my mind – and then a monosyllabic depressive, unable to get up for work in the mornings, incapable of holding down his job.

I'm getting nowhere. The tip of my finger is sore from drawing figures of eight on the rough plastic of the steering wheel. I start the engine and make my way home.

———————

I am in the kitchen making a cup of tea when Claire strolls downstairs.

"How was Robin today?"

"Improving all the time. They're even beginning to talk about discharging him."

She puts her head on one side. "Where do homeless

people go when they leave hospital?" She's studying sociology; I could have guessed she would be interested.

"It's a problem. If they sent him back onto the streets he'd be ill again before you know it. I think the current plan is to wait for a space to come up in a care home where there'd be some council funding."

"That sounds pretty grim." She helps herself to a biscuit.

"It does, doesn't it?"

"And there really isn't anywhere else he could go? None of the hostels or anything?"

"I think they're pretty inflexible." I remember the woman at Hyde Street. "They're just not geared up for people to be there during the day. Health and safety or something."

Claire is wearing her outraged sixth-former face. "But that's so wrong," she exclaims. I nod.

"I know, and Robin's really embarrassed about it too."

"Why can't he come here?"

I am open mouthed. "Claire, you've never met him and I haven't seen him for twenty years; it would be inviting a stranger into our home."

"But you're going to see him every day…"

"That's not the same."

"Yes, but he can't be a stranger anymore."

"Claire, he is. I know nothing about him at all."

"You'd find out if he was here. You said you wanted to." There is challenge in her eyes.

"Not at any price. He could have a criminal record, be a drug addict… anything."

"You told me he was intelligent and articulate."

94

"He is. I'm just not taking any risks with your safety, that's all."

"Hah! So if you were on your own you'd do it?"

I pass her tea and sit down. "Yes, I think I probably would. But I'm not. And that's all there is to it."

"Mum, will you just let me meet him?"

"It won't change my mind, you know."

"I'm not saying that. I guess…" She turns her mug in her hands. "I guess… I'm curious too."

Chapter Nineteen

Robin is sitting in the chair next to his bed wearing a standard-issue striped hospital dressing-gown over an unmatched pair of pyjamas which don't quite reach his ankles. They ride up even further as he struggles out of his seat to greet us. The ward feels unbearably stuffy and I loosen my scarf.

"Please excuse the uncoordinated manner of my dress. Beggars quite literally can't be choosers and I haven't had conventional nightwear in my wardrobe for quite some time."

I don't know where to put myself but Claire laughs out loud. "Mum said you had a sense of humour."

"You must be Claire." He puts out his hand and she shakes it. "I'm very pleased to meet you."

To my shame, I find I am scanning his face for signs of lust.

I swallow hard. "How are you today?" I ask.

He beams at me. "Big improvement. I've hardly had to

use my oxygen and the drip's come out too. They've decided I'm well enough to take my medication in horse-sized tablets instead."

Claire's attention is caught by the newspaper on his bed. "You read *The Times*?"

"Only when your mother's kind enough to bring it for me and even then I can't say I've gone from one cover to the other; I sort of cherry pick."

"So which bits do you like best?" She perches on the edge of the bed, close to his chair. I continue to hover.

"Well, let me tell you the bits I didn't read – it's easier. Sport, for a start, leaves me completely cold and the business news isn't especially relevant to me either. Nor the court circular to be fair. But other than that it's always useful to catch up with what's going on in the world. Gives you a few conversational gambits when you're lucky enough to have visitors. What do you think of *The Times*, Claire?"

"I prefer *The Independent*. They wrote an obituary for Dad. It was really weird reading it but I was very proud, all the same."

"Your mum said he was a musician but I didn't know he was a famous one." He looks up at me and smiles.

"He wasn't exactly famous but he was leader of the Bournemouth Philharmonic Orchestra and credited with developing concert programmes that made classical music accessible without dumbing it down."

"Claire, you're more or less quoting now." I shift from foot to foot; I haven't often heard her talk about Connor, certainly not in this way. Maybe she's making sure that

Robin knows he was a wonderful man. Maybe she's warning him against stepping into Connor's territory?

Robin's gaze drops back to Claire. "Well it must be nice to have a father you can be so proud of."

"What did your father do?" she pounces.

"I don't know. I never knew who he was." I am amazed at both his reply and his frankness. I am about to chastise Claire for her probing but I don't want to appear an old harridan in front of Robin, and anyway, he changes the subject himself.

"So are you musical as well, Claire?"

"No. Dad did let me try his violin a few times when I was little but I couldn't get the hang of it. He thought it was funny but Mum said I made a horrible noise."

"You did too, Claire. All scratchy and—"

"Oh, hello Robin. I see you have visitors." A woman clutching a buff-coloured file has materialised on the other side of his bed.

Robin turns to her, sounding uncertain. "Yes, I have. But... can I help you?"

"It's me who's going to be helping you, Robin. I'm Sylvia. I'm from social services and I've just been assigned to your case."

A flush of colour rises up Robin's neck under his beard. "I'm not sure why..."

"People in your position need support, Robin. We can't just let you go back on the streets when you're discharged." Her voice is like treacle; I can see why it's sticking in his throat.

"No, I'll be fine... I'll... work something out."

"I'm afraid that isn't an option."

"Whyever not?" The sound of my voice surprises me, as does Claire's thumbs up behind Sylvia's back where only I can see.

"Robin is a vulnerable person." Sylvia rolls the last words around her tongue with relish.

"In what way?"

She looks at me with pity. "He's homeless."

"No, he's not." It's all I can do not to gape at Claire as she butts in. "He's coming to stay with us."

"Is that right?" Sylvia clutches the file in front of her as she looks to me for confirmation.

"Yes, yes it is."

Robin reaches for his oxygen mask.

"Oh, well, in that case… I'll just tell the discharge nurse on my way out."

Claire turns and watches as Sylvia retreats up the ward. When Robin looks up he is trying not to laugh. "Thanks for getting me off the hook, but I won't hold you to your offer."

I want to ask him where he thinks he's going to go.

As we're walking past the ward reception one of the nurses stops me and thanks me for giving Robin somewhere to stay.

"It was getting to be quite a problem," she explains. "And he's such a nice man. None of us wanted to see him back on the streets again." She puts her hand on my arm. "You really are a true friend."

I smile and walk on.

As soon as we round the corner I turn on Claire. "Now look what you've done."

She gives me her butter-wouldn't-melt-in-my-mouth look that used to twist her father around her little finger. "What do you mean?"

"Telling that social worker Robin was coming to us."

"But she was awful, Mum. I thought I wanted to be a social worker, but if they're all like that... sticking their noses in..."

"From what I've seen today you're perfectly suited to it."

She sticks her hands in her pockets. "I didn't mean any harm. I just wanted to get her off his back."

"Well you did that most effectively. But now where do you think he'll go?"

"He'll find somewhere... or... he could, you know..."

"Claire, grow up!" I don't even wait for her to follow me down the corridor. I'm out of here.

Chapter Twenty

Given Robin sleeps in the car most of the way to Bishop's Waltham, it was never likely he'd "hop out around the corner" as he so hopefully put it before we left the hospital. As we pull up in front of the house the living room curtains are open and the TV flickers in the grey afternoon. Just as Robin opens his eyes, Claire bobs up from the sofa and waves.

It takes every shred of energy Robin has to cross the drive, but instead of sitting in the lounge for a while he insists he'd be better off in bed. I don't doubt it, but he only gets about a third of the way up the stairs before he loses his breath. I make him sit down and wait.

"I'm a pathetic old man, Izzie," he grumbles. "What the hell have you taken on?"

"Oh don't worry," I tell him. "In a couple of days you'll be running up them two at a time."

He grunts. He's probably too short of air to waste it replying to stupid remarks.

Claire and I move around the house like a pair of church mice until about six o'clock when Robin turns up in the kitchen. His clothes are respectable, if not particularly clean, and it seems tactless to offer to wash them straight away. I'd rather live with a faint tang of sweat than cause offense, and thankfully Claire keeps her mouth shut as well.

I make spaghetti bolognese for tea and soon the scent of garlic and onions fills the kitchen. As I cook I pour myself a glass of wine, but Robin refuses to join me because of all the tablets he's taking. It seems overly cautious and it makes me wonder how long his problems with drink continued. Claire plays the gracious hostess and offers him a cup of tea instead.

Robin eats as though he is savouring every mouthful. In hospital he was surprisingly talkative but the change of environment seems to have silenced him and I remember how he was in the latter part of our relationship. Is the good-natured Robin an accomplished act? I can see Claire is troubled by his manner too.

Once he has finished, Robin pushes himself to his feet and leans on the back of his chair. "I'd offer to load the dishwasher but I need all my energy to crawl up those stairs. I can't remember feeling so bushed. I'm sorry."

I am overcome by guilt for my less than charitable thoughts. Claire beams up at him. "That's OK. The dishwasher's my job. Mind you, I've got plenty of other chores I'd be more than happy for you to take on. Perhaps we can negotiate when you're feeling up to it?"

Robin smiles back and wheezes. "Tomorrow you can give me a list."

Chapter Twenty-One

Robin

I stared at the blue and white curtains, struggling to think where I was. I experienced a moment of waking, being unsure, then pure disbelief as I watched the honeysuckle clamber up and down the stripes. No, not drug induced. I was in Izzie's house. If I listened carefully I could just hear her voice in the kitchen below.

I picked up my watch from the white melamine bedside table. 9:30 on December 31st. Izzie probably had plans for tonight. I needed to be on my way.

My feet landed on the softness of carpet but it didn't help my legs to feel any more stable. I shuffled along to the bathroom like a geriatric and once I'd locked the door behind me, I had to sit on the toilet seat for some minutes just to catch my breath. Standing under the shower was too much and as I sunk into the bath I realised I wasn't going anywhere today – or even maybe tomorrow.

It seemed to take forever to haul myself into my clothes, but Izzie was still in the kitchen, drinking a mug of tea.

"How are you feeling this morning?" she asked.

"Pathetic." I slumped into a chair. "I wanted to be out of your hair today but it's taken me half an hour just to get dressed."

To my surprise she laughed. "Don't you think that's a tad ambitious?"

"I don't want to be any trouble. Certainly not spoil your New Year's."

She stood up to fill the kettle. "Tea? Coffee?"

"Tea please."

"And how would you like it?"

"White, no sugar please."

"Bacon butty?"

My mouth was watering but I shook my head. "I don't want to be any trouble."

"I was going to make one for myself."

My resistance crumbled and I smiled. "Go on then."

"Do you still like ketchup?"

How on earth had she remembered?

I cradled my mug in my hands and watched as she moved around the kitchen. She hadn't changed much over the years; I would have known her anywhere. Maybe the blue of her eyes was softer and of course there were lines around them now... The light from the fridge made a halo of her hair as she rooted around for the bacon and I wondered again if the drugs were making me hallucinate. I shook my head.

"What's wrong?"

"I think it must be the tablets. I feel a bit lightheaded."

"You'll be better once you've eaten."

Izzie was right – although eat and sleep was about all I could manage that day. Claire was going out with her friends but Izzie had no plans to see in the New Year. When I thought about it, I understood.

"I expect you'll be glad to see the back of 2006," I said.

"It's been tough. An awful year. Worst one since... well, for a very long time."

I nodded. "For me too. I... I lost someone as well."

Izzie tried to cover her surprise but the speed with which she looked down at the table gave her away.

"Not in the same way you have," I hurried on. "Not a life partner. But someone precious all the same."

"Really?" Her voice was flat, her eyes full of her own sorrow. Perhaps... perhaps I could distract her.

"I don't suppose you remember Jennifer?"

"Jennifer? The woman who lived by the fairy tree?"

I nodded.

She drew a circle in the crumbs on the table. "I didn't realise... you kept in touch with her?"

"No. I went away. My mother died... anyway, eventually I came back. But it's a long story... Perhaps for another time?"

"Tell me, Robin. Tell me when you came back."

And so I did.

———

The train journey from Newquay to Southampton was disjointed. The closer I got to the south coast the worse the disruption became. I slept on the station at Salisbury then found a bus to Winchester, another to Eastleigh, then walked the rest of the way.

By the time I rounded the bend in the road by the Horse & Jockey it was every bit as bad as I'd imagined: not a tree left standing on the banks of the creek, just a mass of vegetation so tangled I'd have needed a machete to get near the fairy tree.

Instead I walked along the road. It was almost a week after the storm so the pavements were clear, but looking into the gardens I could see small trees and shrubs uprooted and in one place a garage roof had been ripped clean away. The lane next to Burridge Cricket Club was blocked so I walked across the pitch instead, and for the first time had a clear view of the top end of the wood. The damage here wasn't so bad and there were still a number of trees standing. I couldn't see whether the fairy tree was one of them.

I skirted along the edge of the field. Sometimes I had to make lengthy detours around fallen trees but eventually I reached a place where I should be able to see the fairy tree if it was still upright. I braced myself for the worst but there had been some sort of miracle and there it was, climbing from amidst the wreckage strewn around its base. I could see it had lost a branch, torn away by a stricken neighbour, but otherwise it seemed to be intact. I stood at the top of the wood for a long time, just staring at it.

A pheasant's call reminded me I couldn't stand there

forever – it was mid-afternoon and I had next to no money –
so where was I going to spend the night? I had a backpack
full of camping gear and a wood full of fallen trees so I
scrambled down the slope, past the thin ends of horizontal
branches, and into the scrub below. The air was heavy with
the sweetness of sap; every time I've split a log since I've
remembered it.

Close to the fairy tree the tops of two beeches had
crashed together in a massive tangle. I took off my rucksack
and burrowed underneath. Progress through the labyrinth
of branches was slow as I had to snap off twigs left, right,
and centre. A few feet in, I found a gap which could be
made just about big enough to sleep under, but when I
rolled on my back it was clear that the shelter it would
provide from any rain would be minimal. In a reversal of
their normal uses, I stretched my waterproof groundsheet
on top of the branches and used my tent to cover the
crushed vegetation that had become my floor.

Having constructed a makeshift shelter, my next priority
was food and drink. Daylight was fading fast and my way
down to the Hamble was so blocked that I knew it was
pointless even trying. I had a packet of biscuits in my
rucksack but I was getting thirsty. I thought for a while then
remembered seeing a cattle trough in the field. It was almost
completely dark when I slipped out and filled my billycan. I
came back, boiled the water, sipped most of it while it was
hot to keep out the chill, ate a few biscuits, then wrapped
myself in my sleeping bag and fell asleep.

Over the next few days I was able to make some
modifications to my new home – including the addition of a

corrugated plastic roof which looked as though it had blown off someone's shed. I also beat a path down to the Hamble for water, but the issue of food loomed large. I counted out every last note and coin I had; it totalled £42 and even carefully eked out it wouldn't last long.

I knew I couldn't live in the woods indefinitely but I couldn't think of anywhere else to go. I must have known a couple of dozen people living within a few miles but on not one of their doorsteps could I imagine turning up, filthy, homeless, and out of work. Not even Auntie Jean would have wanted to see me like that.

I tried fishing in the Hamble but to no avail. Then one day I found a rabbit caught in some barbed wire. It was barely alive so I knew the kindest thing was to finish it off, and although it was a skinny little thing it was a welcome source of protein to supplement the bread and cans of cut-price baked beans I'd bought from the local shop. The way it met its end got me thinking and I spent hours trying to create what I hoped would be an effective yet humane snare from a piece of wire I borrowed from the cricket club fence.

Effective it was – humane it certainly wasn't. The very first morning I was confronted with a snarling fox, its foreleg almost torn right through in its struggle to escape. I was mortified, and I stood for a long time trying to work out what to do. I jumped out of my skin when I heard someone say, "I hope you're not thinking about setting it free; that old bugger's been in my chicken coop one time too many."

I looked up and about ten yards further up the slope was a woman in a hooded anorak. I couldn't see her face but I knew her voice instantly. It was Jennifer. I just hoped she wouldn't recognise me.

"I don't know what to do with it, to be honest," I told her.

"Then don't do anything. Just wait while I fetch my gun."

It didn't even cross my mind to run away; she had told me to stay and I did, watching the fox lick the open wound. At least it would be out of its misery soon.

When Jennifer came back she told me to climb the slope and stand next to her.

"I'd hate to smatter you with shot too," she told me. Once again I did as she asked and she dispatched the fox with startling efficiency before turning back to me. "I wondered who was living in the woods when I saw the corrugated roof. It's Robin, isn't it?"

I nodded.

"Well I have to say that you look very cold and wet, and if you were hoping to catch some breakfast in that snare you're probably hungry too. Come up to the house, get yourself and your kit dry, and have something to eat."

"I c-can't," I stammered. "It's too much."

"Nonsense. It's the very least I can do for you."

I was wet, cold, and hungry and satisfying those basic instincts had almost taken over, but still I hesitated. She gave me a little push.

"Go on then, get your stuff – all of it, mind – but don't take all day because I don't want to catch my death waiting for you."

I scrambled down the slope and crawled into my lair. I

had some dry clothes in a bag at the bottom of my rucksack and I rolled up my tent, sleeping bag, and groundsheet and stuffed them on top, grabbed my billycan and raced back to where Jennifer was waiting.

She nodded her approval. "Come on then," she said, and tucking her gun under her arm she led me to the top of the wood and out over the field towards her house. I followed in silence.

Once we were inside she showed me to the same bathroom I'd used that day with Izzie. Reluctant to go in, I waited while Jennifer fetched shampoo, conditioner, soap, towels, and a dressing gown.

"Do you have clean clothes?" she asked, and when I nodded she told me to give them to her. "They're probably damp. I'll hang them over the Aga to air while you get cleaned up. Then we'll put everything else in the washing machine."

I showered as quickly as I could then put on the dressing gown before going downstairs. I stopped at the closed door of the kitchen. On the other side I could hear Jennifer moving around and smell onions cooking. I felt frozen to the spot.

We both jumped when she opened the door and saw me standing there.

"Robin, are you all right?"

I managed a "yes" and propelled myself past her. My clothes hung on the rail above the Aga. I tried to work out the possibility of grabbing them and making a dash for the door.

"Right then," said Jennifer, "we'll have some soup. I

hope you don't think I'm being mean but it's not a good idea for you to eat too much – your tummy's probably not used to it. So we'll have a proper meal later on. Go on, sit yourself down while I dish up."

I perched on the edge of a chair and watched while she ladled out the soup. Onions and herbs filled the air, making my mouth water. When she put a bowl in front of me it was all I could do to stop myself from falling on it like some sort of animal, but I waited while she cut us both a chunk of bread and sat down herself.

"It's OK, Robin, you can start," she told me. But instead of eating I put my head on the table and wept.

I heard her chair scrape back and felt her hand on my shoulder.

"Oh, you poor boy," she murmured, and that made me cry all the more. She moved my bowl away. "Don't you worry," she told me. "You get it out of your system and we'll eat when you're ready."

Eventually I did stop, but I didn't know how to lift my head. It was Jennifer who told me to go and wash my face while she reheated the soup, and this time I did eat it, sipping it slowly through chattering teeth.

When I had finished she made a pot of tea while I rescued my clothes from the rail and got dressed. Jennifer emptied the washing machine and once again the space above the Aga was festooned with my belongings. Then she rooted around in my rucksack and pulled out my sleeping bag.

"This next."

I found my voice. "I need it tonight," I told her.

"I think you should stay here tonight."

"No way. You don't know me." I stared at the knots in the table.

"Well you're not going back into the woods so we'll just have to think of a compromise."

The compromise was the summerhouse. Jennifer led me down the path and, towards the end of the lawn, was a wooden building with a small veranda on the front. It had a gabled roof, a door in the centre, and a window either side, rather like a child's drawing. Inside, it was full of cobwebs. Jennifer gave me a broom and a duster while she went up to the loft to look for a camp bed and an electric heater.

Chapter Twenty-Two

Y ou would have thought that with a full belly and a roof over my head I would have slept like a log, but I didn't. I was probably too tired. I lay awake most of the night wondering why I felt so completely devoid of any emotion. I knew nothing about depression back then and it didn't cross my mind I was ill – I just thought I was being pathetic.

Next morning I stayed in bed until Jennifer knocked on the door.

"I'm off to feed the chickens and collect the eggs. Want to help?"

To be honest, I didn't; I just wanted to lie where I was. But I knew I should do everything I could to be useful so I crawled out from under the blankets, pulled on my jumper and the anorak Jennifer had lent me while mine dried, and followed her across the lawn.

I watched while she released thirty or so chickens from

their coops. Then she explained how much corn they were given and sent me to the outside tap to fetch some water. I broke the ice on top of the two enamel basins they drank from, emptied out the dirty stuff and filled them with fresh water. I spilt some of it on my trousers and the chill seeped through to my legs.

Last of all we collected the eggs. Jennifer looked at me.

"Guess what's for breakfast?" she smiled.

It was as I watched her cut her toast into soldiers that I started to cry again. It was what Mum and I had always done and the memory sliced through me.

Jennifer made no comment until I was calmer. "You seem very sad, Robin," she said.

I shook my head. "No, I don't feel anything and then I cry."

"And how long have you felt that way?"

"I haven't before... Not really."

She dusted the crumbs from her hands onto her plate. "Then what happened to change things?"

What, indeed? I turned my egg cup around on the table again and again before I finally picked up my spoon and cracked the top open, the white and the yellow of the yolk merging into grey.

After breakfast I went to the utility room to look for my tent and rucksack; it was time I was moving on. But they were missing.

"Oh, I'm drying them out upstairs," Jennifer said. "Anyway, you don't need them just yet. I was rather hoping you could help me clear some wood. That dreadful wind knocked down a couple of my apple trees and it's a shame to waste such good fuel."

My labour was the only means I had of thanking Jennifer for her kindness, so I wielded her ancient petrol-driven chainsaw while she stripped away the remains of the leaves and took them off to the compost heap.

Jennifer's land amounted to almost two acres. The chickens had a substantial wire-fenced run but very often escaped into the rest of the garden, scratching around on the lawn and sometimes leaving their eggs in the overgrown shrubbery. All this was on the Hamble side of the house, facing the woods. Most of the rest of the land was to the left as you looked towards the river and half of it was covered with fruit trees. Nearer the house itself was a huge vegetable plot and further away a neglected paddock.

Apart from the vegetables, the only part of the garden which was in any way well looked after was the relatively narrow strip between the front of the house and the road. Behind high beech hedges were a neat lawn and a long rose border. Roses, I was to discover, were one of Jennifer's passions. But back then, in those short November days, I knew as little about her as she did about me.

It took us quite a while to deal with the apple trees. I still felt numb but at least I didn't cry again. Then, while we were having lunch on the third day, Jennifer's phone rang and it was one of the neighbours who'd noticed our tree clearing and wanted to know if I could do some for him too.

"What do you think, Robin?"

"Of course I'll help out." I didn't have anything else to do anyway.

"How much will you charge?" I was stumped. I had no idea and I told her so. "All right," she said, "I'll tell him £5 an hour."

"That's way too much."

"No it isn't; getting people to clear wood at the moment is like hen's teeth. You're a hard worker and he's a pretty wealthy man."

I knew I wasn't worth such a princely sum but the neighbour seemed happy to pay it so I set off up the street with Jennifer's chainsaw. I spent four long days sorting out the mess that two pine trees had made of his shrubbery and came away with £160 in cash. I passed it straight across the table to Jennifer.

"For the use of your chainsaw and my keep."

Carefully she counted out £40 and gave the rest back to me. "I think perhaps twenty-five per cent of what you earn is about the right amount."

I shook my head. "This might be all I earn. You take it; you've been so kind."

"I doubt it. Two more people phoned this afternoon. News of a man with a chainsaw gets around."

I felt myself smiling although I couldn't have said why.

"It's amazing what the ability to earn does for a man's self-respect, Robin. But I suspect the actual working also makes him hungry. Go and wash your hands and I'll dish up our tea."

Over the next few weeks my tangled emotions started to settle down. I felt flat, but it also brought a sort of calm – or perhaps that emanated from Jennifer. Although, as I was to find out, she had troubles of her own.

It was as Jennifer was opening the first of the Christmas cards to tumble through the letterbox that I asked her if she would be seeing her family over the festive season. She set down her paper knife and looked across the table at me, shaking her head.

"No, not anymore." There was such sadness in her voice that I put my toast back on my plate and gave her my full attention.

"Why, what happened?"

"It was after you rescued the boys from the river. Susan was furious with me – said I wasn't fit to be a grandmother and she wasn't going to let me near her children again."

"But surely that was just the heat of the moment. She couldn't really mean it."

Jennifer's voice was even. "She did. Every time I tried to phone she hung up on me."

"That's awful. Doesn't she realise she'll only ever have one mother? It's not worth splitting a family apart for. The boys were OK; it was just a bit of mischief."

"It wasn't just that, Robin – although it was the final straw. Susan and I weren't close anyway and when her father died I did something she found very hard to forgive." Her long fingers reached for the paper knife but she quickly put it down again.

"Am I allowed to ask what it was?"

"I sold most of our land. We had quite a sizeable

smallholding and I couldn't cope with it on my own. But Susan said it had development potential and I'd done the family out of millions of pounds by my stupidity. I hadn't, although she never listened long enough to find that out. But there's no chance of the land going for houses anyway – not this close to a protected wood."

"Falling out over money… That's even worse."

Jennifer shrugged. "That's Susan."

"But what about the boys?"

"They're too young to understand but I miss them dreadfully. They'll forget all about me in time – she'll demonise me, and that will be that." She started to stand.

"Then don't let her."

Her fingers gripped the back of her chair. "How can I not?"

"Write to them. Send them cards and pictures and letters about your life. Perhaps she'll stop them reading them, but maybe she won't. Maybe they'll get to watch for the post. You never know…"

"Do you really think so?"

I wasn't completely sure but I wanted to give her hope. "It's worth a try," I said. Then I got up and walked around the table and gave her a great big hug. It was the moment we started to become close. Never quite a mother and son relationship, but all the same…

But the warmth of the kitchen now was Izzie's not Jennifer's, and I had talked myself to a standstill.

"Izzie," I faltered. "I really am much too tired to carry on. Anyway, I must be boring you rigid."

"No, it's fascinating – but it will keep." Her eyes were full of sympathy. It wasn't what I wanted to see.

I hauled myself up from my chair and shuffled out of the kitchen like an old man.

Chapter Twenty-Three

It made no sense. The trees were bare, a chill mist hanging between them, yet the fleeting glances of Izzie that I caught against the milky sun were yellow; she must be wearing her summer dress. I wanted to catch her. No, I needed to catch her, but in the way of dreams I couldn't. My legs were heavy and lumbering as though they were encased in mud. But I had to reach her, had to stop her. I started to shout her name.

Then her hands were in mine, her voice low and urgent. "Robin, are you all right?"

The strip of light from the landing beat a path to my bed, and sitting on it was Izzie, wearing a pale-blue dressing gown. I couldn't work out why.

"Robin, what's wrong? You were calling me."

"It was a dream," I gasped between breaths that were every bit as laboured as if I had actually been running. "Give me a moment, I'll be OK." But I didn't let go of her hands; I wanted to remember the small coolness of them.

She didn't withdraw either, holding my fingers in hers as I struggled to control my breathing. In the end I started to cough and I had to let go to cover my mouth.

When I recovered myself I apologised for waking her.

"It must have been some dream." It was a question rather than a statement.

"I can't remember. Probably just as well."

A car drew up outside and we heard Claire call her goodnights. Izzie jumped from the bed.

"I'm fine now. Sleep well, Izzie – and thank you."

"And you."

She shut the door behind her and I heard her scurry along the landing.

I listened as the front door opened and shut. Claire took two steps across the parquet floor of the hall and then there was silence until the tap started running in the kitchen beneath me; she must have taken off her shoes. After a little while I heard a creak on the stairs and a click as the strip of light disappeared from underneath my door.

I lay awake for a long while, remembering Izzie's hands in mine and wondering how such strong feelings could survive, untended and largely ignored, for almost half my life. The whole of my life with Jennifer. Talking to Izzie about the early days had been like stirring a muddy pool then watching the silt shift beneath the surface. Shadows and leaves... golden and russet oak leaves... jewels of colour in an otherwise murky world.

I don't remember the date Jennifer took me to find our first Yule log but I would wager it was the 21st of December. It was a bright, frosty morning and I was splitting firewood. The chickens scratched nearby, pecking in the sawdust for the grubs and bugs that my work occasionally released. They were undemanding companions.

I stopped to stretch my back and saw Jennifer approaching across the lawn, carrying a garden trug.

"Fancy a break, Robin? I thought we could walk down to the wood and see if we can find a Yule log."

"Of course, Jennifer. That would be nice." I replied. There was no enthusiasm in my voice but I expect she'd become used to that.

As we walked around the edge of the field I asked her what sort of log we were looking for.

"Oak is the best," she told me. "But ash would do nicely as well. The most important thing is that it fits in the fireplace. We'll know it when we see it."

I remember thinking that it didn't really matter what size it was; one swift blow with my axe would make it fit anyway.

At the corner of the field where the track led down to the Hamble was a holly bush and Jennifer took her secateurs and cut half a dozen pieces, mainly without berries.

"I know people think they're pretty, but they're for the birds really, not for us."

We wandered on towards the Hamble past a mass of fallen trees.

"There were a couple of big old oaks near here," Jennifer

told me. "When they fell, their top branches ended up in the river so I suspect some of them have been washed away."

The tide was on the half and the mud golden with oak leaves. It shimmered in the sun and I turned my eyes skywards, seeing only blue. The white of an egret's wing flashed across the river and as it called, something began to resonate inside me. Colours. I was seeing colours again.

Jennifer led me between the fallen branches, weaving our way beyond the high-water mark. She prodded one piece of wood after another.

"That one looks about the right size," I offered.

She shook her head. "I'll know it when I see it."

She hunted for a little longer while I stared up, up, into the amazing blue, only coming back to earth when she exclaimed, "Robin, that's the one! The one sticking up with mistletoe on the end."

I looked. It was some yards ahead of her, pointing proud towards the sky, a trail of berries wrapped around it like Orion's belt.

I moved forwards. "It'll be easier for me to reach it than you."

"No, Robin. Stop a moment. We have to ask the tree first."

I looked at the devastation around me. "It doesn't look as though it's in much of a position to refuse."

Jennifer's head jerked up and then she began to laugh. Underneath my beard I felt my facial muscles contorting into an unfamiliar pattern.

Jennifer looked at me for a long moment then touched my arm. "I have always believed that human beings are

123

better off when they are in tune with the turning of the earth."

I was getting used to smiling now. "And I'm in tune because it's a bright day and I can feel the greyness lifting?"

"Something like that. Now let's ask the tree, then you can collect our log."

"Ask out loud?"

She shook her head and we stood in silence for a few moments. A pheasant's call split the air, answered by another across the river. Jennifer said nothing more but I knew the moment to edge into what would have been the canopy of the oak. I grasped the log in both hands and brought my weight onto it. It snapped from the trunk with a loud crack and, gathering the trailing mistletoe, I carried it back to Jennifer.

"In the autumn I made some cider," she told me. "I thought I would be drinking it alone to celebrate my Yule log but I'm glad I will be sharing it with you."

I bowed my head.

"Thank you, Jennifer."

Her words meant the world to me.

Chapter Twenty-Four

I slept long into the morning. Izzie was alone in the kitchen when I finally made my way downstairs.

She looked up from her newspaper and smiled.

"Hello, Robin. How are you today?"

"OK, thanks. I thought I might take a walk up the road, get some fresh air. Start my rehabilitation."

"I've got a better idea. How about we have some lunch then go to Netley for a stroll along Southampton Water?"

I hesitated. "It sounds nice, but I'm not sure I'm up to a proper walk and I don't want to spoil it for you and Claire."

She laughed. "I'm not proposing a three-mile hike."

"I reckon I'd be pleased with a three-hundred-yard one."

"OK, then we'll take a flask and the paper and you can do your bit then sit in the car while Claire and I step it out." She stood up and walked towards the kettle.

"No, really, Izzie. I'll just go around the block. You're already doing too much for me."

"It's nice to have you here."

How nice? I sat down with my head in my hands.

"Robin, what is it?" she asked.

I tried to gather my thoughts. "It's all too one-sided. My life's a bit of a mess at the moment – not really the best time to see you again."

There was a short silence before she replied. "I was thinking about it last night. I'd kind of assumed you'd been homeless for ages, but if Jennifer died so recently that's not the case, is it? What happened? Did her family finally show up and chuck you out?"

"No. Not at all. Stephen—remember, the older boy?—he came back years ago." I paused. The memory warmed me a little and I managed to look up. "It was when he was eighteen. He'd quite deliberately chosen to come to Southampton to go to university and practically the first thing he did was come to find his gran.

"It was a beautiful October morning and I was up a ladder at the front of the house pruning one of Jennifer's climbing roses. I didn't hear him come up the drive, but when he spoke and I looked down I knew who it was instantly. In most ways he hadn't changed since he was a small boy – still had that very earnest look and a nose covered in freckles.

"'Stephen', I said, and he looked amazed. I climbed down and introduced myself as his grandmother's lodger, saying I recognised him from her pictures. Then I took him to the corner of the house. Jennifer was cleaning out the chicken sheds and I sent him off across the lawn before going inside to leave them to it."

"So was Stephen jealous of you? Is that what went wrong in the end?"

I shook my head. "Not at all. Over the years we became great friends. No, my current situation's completely of my own making. Just like it was last time."

"It wasn't entirely your fault last time."

It was a comforting thing for her to say, but of course she didn't really have a clue. I was saved from further embarrassment by Claire's footsteps running down the stairs.

In the end we compromised on my exercise. I pottered down the road and back again with Izzie strolling next to me. Then she and Claire would go off for a proper walk.

Afterwards I didn't feel too bad. "When you take the car I'll sweep the drive," I told her. "It's about time I started to earn my keep."

"Oh, no, Robin, it's cold. You have a rest."

"I will after it's done. Now, where d'you keep the brush?"

We went back into the hall and she led me into the garage which was built into the side of the house. It smelled musty and metallic, and to my surprise was almost completely filled by an elderly VW Beetle.

"It was Connor's car," Izzie explained. "Claire wants it for when she learns to drive but no one's touched it since the summer. I need to ask the garage to tow it away to get it going again but I just haven't got around to it."

"Why, is there anything wrong with it?"

"I don't think so – just lack of use. I doubt the engine even turns over now."

"I'll have a go with it, if you like."

Izzie looked doubtful and I backpedalled. "Listen, I know this car is precious to you, but I wouldn't do anything to damage it, honestly."

"It's not that. I'm just surprised you know how."

"I can turn my hand to a lot of things, Izzie."

She tilted her face towards me. "Robin, what have you been doing with your life?"

I bit back a quick-fire *Waiting for you* and told her. "Gardening mostly, but also decorating and general maintenance. Anything anyone would pay me to do, really. And that included keeping a vehicle on the road. Jennifer hated getting ripped off by the garage so we invested in a manual and I learnt to do it myself. For years she had a lovely old Ford Escort estate and when that finally died we bought a nice little VW van between us."

"What happened to it?"

"Eventually it became too difficult to take Jennifer out, certainly on my own. So I sold it. It was a big house; we needed to pay the bills."

"Too difficult? What happened to her?"

I shook my head. "Alzheimer's. It's the cruellest thing, Izzie, to lose your mind."

She touched my arm. "You told Stephen you were her lodger, but you were more than that, weren't you?"

I nodded. "I was so lucky. Most people... another

mother… especially— Come on, Izzie, show me where this broom is and get off on your walk. Then I can make a start on the front garden."

Chapter Twenty-Five

I was still abusing Izzie's hospitality when the first day of term yawned empty ahead of me. I could only lie in bed for so long, listening to the silence that descended after the front door closed behind Izzie and Claire. Water trickled into the tank above me in the loft, and after a while I heard the soft thud of the boiler bursting into life. The coughing fit that assailed me as I put on my dressing gown reminded me why I couldn't make more of it.

Izzie had left a cheery note on the kitchen table but the house didn't welcome me. I took my mug of tea to the living room and perched on the edge of one of the sofas. The coffee table was strewn with junk mail and magazines but I resisted the urge to tidy it. As I looked around, the family pictures on the mantelshelf caught my attention.

Connor, of course, was in every one. The first was of when Claire was a tiny baby, held in the arms of an Izzie who looked less like the girl I remembered than she should have. Same fine blonde hair, just reaching her shoulders, same little upturned nose, but her face was thin and her eyes seemed haunted. But she had a new baby – it must have been lack of sleep. And there was Connor, crouched next to them, a mop of dark hair, a firm jaw and a delighted smile.

I tried to get the measure of the man from the photographs. He wasn't particularly tall; he stayed fairly slim over the years, and he seemed very affectionate given he had his arms around Izzie or Claire in just about every picture. Affectionate or possessive? If it was the latter then maybe it was his presence making me feel unwelcome. It was his house, his wife, his child. I shook my head – that was nonsense. He was gone.

I felt much better once I started work on the Beetle and Connor's malevolent ghost, real or imagined, drifted away. Early in the afternoon I took a walk and managed about three times further than I had the day before. It was progress, but not enough. Certain very important tasks were long overdue.

Claire came home at about four o'clock. The garage door was open and she walked straight in from the dusk, making me jump.

"Hello, Robin," she beamed. "How are you getting on with my car?"

"OK, Claire. She needs a couple of brake pads and I'll have to jump start her off your mum's, but other than that she should be fine."

"Won't she need servicing?"

I wiped my hands on an old duster I'd found under the

sink. "I've done that. There was some oil in the boot, and all the filters and that looked OK."

"Wow. I never had you down as a grease monkey. Dad wouldn't have known which end to hold the spanner."

I laughed. "I gathered that when I finally unearthed the tool kit with the spare tyre – it didn't look as though it had been touched. But if he was a violinist perhaps he didn't want to risk damaging his hands."

She wrinkled her nose. "I never thought of it like that. He was pretty useless around the house and—" She ground to a halt.

I rested back on my haunches. "Is it good or bad to talk about him?"

"Good… I think. It's just that no one seems to want to. It's like he's been forgotten, and so quickly."

"People are embarrassed I expect. They don't know how you'll react if they mention him. But if you start the conversation, I reckon they'll be happy to join in."

"What, even Mum?" Her chin jutted out at an angle of challenge.

"Have you tried?"

"Only once or twice and she always changes the subject. And I don't want to stress her out and make her ill again." She started to unwind the multi-coloured scarf from around her neck.

"What happened last time?"

Claire stopped unwinding and bit her lip. "They said it was depression but it was weird. I suppose I thought depressed people moped around being miserable and crying a lot but she wasn't like that; she just got very forgetful and couldn't cope with anything. Not even everyday things like knowing when to eat, and certainly not work. And she was drinking too much – that couldn't have helped."

"Depression takes many forms, Claire. And I suppose everyone reacts differently to grief." I stood up and stretched. "Come on, if we want to keep Izzie as stress free as possible let's have her tea on the table when she gets home."

Claire beamed up at me. "You're very good for Mum, you know," she said. "The best thing that could have happened to her."

Before I could reply she raced off upstairs to get changed.

Chapter Twenty-Six

Each day I walked a little further; sometimes I went out three or four times. Wearing two jumpers, a scarf, and my coat, even so the frost still bit into my lungs and made me cough. But my muscles were lurching into life again and on Thursday the air smelt different; for the moment, at least, the iron grip of winter was coming to an end.

Friday dawned damp and blustery and I knew I had to take my chance before the weekend. As soon as Izzie and Claire left the house I hurried to get ready and after a quick breakfast of tea and toast I walked down into the town to where I had spied a bus stop.

It was not a long journey to Botley but there I had to wait for another bus to take me towards Curbridge. To pass the time, I mooched around the shops and bought the notepad and pen I needed. I had a little cash but it was running out, though if today went according to plan then I should be able to get by for a while longer. The problem was I had no idea what I would find and the very thought brought a tightness to my chest. I started to cough again.

I got off the bus at the Horse & Jockey and made my way into the wood. The drizzle had stopped but a bank of grey cloud hung over the tree tops, muffling every sound. A lone heron fished on the far bank of the river.

This was not my normal approach to the fairy tree and I was surprised to find how far away the cohorts of little plastic guardians began their watch. It fascinated me, the way children and sometimes adults brought these offerings – things they had treasured but were prepared to leave as a gift for the fairies. It was a nod to paganism that I'd wager few of them would recognise or understand.

The first time I made the link was on a clear February night when I'd followed Jennifer across the garden and down the slope to the woods. When I saw her kneel before the fairy tree I had stopped, hidden by the shadow of the hedge, my mind in turmoil. But then I'd told myself that faith was very personal and so I had crept away.

I'd jumped out of my skin when I heard a knock on the summerhouse door. Jennifer stood there, her anorak hood pulled close over her head and a lighted candle in her hand.

"It was you at the top of the woods?"

I hung my head. "I'm sorry. I went away as soon as I realised it was private."

"It isn't, not really. In the old calendar today is special and I like to mark such things."

I frowned. "Special?"

"It is said that from now on, winter's grip will be less tight on the land, and the days will begin to get longer."

I looked past her into the freezing darkness. "I don't know about that but it's certainly too cold to be standing outside. Come in."

She shook her head and put the candle into my hand, closing my fingers around it. "No, I just came to give you this. Put it in the window and let it burn. My wish, more than anything, is for it to send light into the darker corners of your mind."

I didn't understand but I watched it flicker as I lay on my bed and I think perhaps it soothed me. The next day I returned to the fairy tree and discovered that Jennifer had not only been communing with nature at its foot.

And now I was here on the same mission: not to worship, but to kneel by the little box to collect the children's letters. Although I found out what Jennifer was doing that night, she didn't tell me herself until years later when she slipped on some ice in early December and broke her wrist. She had no option then but to share her secret because at that time of year it was more important than ever the letters were answered.

This Christmas I had let the children down. The box was full to bursting point. I eased the bundle out and stowed the letters in the inside pocket of my anorak. That was the simple part; the next stage of my plan was very much riskier.

Even from the back, the house had a neglected air and I guessed it was probably empty. It wasn't in a bad state of repair – I'd been able to keep that side of things pretty much together – but when you've known a house for years you can tell when things aren't right. I don't remember actually noticing the lack of smoke from the chimney, or the back bedroom curtains still closed at noon, but there was a general sadness about the place that felt infectious.

I stole into the garden, keeping to the line of the hedge. Only the occasional car on the wet road at the front broke the silence. This space had always been alive with clucking and I wondered what had happened to the little flock. Jennifer and I had never fallen into the sentimentality of giving them names, but all the same they had been a big part of our lives and the unexpected emotion I felt at their loss almost drove me back into the woods.

Nevertheless, I crept up to the summerhouse and turned the handle. It was locked. I peered through the window; the dusty furniture and piles of boxes were untouched and that confirmed my impression that the house had not been sold.

The key to the back door was in my pocket and I slipped into the kitchen. The chill air rushed to meet me. All the years I had lived here, the Aga had filled this room with warmth. There had always been flowers too – something seasonal from the garden to cheer and bless our home. I told myself to get a grip. There was no point in crying for Jennifer; in the end, hers had been a blessed release.

I didn't dare put on the light to relieve the gloom. I ran the water for a while, filled the kettle, and made myself a mug of black coffee – mainly to warm my hands. I left it steaming on the table while I went through to the hall.

The pyramid of post spreading across the doormat told me the house had not been visited for some time but I ignored it and made my way upstairs. At the end of the landing Jennifer's bedroom door stood open, the light from her windows spreading across the faded roses on the carpet. With a heavy heart I turned away.

My own room was as I had left it: the plain blue duvet square on the bed, the photo of Mum and me on the chest of drawers next to my deodorant and radio. On the corner nearest the door was an envelope addressed to me in Stephen's handwriting. I fingered it for a while, before pushing it into my pocket.

I was almost afraid to open the drawer. The wood caught on the runners but I gave it a tug and it fell out completely. It didn't matter because there, among the socks scattered across the carpet, was my wallet. The brown leather fell open as I picked it up revealing my bank card, my credit card, two ten pound notes and a book of stamps. Dizziness overtook me and I slumped onto the bed, coughing.

I had what I wanted so I could get out of here. But first I had to do my duty by the fairies. I returned to the kitchen and pulled out the children's letters and my notepad. Each reply had to be different, but they all began with the same apology: the fairies and elves of the forest had been called to help Father Christmas in Lapland and had only just come back home. In the chill of the kitchen I felt the warmth of Jennifer's hand.

It took me a long while to write all the letters, and by the time I left the house it was drizzling again and what little

daylight there had been was fading. Sheltering next to the
garage wall were some snowdrops, so I picked a handful
and set them in a little vase by the silent Aga. Then I locked
the back door and slipped along the line of outhouses,
across the hedge, and into the wood.

Chapter Twenty-Seven

I wondered why someone was tapping a nail into the fairy tree but, as I came to, I realised they were knocking on my bedroom door.

"Robin, are you all right?" It was Izzie.

I struggled to open my eyes. "It's OK, you can come in."

She peered around the door. "I was just a bit worried, that's all."

"No, I'm fine, just overstretched myself today I think."

"You've been into town – shopping, by the look of it." She folded her arms.

"I wanted to say thank you to you and Claire."

"You shouldn't have. You've worn yourself out and spent far too much money. It's not necessary."

The inflection in her voice put me on my guard. I asked her what was wrong.

"Nothing. It was just odd, that's all, coming home to a dark house with... with flowers and wine and chocolates in the kitchen and not you."

"Well I'm here."

"I didn't know that," she burst out. "Your coat wasn't on the hook and I thought... I thought... you'd gone away... especially when I saw that stuff. It was a horrid trick to play."

"Izzie, it wasn't a trick. I was just so exhausted I—"

But she was gone, running along the landing and slamming her bedroom door behind her.

I looked at my bedside clock: half past seven. I wondered where Claire was, then remembered that she was at the cinema with her friends. I stood and stretched, picked up my anorak from the bedroom floor, and hung it in the hall on my way to the kitchen. If Izzie hadn't eaten then my very simple plan was to cook a meal to entice her back downstairs.

She may not have eaten but she had certainly had a drink. Although the bottle of wine I'd bought was untouched, a tumbler was abandoned on the draining board next to a bottle of tonic water. I picked it up and sniffed it. Gin.

In the fridge were a couple of peppers and some eggs. I found an onion in the vegetable rack and started to fry the vegetables. Once they were ready I turned off the gas and went to find Izzie.

To my surprise she was sitting in the darkened living room.

"Are you hungry?" I asked "I'm making an omelette as a peace offering."

"It's me who should say sorry." The only light came from the kitchen and it was impossible to read her expression.

"No, I should have left a note. I should have realised you'd come in and wonder, and that you'd be tired too after your first week back at work."

"It was fun to be back at work," she replied, tilting her chin. "But it was knackering all the same."

I put my hand on her shoulder. "Come and have something to eat."

She nodded and followed me into the kitchen and poured herself a glass of wine.

While I finished the omelette she put the tulips in a vase. "They're lovely, Robin. I can't remember the last time anyone bought me flowers, but you really shouldn't have spent the money."

"It's OK. I have some money now – just a bit, but enough for me to buy some thank yous and to pay my way."

Izzie's eyebrows furrowed. "But if you had money, why were you on the streets?"

"I have some money now – I didn't then. Well, not enough." I forced a laugh. "I had all of sixty quid in my pocket and that wasn't going to get me very far."

"But what happened today? How come you've got money now?"

I somehow managed to overcome my embarrassment. "I finally plucked up the courage to go back to Jennifer's and pick up my bank card."

"You mean you actually lived on the streets rather than go back there? Why the hell would you do that?"

I focused my attention on the omelette, taking it off the

gas and halving it, sprinkling some grated cheese and putting it on our plates.

"Why, Robin?"

"I just didn't feel I could." It was only half the story, but it was the best I could manage. To deflect her attention I asked her about her day.

"You don't want to tell me, do you?"

I put down my knife and fork. "It's not that I don't want to tell you," I lied, "I just don't want to talk at all at the moment."

"When it was bad, you never did."

I didn't understand what she meant but I guessed she was still spoiling for a fight. "Izzie, please, let's not argue. We're both tired and it isn't worth it. Ask me again when I've got a bit more mental energy and I'll tell you exactly what happened, I promise."

She drained the last of her wine and stood up. "You have changed, Robin, but for the better. I'm off to bed now. Goodnight."

I was left staring at a half-eaten omelette, listening to her footsteps on the stairs, and puzzling over her words.

I was still there when Claire came home. Immediately her eyes fell on the almost empty bottle of wine.

She was characteristically direct. "If you don't mind me asking, how much of that did you drink?"

"None of it."

"Do you not drink for a reason?"

"You mean, am I a recovering alcoholic? No. I've just got out of the habit really – although I have to admit I was toying with the idea of polishing that one off." I picked up

Izzie's plate and started to scrape congealed omelette into the bin.

"Where's Mum?"

"She's gone to bed."

"Was she very drunk?"

I straightened up. "I think she was just very tired."

"You can tell me if she was drunk, you know. I've seen it all before."

"It worries you, doesn't it?"

Claire sat down at the table. "Yes, because she's using it as a crutch and I know that's not a good thing. Do you think that between us we can get her to stop?"

"That rather depends on whether she wants to."

"Well of course she doesn't want to or she wouldn't do it."

I returned to my seat. "Sometimes it's not that simple. We don't know her reasons for drinking and perhaps neither does she. Maybe she doesn't even know you think it's a problem."

"Well I've told her often enough."

I smiled at her. "I expect you have. But I also suspect she wasn't listening."

"She'd listen to you; you're not a child."

"No. I'm a homeless man who up until today was entirely dependent on her charity."

Claire sounded cautious. "What happened today? You're not going anywhere, are you?"

"Today I finally managed to get access to my bank account. I bought your mum some flowers and a bottle of wine – which on reflection might have been a bad move –

and I bought you some Maltesers." I pushed them towards her. "I hope you like them."

"That doesn't mean you're leaving, does it?"

I leant back. "I haven't had that conversation with your mother yet."

"Please don't go, Robin. I... I'm not sure I can cope with Mum on my own anymore."

Her voice was breaking and I reached across the table, her hand vanishing under my own. It hadn't occurred to me what a responsibility it had been for a sixteen-year-old to be living with a mother with depression – especially when she was still struggling to come to terms with her own loss.

"Claire, I don't want to go, but I can't live on charity either. I need to get back on track – get working, earning some money. And I'm pretty much well now. She mightn't want me to stay."

"She will, I know she will," she sniffed.

"Well let's see what she says."

"Will you talk to her tomorrow?"

"I don't know, Claire." I wasn't sure I would be ready to have the whole conversation Izzie would want just yet.

"Oh please, Robin, promise me." She looked so young, so vulnerable, her big grey eyes swimming with tears, that the only thing I could say was 'yes'.

Chapter Twenty-Eight

S aturday dawned crisp and cold, and Claire lost no time in suggesting that Izzie and I should make the most of the weather by going for a walk while she got on with her homework. It sounded like a most obvious ruse to get us out of the house together and I thought Izzie would be suspicious, but instead she said it was an excellent idea, provided I was up to it. With Claire looking daggers at me from under her fringe I had no option but to agree.

We went to Swanwick. It was only a few miles down the Hamble from the fairy tree but it was over a year since I'd been there. Towards the end of her life, Jennifer had been reluctant to leave the house, imagining burglars – or worse – would descend the moment we did, so my world had shrunk to the size of hers.

We parked the car at the top of the creek. The tide was up and two swans glided down the river as we walked along the path to the marina. So we talked about birds, and the boats moored on the opposite bank, and how Izzie had given up rowing when she was expecting Claire – anything to avoid the conversation I knew would have to come. I didn't even know how I was going to start it.

I shouldn't have worried; the moment we decided to go into the coffee shop, money reared its ugly head.

"I'll get these," I told Izzie and immediately she started to argue, right in front of the counter.

"For God's sake, woman, let me have some pride," I hissed and she retreated to a table in the far corner.

I apologised even before I put the tray down in front of her.

"I have some pride too," she told me. "Don't ever speak to me like that again."

"I'm sorry, Izzie," I said. "but I'm getting too uptight about this. We need to sort the money side of things now I'm in a position to do so."

"So how much money do you have in your bank account?" I could see where Claire got her directness from.

"I don't know. A few hundred pounds, I think. I need to get earning again but to do that I need a proper base."

"So you're going to move on?" She started to take our cups off the tray.

"I can't live on your charity, Izzie. You've been amazing already, taking me into your home and letting me get well. And I've loved being with you and Claire, but—"

She cut across me. "You don't have to go."

"Then we need to come to some proper financial arrangement."

"It's really not necessary. Connor's life insurance paid

off the mortgage and I'm on a good salary. I don't need a contribution from you."

"But I need to make one. Can you understand that?"

She was stirring her cappuccino, her spoon scraping the edges of the cup, mixing the froth into the coffee. She looked up at me. "Tell me why you had to leave Jennifer's house in the first place." It wasn't a question, it was a command. But I wasn't ready to share those awful moments yet.

"You know when… when something hurts so much…" And then I thought of Claire.

"You're not going to tell me, are you?" Izzie filled my pause.

I shook my head. "I am. You'll just have to bear with me if I struggle."

In truth it was hard to know how to start. I knew when, of course. It was the moment I found Jennifer dead on her bedroom floor, buttocks and stick-thin legs protruding from under her faded pink nightie. There in the café I could see her; I could hear the hiss of the coffee machine but all I could see was that awful indignity.

"What did you do?" Izzie prompted.

"I picked her up and put her on the bed. Just to be sure… I mean, I knew, somehow, but all the same… It sounds silly, but I tucked her in, and then I went downstairs to phone Stephen, and then the doctor.

"He seemed to come almost at once but I think that was because I'd lost all sense of time. I know that because Stephen and his partner, Gareth, arrived just afterwards and they'd driven all the way from Brighton. I was still in my dressing gown. Stephen was in tears. Gareth kind of took over with the GP but before he left he asked me all sorts of questions. I told him I'd found her in her bed.

"A while later, Gareth suggested I get dressed. Jennifer's bedroom door was closed and I went in one last time and sat beside her. There was peace, Izzie, peace in that room. She had gone and it was right. It made me feel better so I had a shower and wrapped up warm ready to go and feed the chickens.

"When I went back into the kitchen, Stephen had stopped crying and Gareth was explaining that they would be coming to take Jennifer's body away shortly, and asking if he wanted to see her first. I tried to reassure him, telling him she looked very peaceful, but he was unsure, asking Gareth what would happen next. The answer was a post-mortem."

I coughed a few times then cleared my throat.

"You couldn't get me another coffee, could you?" I asked Izzie.

The word *post-mortem* had not so much stopped me in my tracks as sent me hurtling back twenty years. Uncertainty. Suspicion. But Jennifer was old, wasn't she? She'd had Alzheimer's. I asked Gareth why and he said it was routine under the circumstances. What circumstances? But I didn't ask. I put on my anorak and went outside.

The crack as the ice broke on the water troughs in the coop took me back to my first morning at Jennifer's. I almost heard her voice, but when I looked up, of course she wasn't there. Instead an insidious thought took root: I'd found her on the floor, not in her bed. I'd lied. Suspicion. Questions. I couldn't go through it again.

I jumped when Izzie put the mug down in front of me.

"You did look miles away."

"Not miles, years." I sighed. "The long and short of it is that I lost it. I went out to feed the chickens then I decided to go for a walk by the river. When I got back there was a dark-green ambulance in front of the house so I just kept going. I suppose I cracked up again. I never went back."

"But why not? You could have waited until they'd gone out and…"

I smiled at her. "That assumes I was acting even half rationally. And I wasn't. I guess now I've told you, you'll want to think again about asking me to stay."

"Not at all. You mustn't be so hard on yourself, and anyway, you've pulled yourself out of it much quicker than you did after your mum."

"I'm older and wiser. And this time I've found a very good friend."

Izzie looked at the table, her finger tracing a delicate figure of eight. "Last time… I could have supported you better… I…"

"I never gave you the chance."

We sat in silence for a while, lost in our own thoughts, but more than anything I knew I didn't want to lose her again.

In the end she said, "So will you stay with Claire and me?"

"I'd like to, yes. But you must let me pay my way as far as I'm able."

She gazed out of the window towards the river. "Friends don't have to pay."

"Friends share burdens. Friends need to feel like equals. Look at me, Izzie; this is important."

"Did Jennifer always take twenty-five percent of what you earned?"

"Yes."

Finally she turned her head. "Then I'll do the same."

Chapter Twenty-Nine

Izzie

As Robin holds open Jennifer's kitchen door, it seems only a fraction less damp inside than out. Although the scrubbed pine table dominating the room is empty, there are papers and magazines piled to one side of the Aga. On the other is a vase of wilting snowdrops.

Robin looks around and sniffs the air. "Best get that lighted if Stephen's planning to stay." He drops to his knees and starts fiddling with switches and dials. There is a click and he sits back on his haunches.

"Is there anything I can do?" I ask.

"Run the cold water? I'm going to find a fan heater."

It has taken me most of the week to persuade him to come back to collect his possessions but he finally saw sense because if he is to restart his business then he needs his tools. And then, when I came home on Thursday, he told me it was all arranged, and he would meet Stephen at the house on Saturday. Stephen had been pleased to hear from him, he said, and he sounded surprised that that might have been the case. Personally, I suspect Stephen has been very worried about Robin.

As we wait, I wander around the house. In the dining room the table is pushed back against the wall and there are two easy chairs in front of the French windows. I sit down in one and look out at the unkempt garden. Robin follows me, but remains standing.

"I need to get this place straight," he mutters.

"It might make it easier to sell."

"Stephen may not want to sell."

Oh dear. It's not that he's spoiling for a fight, exactly, but he isn't going out of his way to avoid one either. I stretch out to take his hand but he pulls it away and thrusts it into his pocket.

"Don't be like that. I was only trying to… to reach you."

He shakes his head as though he is trying to clear it. "God, I'm sorry Izzie. I'm a nightmare this morning. I'll be OK once Stephen arrives but until then I feel like I'm trespassing."

"I don't see why. It was your home, not his."

He shrugs and turns away.

Luckily, it's not long before we hear a car in the drive. Robin was right when he told me that Stephen hasn't changed since he was eight years old: the same round freckled face with a ready smile, the same sandy hair. He is not a tall man and this adds to the impression of a slightly overgrown schoolboy. He embraces Robin like the long-lost brother he probably feels he is and like me, he only comes up to his chin. If he recognises me as the girl in the yellow dress whose hand he held coming out of the river, he doesn't let on.

Stephen's partner, Gareth, is quite short too, but stocky and dark and reminds me of a pit pony. His strong Welsh accent only re-enforces the image, as does the solid way he pitches in with everything he's asked to do. I like Gareth. And, of course, I like Stephen – especially as his respect and affection for Robin are tangible.

Robin boils the kettle and makes us coffee while Stephen explains why the house has been abandoned.

"My mother's contesting the will. I'm so glad you've shown up again, Robin, not only because, well... but we need all the help we can get to show that Grandma was of sound mind when she made it."

"Of course she was. We got a letter from her consultant to prove it. Your boss insisted on it before he drew it up."

"I know, but we can't find the letter – only a photocopy. Or the original will, for that matter. I think Mother must have hunted around and found them."

"Not a chance. If I'm right about where they are, she'd have to have been quite literally taking up the floorboards."

And with that, Robin disappears and we listen as he races up the stairs two at a time.

Stephen turns to me. "So is Robin all right? I've been so worried about him. He took on so much looking after Grandma and, as the weeks went by and I heard nothing, I began to fear the worst."

I am careful in my response. "From what he's told me he was just exhausted, and then he got ill with a chest infection. I bumped into him just before Christmas so at least he was able to convalesce at my house and he's pretty good now. But how are you coping, Stephen? You've had a big loss too."

"I've got Gareth – that really helps. But then Robin's got you now, hasn't he?"

I'm just pondering his words when Robin gallops back into the room, waving a large brown envelope.

"Here we go, Stephen. I'm sorry but I never gave this a thought. I have to say I'm not a hundred percent sure about what's in here but Jennifer made me hide it when she was going through a particularly paranoid phase."

Stephen spreads the contents on the table. There are three bundles of papers. He unwraps the largest and scans the contents with his quick lawyer's eyes.

"Deeds to the house... brilliant. And the undertaking over the land she sold when my grandfather died. Just as well Mother never found that or we'd never get her tentacles out."

"Why's that?" I ask.

"Because my mother is a grasping, old bat, and if Barry Westland ever sells his fields for development it could be worth a fortune. Now, what else have we here?"

The next bundle contains the will and letters from both Jennifer's consultant and her GP. Stephen sits back in his chair and takes a sip of coffee as he reads them. Then he opens the final parcel of papers and turns to Robin.

"This one's for you; it's Grandma's life insurance policy."

Robin sounds cautious. "What's that to do with me?"

"It's written in your favour. It was sound advice to keep it out of her estate. Apart from the tax considerations, I think she always knew Mother might contest her will and she wanted you to have access to some funds straight away."

"I can't take the money, Stephen. I'll happily help you get what's rightfully yours, but I don't want anything for myself."

"I won't let you go against what Grandma wanted." He looks towards the snowdrops. "I can see you respect her memory, Robin, so respect her wishes too."

Robin looks at the table. "Let me think about it."

"OK, but let me tell you what there is. First, there's the life policy – it's worth about ten grand and that is yours completely without argument. Then, although the house is left to me, the contents are yours. As you know, Grandma didn't have a lot of cash so the residual estate amounts to the few shares I didn't need to sell before she died and the undertaking over Westland's fields – which will probably never amount to anything – and that's split between us. So I have the lion's share anyway."

"Why is your mother fighting the will if the house stays in the family?" I ask.

"Because her precious Toby doesn't get a bean. He never came to see Grandma so she didn't see why he should. And I'm certainly not family anymore as far as my mother is concerned."

"Oh, Stephen, that's so sad. I could never do that to my daughter."

Stephen shrugs. "I'm used to it."

Robin almost topples his chair when he gets up. "I'm going for a walk." I make to follow him. "No, Izzie, on my own." But he sees the expression on my face and his voice softens. "I won't be long, honestly."

I have my back to the window but Gareth stands and I assume he watches Robin cross the lawn.

"He's off to the woods," he says.

Stephen shivers. "Last time I saw him go that way he didn't come back. I wish I'd followed him then."

I draw an arc on the table, my index finger tracing the scratches and knots. "It's what he does. He did it to me... years ago."

Gareth leans against the Aga. "People like Robin don't do it to hurt, or for effect – I've been trying to explain that to Stephen. They walk away when they're so low that they don't believe they matter to anyone. And he seems fine this morning, back to his old self."

Stephen raises his eyebrows. "Ga's a psychotherapist. He can't help himself."

"I was only reminding you, and trying to explain to Izzie, what I think is going on."

I smile at him. "It's interesting. Do you psychoanalyse everyone?"

Stephen laughs. "Of course he does – just not to their faces."

Robin is gone no more than half an hour and when he comes back we walk down to the Horse & Jockey for lunch. We find a table next to the window and when Robin and Stephen go to the bar to order, Gareth excuses himself and heads for the gents. From my seat I can see Robin's back; his fleece stretches across his shoulders and they shake a little when he laughs. As he leans forward his bum juts out slightly, filling his jeans, firm and slightly rounded. I want to touch him, to feel the fabric under my fingertips. A warmth spreads, low in my stomach. I have forgotten this feeling.

He turns his head to speak to Stephen; I see his slightly hawkish nose, chin hidden by his beard. He has a pint in his hand. That surprises me too. I've not seen him drink so far this time, although of course, before…

It was New Year's Eve and I thought the beginning of 1987 would be a good time for Robin to stop moping around and get his act together. We'd had a miserable Christmas; he had refused to come to my mother's but I had flounced off anyway and goodness knows how grim those days were for him, all alone in our tiny flat. From the state of it and him when I came back, I surmised he'd hardly got out of bed. There were two empty whisky bottles in the kitchen.

I flew off the handle when I saw them but Robin didn't fight back. He just sat on the sofa in a daze and then said I was right, he ought to try harder, and he promised he would. I softened towards him then and we had a few days of relative peace so I arranged to go out with friends on New Year's Eve. I even bought a new dress to wear and a new shirt for Robin and he seemed quite pleased.

But on the afternoon of the 31st he refused to go. He didn't give me a reason, just put on his anorak and stormed out of the flat when I started to yell at him. I cried for hours and hours, but I was feeling sorry for myself, not for Robin.

If only I had understood. I went out but it didn't feel right so I came home well before midnight. Robin wasn't there. Eventually he came back, took one look at me pretending to sleep, and spent the night on the sofa.

Before he went out the next morning, he left me a note saying he was a worthless shit and he was sorry for messing up my life. I walked the streets looking for him and eventually found him in the local pub. We spent a couple of hours getting drunk together but it was the beginning of the end.

Chapter Thirty

I push my pillow away for the umpteenth time and swap it for the cooler one beneath. No joy. After a while I pick up my alarm clock and the faint green glow of the hands tells me it's six o'clock. Thank the lord for that. Rain patters steadily against my window; Robin will be able to stay in bed. Lucky him.

A bedroom door clicks open – Claire's. Her footsteps pad along the landing, then not to the bathroom but down the stairs. If she's awake too then we might as well have a cup of tea together. It'd be a good start to the week. I tip my legs over the side of the bed and head for the en suite to clean my teeth.

Light shines from under the living room door but Claire is in the kitchen. I catch her reflection in the dark glass of the window as she stands at the sink. She scrabbles to wrap her dressing gown around her.

"What's up?"

Her head jerks away. "N-nothing."

The evidence on the draining board is slim and hard for me to piece together. A small china bowl and a carton of salt. She has something scrunched in her hand. Her eyes look feverish before they drop away. Drugs? I sink onto the nearest chair.

"Claire, tell me."

She shakes her head. "You'll get mad at me, I know you will."

"Try me."

"What's the point? You go off on one for nothing, so what will you do when it's something?" Her voice is breaking and she rushes past me, but I leap to my feet and grab her arm.

We are eye to eye. How has my baby grown this tall? How come her heaving chest is bigger than mine? But her face reveals a vulnerability that hasn't changed at all.

"Come on," I tell her. "Let's sit down. I promise I won't... go off on one, as you put it."

She crumples onto the chair in silence. I walk over to the draining board and put the kettle on. It's already full of hot water – as is the china bowl. I pick it up and bring it to the table.

"What were you doing with this?"

No answer.

"Claire?"

Without looking up she opens her dressing gown and lifts her pyjama top. The bottoms are pushed down and I can see why; the skin around her tummy button is red and puffy, its anger centred on a tiny diamond stud.

"Where did you have this done?" I fire at her.

"You said you wouldn't go off—"

"I'm not."

"You are and you promised…"

"Don't make this my fault. I'm not the one who went to some filthy backstreet place to get themselves mutilated."

"See! I was right. You don't want to help me, you just want to… I don't know what you want…" Her head falls into her hands and she starts to sob.

"Claire, come on, I'm more angry with whoever did this than I am with you. But that's not the point. I do want to help you, of course I do. I'm your mum. Come on, let me have a proper look."

"It hurts so much," she sobs, "and it's making me feel sick and—"

"Come on, sit up."

She does as she's told. Her skin is hot to my touch and she flinches. The wound around the stud is oozing, but at least the sticky liquid is clear.

"Why the salt water?"

"I texted Sasha last night and her mum said."

Just in time, I bite back more vitriol. I steady my voice. "I think TCP might be better; there's some in the bathroom. And perhaps take some Nurofen too. You sit quiet while I get them."

But she doesn't listen even to that. Instead, by the time I've come back downstairs there are two mugs of tea on the table. It's a peace offering, so once again I bite my tongue. Claire is brave as I dab on the TCP. I want to take out the stud but she won't let me. If I push it, she'll only argue.

Instead, I hold her hand as we drink our tea in silence.

Chapter Thirty-One

The corridor from the staffroom to my class flips into an upside down tunnel. Strip lights on the ceiling form white lines down the road. I recognise the feeling and stop in front of a notice board. *Breathe, damn you, breathe.* I read the list of names signed up for football. I follow the rungs of the squash ladder. Four weeks into term – seven weeks to go.

The roar of footsteps quietens behind me and I look at my watch. Three minutes past. I have to move. One, two...

"Hello, Mrs O'Briain. I thought I was going to be late. I forgot my homework."

Went out for a sneaky fag, by the smell of his jumper. "You will be late, Alex. Just no later than me."

"Don't you want to give me a head start?" I'm used to his cheek. It's harmless.

"No, but I'm not going to race you either."

He laughs and we set off together, my strides matching his as though my life depends upon it.

The strangeness lurks in my head until I get home. It's not an ache, nor the stuffiness of a cold, nor the lightness of fever. I don't know what it is – but it's there. And it shouldn't be. I need an anchor; I need Claire. I need to know she's OK. I need a hug.

It's Robin who reminds me that Claire's gone to a party and will be staying at Sasha's house.

"Oh… I wondered if she would. She's… not been too well this week."

"Hmmm. She told me yesterday what she'd done. She said the college nurse reckons it's OK though."

"Yes. I was glad she went to see her. I think she was very good with her after Connor died."

Better than I was, probably.

The kitchen smells of mince and onions and there are three five-pound notes on the table. I sit down on the opposite side to them.

"How was the major?" I ask him.

He seems pleased that I remembered. "Suffering with his arthritis, poor old soul. But he's got me another morning with one of his mates from the bridge club."

"That's good."

More fivers to add to the pitiful stash in my bedroom drawer. But on the other hand, perhaps they will fund a few days away at half-term. A break would do me and Claire good. A cottage in Devon or Dorset, perhaps. Maybe Robin would come too. I glance across at him now, one hand clasped around a bottle of wine, the other gripping the corkscrew. I want him to put the bottle down and wrap those arms around me. I want it so much I daren't let it show.

I continue to watch him as he bends to put a homemade lasagne in the oven.

"Do you mind?" I ask him.

"Mind what?"

"All this... domestic stuff?" I pick up my glass.

"Not at all. I feel like I'm pulling my weight. Especially 'til the business takes off again."

"But don't you want more from life, Robin? More than gardening and odd jobs and housework?"

He leans against the sink and folds his arms. "Once upon a time, you know I did. But it's too late for all that, Izzie. My degree's twenty years out of date, for a start. Why do you ask? Would you respect me more if I did?"

The question is a bolt from the blue. "Oh, Robin, I didn't mean anything by it. It was just idle curiosity, that's all. And if you must know, what you did for Jennifer is one of the most remarkable things I've ever heard."

He shrugs his shoulders. "It's nothing when you care for someone." And then he finds all sorts of little jobs to do around the kitchen while I drink my first glass of wine.

Tonight he shares my bottle – he doesn't always, but it's nice not to drink alone. I wish I could tell him what happened in the corridor today, but how do you share those things? I wouldn't know where to start. I wish I could tell him how bad I am at being a lone parent, but that would sound too needy. If I drink any more, these awful words might just spill out and then where would I be? I decide to go and do some marking instead. Numbers. Nice and safe.

I ask Robin if he minds and he doesn't. He says it would be good for me to have a clear weekend and the weather forecast is dry at least.

"Let's have a day out on Sunday," I suggest. "Let's take Claire to Kimmeridge – she's never been."

"Well, in which case it can wait until summer – it'll be pretty grim there now. If you fancy some sea air, perhaps we could go to Lymington. It's much closer."

He doesn't want to go back. "Wherever," I shrug as I pick up my wine and trudge upstairs to the study.

I straighten the pile of scripts and take the lid off my pen. I gaze at the curtains in front of me. They are plain grey but the weave of the fabric is suddenly fascinating. I consider trying to count the threads. Sip by sip, my wine glass empties. Eventually I hear Robin come up the stairs.

"Goodnight, Izzie," he calls.

"Night, Robin," I reply.

It brings me out of my daze. I need another drink so I go downstairs and open a second bottle. There's only trash on TV – Friday night chat shows peopled with minor celebrities – but it's company of a sort. It stops me looking at the pictures of Connor when all I want is for Robin to hold me. Connor would hate the way I feel; he was very possessive, but I never minded before because I didn't want anyone else.

There could never be another Robin.

I didn't want Connor at first either, but he was persistent. I moved out of the flat I'd shared with Robin very soon after he left. Much as I'd want to rush home every night with my heart in my mouth in case he'd come back, or maybe sent a letter, once I was there on my own I hated it with a vengeance. I couldn't afford it anyway and we'd got behind with the rent. My mother agreed to bail me out on condition I applied for teacher-training college so I did what I was told. I guess I was too numb not to.

So when I met Connor I was sharing a house with two other girls. They thought he was lovely and that sort of chivvied me along. And he did have a lot going for him: he was boyish and fun, always laughing, always in the middle of the party – and for some curious reason it was me he wanted.

I gave in after a few weeks and we started to go out together. I didn't mind the way his fingers gripped my shoulder when another man spoke to me; he kept them at bay and gave me a safe harbour. He would never need to know that he was second best; he deserved more than that. I hope I gave it to him.

I tried very hard to be who Connor wanted and on St Valentine's Day 1988 he asked me to marry him. I had no reason to refuse and he booked the registry office for the day after I finished my exams. Within sixteen months of Robin walking out of my life, I was Mrs Connor O'Briain. If it sat uncomfortably at first then out of respect for Connor I hid it, and over the years we built a life based on something more reliable than romance.

Claire came so quickly we hardly had any time together anyway. Being a good wife became an extension of being a good mother, and that was easier. Nothing had prepared me for the intensity of love you feel when you hold your child – it blew me away. So much so that when Connor wanted more children I prevaricated, made excuses, and generally kept putting it off. I didn't think I could cope with feeling that way twice over and I was secretly scared that perhaps I wouldn't, and a second child would never be loved quite as much.

I pushed Robin to the back of my mind; I couldn't bear to think that he was out there, somewhere, living a life without me. Or not living one. Kind of suspended in a place of booze and darkness where I hadn't wanted to follow, and even if I had, I hadn't been able to reach. It was far better to pretend nothing had ever happened.

I managed – kind of. But Connor and I took Claire to see the fairy tree when she was just three years old and it all came flooding back. Connor was beside himself; he'd never seen me so upset, but I knew I could never tell him how much I loved Robin so I only told him the bad bits – the moody, unreasonable, drunken man he'd become. And Connor held me to him and told me the past couldn't hurt me now and I should just wipe it all from my brain.

I refill my wine glass and sit back on the sofa, my finger smoothing the fabric in figures of eight. It's been a shitty, shitty week, what with Claire... Do all mothers say and do the wrong thing? Of course they don't. It was Sasha's mother she'd turned to, after all. If I knew Angie better I'd ask her how do I do this right? But I can't. I'm meant to know. Why don't I?

I think of Robin as he is now, hair and beard flecked with grey, deep lines around those sun-specked hazel eyes. My female colleagues laugh about how unfair it is that men get sexier with age, and in Robin's case it's true. His hands have been toughened by his work and a scar runs the length of his thumb. How would it be to be touched by him now? I can almost feel the pads of his fingers circle my nipples. Red wine splashes on a discarded newspaper as I reach for a top-up.

This has gone on long enough. I have to know if he feels the same about me; if he doesn't I will not go on torturing myself and he will have to leave. That's the end of it. And if I make a fool of myself tonight then at least Claire isn't here to see it.

I drain my glass and stand up. I somehow manage to curb my desire to run straight to his bedroom. I need to clean my teeth and check my face – put on some lipstick, at the very least. So up the stairs I go, a bit slower than I'd planned because my legs aren't behaving quite as they should. Each step gets bigger and bigger and near the top I miss my footing because they've got so huge and I slide back down a few.

I cry out in shock and frustration.

Nothing hurts but I don't think I can get up. My arm gropes for the banister but can't find it. Then I hear Robin say, "Izzie, are you all right?"

"Think so."

He comes down a few steps to my level and I reach out for him. He crouches next to me, his dressing gown smelling of washing powder. I bury my nose in it.

"Come on, I'll give you a hand." I look at him and there is concern in his eyes, but he is smiling just a little bit. That's good – he must still like me.

I put an arm around his shoulder and he hauls me up. I

lean on him and he kind of drags me up the last few steps. We reach the landing and he takes me in his arms and carries me to my bedroom. It's rather romantic really. He's very strong.

He puts me down on the bed and takes off my slippers. "Can you manage to undress?" he asks.

I pout in what I hope is a sexy manner. "I'd rather you did it for me."

He smiles and shakes his head. "Oh, Izzie… Come on then, sit up, then I can take off your jumper."

I do as I'm told then flop back on top of the duvet.

He stands back. "Are you sure you can't manage your jeans?"

I giggle. "Nope."

So he undoes the button and unzips the fly. His fingers brush my stomach and thighs and they are softer than I imagined. I don't want him to stop. But once my jeans are folded on my bedroom chair he pulls the duvet over me.

I grab his hand. "Robin, please stay." What's in his eyes? "I need you. I want you to make love to me."

He sits down on the edge of the bed and squeezes my fingers. "No, Izzie, not tonight."

"Why not?"

"Because you're drunk as a skunk and you might regret it in the morning."

"I won't. I know I won't."

"You might, and I couldn't bear that. Ask me when you're sober. Ask me when I can be sure you mean it – then I won't turn you down."

He stands to leave, but he is still holding my hand. I try

to make sense of his words but they won't stop spinning around my head. He stoops and kisses the tips of my fingers before tucking them under the duvet.

He turns off the light and the click of the door latch tells me he's gone.

Chapter Thirty-Two

I deserve a serious hangover. Perhaps it is because I slept like a log that I don't have one. I have no idea how long I did sleep; it's half past seven now but who knows when I went to bed. I think I know how I got here though, but for a moment I wonder if I dreamt it. I raise myself on one elbow; my jeans are folded on my bedroom chair. It isn't where I'd have left them after a few glasses of wine.

As well as a hangover, I deserve nothing but shame and embarrassment. I feel neither. I feel strangely calm, because the thing I remember most about last night is Robin saying that if I asked him into my bed when I was sober he wouldn't turn me down. Perhaps I did imagine that, but no, it is there, along with the memory of his touch on my leg and my jeans on the chair.

The house is silent; Robin must still be asleep. The pump of my shower might wake him so instead I wash with warm water from the basin, brush my hair to get the tangles out, and clean my teeth. I have to admit that my mouth is not at its best this morning. I gulp two glasses of water from the cold tap, the chill of it gripping my throat.

I look myself up and down in my bathroom mirror. My buttocks are almost nothing but at least my breasts are pert. Still, it isn't the greatest of bodies these days – I am forty-four, after all – and I don't quite have the gall to go to him naked. Instead, I pull a candy-striped nightshirt over my head; it looks casual but it's short enough to help me feel sexy. Lord, I need that help right now.

With every step along the landing I expect to lose my nerve, but the thought of what might happen if I don't do this is driving me on: at worst, a lifetime of what ifs; at best, a day of not looking each other in the eye.

Robin is lying on his back with his hands behind his head. He doesn't move when he sees me, but a muscle under his beard twitches.

"How are you feeling this morning?" he asks.

"Better than I deserve. And I'm sober."

The word hangs between us but he says nothing.

"Did you mean it?" I blurt out.

His Adam's apple bobs up and down. "Did you?"

"Yes."

Before he has a chance to reply, I slip under the duvet. In a single movement he turns and pulls me to him, holding me as tightly as he can. His naked skin is warm and I sink into him, an enormous sense of safety filling me from head to toe. I have found him; I've found my Robin again.

Of course we make love. I expected it to feel familiar, but instead it is shiny and new, as if we have never done this before. Robin recognises it too. It must be what prompts him to tell me he has waited a lifetime for this moment. Was it worth the wait? When he tells me yes I purr like a cat. He laughs then starts to kiss me again, his beard a soft tickle on my skin.

Later, he pulls me out of my reverie by asking what time I have to pick up Claire. We are scarily close to it and he leaps out of bed saying he will go and I should finish my marking so we can all have an outing this afternoon.

"Where to?" I ask him.

He pauses, one leg halfway into his jeans. "Not Kimmeridge. That's just for us."

I feel myself glowing. "I didn't understand last night."

He frowns. "I'm not sure I understand this morning either, so let's hold off on telling Claire until we've had time to talk."

My glow stops. "You're not regretting it, are you?"

He zips his fly and walks back towards the bed, then stoops to kiss me. "My only regret is that we didn't do it twenty years ago."

And that leaves me feeling very puzzled, because we did.

Chapter Thirty-Three

Robin

The day Izzie and I first made love was unreal. I had to keep pinching myself to make sure it was actually happening.

That afternoon we went to Highcliffe to hunt for shark teeth. Izzie and Claire didn't believe me, but as we scoured the sand at the edge of the tide I found one within minutes. They gathered close, marvelling at its sharpness, and I told them about the Jurassic Sea and the animals that swam in it fifty million years ago. Izzie's hand touched mine as she took the tooth from me and slipped it into her pocket.

Claire and I trawled the beach for more hidden treasure while Izzie sat on a bank of shingle, watching the surfers.

"I've never surfed," Claire said when we joined her, "but it looks awesome. Have you, Robin?"

"Yes. When I was a student and then... one summer... I

went to Newquay and worked in a surf shop and for a surf school. I was on the beach a lot that year."

"Wow. I'd love to go to Newquay." Claire looked at Izzie from under her fringe. "Actually, Mum, Sasha and some of the others from school are planning a week there after our exams. Do you think I could go with them?"

I watched Izzie's fingers clench around the shingle she was sifting. "Who's organising the trip? Will somebody's parents be going?"

Claire shook her head. "We'd be staying in a hostel with other groups and doing a proper surf course, so we'd be supervised, but the idea is that we go on our own."

"Oh, I don't know, Claire. If you want to learn to surf perhaps Robin could teach you instead?"

"Well, I'm very rusty, but whether or not Claire goes to Newquay I'll certainly take her out a few times to get the feel of it. But not until the weather's warmer," I added. "Those guys out there today must be nuts – it's freezing."

"That's great, Robin. Maybe Mum would worry less if I could already surf."

"What I don't like is the idea of you going away on your own. You'll only be seventeen, after all." Izzie wrapped her coat more tightly around her.

"I bet driving a car's more dangerous than surfing," Claire muttered.

"Then perhaps I won't let you do that either," Izzie snapped back. She looked up at me, eyes pleading for support.

"Listen, Claire, it's unreasonable to expect your mother to say yes when she knows nothing about this trip and it does all sound a little vague. Why don't you get some more information together? When do you have to decide?"

Claire picked up a pebble then dropped it. "Not for a little while – next month probably. But what's the point if Mum's going to say no anyway?"

Izzie sighed. "I'm not going to say no anyway. Robin's right, I need more information and more time."

That pacified Claire – sort of. As we walked up the cliffs to the car park she dragged behind us and kept turning back to watch the surfers.

Izzie touched my hand. "So when did you go to parenting class?"

"Did I overstep the mark?"

"Not at all. I don't feel such an inadequate lone parent when you're around."

I wanted to hug her but I couldn't. We would have to tell Claire about us first.

On Sunday morning we strolled into Bishop's Waltham for coffee while Claire got on with her homework. Over lattes and croissants, Izzie's hand stretched across the table and crept into mine.

"I missed you last night."

I lifted her fingers to my mouth and kissed them. "I missed you. I want this settled today, Izzie. It's too hard when we've waited this long."

"But what is there to settle? We just need to tell Claire then everything will be fine."

"But what do we tell her? What are we, Izzie?"

Two little furrows appeared between her eyebrows. "I'm not sure what you mean."

I set her hand free so that she could pick up her mug. "Well, if we weren't living under the same roof already there would be a period of courtship. We'd go out a few times, then perhaps you'd ask me to stay, and I would, but not every night. Then, after a while, if it was all going well, maybe we'd talk about moving in together. But the reality is we're already there."

"I don't see why that's a problem."

"I'm not saying it's a problem, but we need to know where we are on the continuum." I grinned at her. "What I really want to know is, am I courting you from the spare room or are we going to be tucked under the duvet together every night?"

She laughed and looked at me in a way that took me straight back to Jennifer's bathroom in 1986.

"You come to my room tonight, mister, and I'm not letting you go. Even if I have to chain you to the bed. But seriously, Robin, it's not like we don't know each other. And Claire likes you so it's not going to be an issue. I know we can make it work this time."

"Last time we didn't have a chance. Mum died and… it felt as though it was all my fault. I couldn't cope, Izzie. I ran away. I didn't deserve you."

"Oh, Robin. I was just as much to blame."

It was an odd comment but I ignored it. I didn't want to keep looking back over my shoulder at the past.

Izzie wanted us to tell Claire together but I was adamant she should do it alone because if I was there it wouldn't give Claire the opportunity to express her concerns. And she was bound to have them; her father hadn't been dead six months – this was frighteningly fast by anyone's standards. So when we got home I put on my gardening trousers and my wellingtons and went outside while Izzie climbed the stairs to Claire's bedroom.

It's hard to find things to do in a garden at the end of January so I took the bird feeders off the apple tree and gave them a good clean under the outdoor tap. As I was blowing on my fingers to warm them I noticed that there was a corner of the lawn which looked particularly damp so I got a fork out of the shed and started to spike it. I was just finishing when I felt someone watching me.

I turned around. "Well, what do you think, Claire?"

"You've missed a bit – just behind your left foot."

I speared the ground again. "You know that wasn't what I meant."

She smiled. "You and Mum? I'm OK about it. No, that's wrong. I guess I'm pleased. It's the best thing for her."

"But it's too soon after your dad?"

She shook her head. "No, Mum needs you now. Time wouldn't make any difference. It's just, well, a bit odd."

I folded my hands on my fork. "I will never take your father's place Claire, nor would I want to."

She smiled at me. "No, what's odd is I think my father took yours."

That took me aback all right. "Oh, come on, Claire…"

"No, really. Mum said you were old flames and the way she lights up around you, the way she looks at you… it was never like that between her and Dad."

"That's just the difference between a new relationship and an old one. Let's face it, Claire, by the time you were old enough to notice how your parents were with each other they'd have been together more than ten years. Your mother and I have been together about ten minutes."

"But what about before?"

"We never even got off the ground. It was all just starting when my mother died and it pole-axed me completely. I was in no fit state to be any good to anyone."

Claire frowned. "That's funny. Mum gave me the impression it was more."

I looked back towards the house. "Inside our hearts I think it probably was. I was head over heels in love with her, Claire, and even if she felt half of that for me it would have been a pretty big thing. But that's all ancient history now and everything happens for a reason. We've been given another chance, that's what matters."

Out of nowhere, Claire hugged me. "You're going to be so good for Mum. Thank you, Robin. I'm so happy it's you."

Chapter Thirty-Four

I was just finishing setting out the elements of my surprise for Izzie when I heard the hiss of tyre on the drive then the engine cut out. But there was a longer than normal pause before the car door slammed and a blast of icy air from the hall heralded Izzie's arrival.

"The fairies have got a treat for you," I called.

There was no reply.

"Izzie?"

Her briefcase thudded onto the parquet. "What?"

I was about to repeat myself but one look at her face silenced me. I reached towards her and traced the lines under her eyes with my index finger. "What's wrong?"

For a moment I thought she was going to cry but she blinked and shook her head. "Nothing... I mean, I think I might be coming down with something." Her eyes glanced past me and locked onto the coffee table. "Champagne, Robin? Have you won the lottery?"

"Some days I think I have."

She cuffed me on the top of my arm. "Idiot. What's it in aid of?"

"A half-term safely navigated, a table booked at Regginas for eight... but I can cancel it if you don't feel well."

She looked down at our feet, hers neat in their black court shoes, dwarfed by my sprawling socks.

"Look, I'll call them now. We can go another time – it doesn't matter."

"Robin, I'm sorry, it was a lovely thought too." When she finally looked up, her eyes were red rimmed.

"You do look full of cold."

She sniffed. "Yes, that must be what it is. Two of my tutor group have a real stinker and I bet I've caught it."

I moved to hug her but she turned and started up the stairs. "I think I'll have a soak in the bath. I might feel more human after that. Glass of champagne might help too."

"How about I bring you one then pop down to the village for some fish and chips?"

"Perfect."

It wasn't until Izzie was halfway through the bottle that I discovered what was wrong. As I unwrapped our supper she asked, "What time's Claire coming back?"

I frowned. "I'm not sure, exactly. I can't recall her saying when the film finished. Didn't she tell you when you dropped her at the station this morning?"

Izzie picked up a chip and nibbled at it. I poured myself a glass of champagne.

"We weren't exactly speaking by then. We had a bit of a row, if you must know."

"Can I ask what about?"

Izzie put her head in her hand. "Newquay. Bloody Newquay."

"Oh."

"She won't let it rest, Robin. She's like a dog with a bone. It's driving me mad."

"So has she got the info she promised you?" I picked up the vinegar bottle and sprinkled it liberally over my chips.

"No. Well… some of it – but not nearly enough. Only the dates, and the name of the hostel and how much it's going to cost. But I need to know who's going Robin, how they're getting there, what sort of supervision they'll have… I know nothing that really matters."

"And does she understand that's what you need?"

"She says I'm being unreasonable."

"Well you're not." I put my hand on hers but she shook it away.

"I don't need you to tell me that."

I turned my attention to my fish but it felt like greasy cardboard in my mouth. I swigged some more champagne but that tasted flat too.

Eventually Izzie said. "I am being unreasonable with you, though."

"I just don't understand what you want me to do, that's all."

"I'm not sure I do either. Just listen, I suppose – and if Claire says anything to you then back me up."

"Sure."

After a while Izzie picked up her glass. "It's lovely

champagne, Robin, but why did you buy it? It wasn't just about half-term, was it?"

"Partly. But also because Stephen called to say that Jennifer's life insurance has paid out. He's bringing the cheque down tomorrow. I don't want the money, Izzie, but if I have to have it then I thought I'd treat you. But I'll rebook Regginas for one night next week when you've had a chance to rest."

"You don't need to wrap me in cotton wool, Robin. I'm all right."

I shared the remains of the champagne between our glasses.

Chapter Thirty-Five

Izzie wasn't all right. The next morning her cold was so bad she stayed in bed but Claire was eager to come with me to Jennifer's house. It was a crisp, clear day and the sight of the garden looking neat and tidy with the crocuses starting to push through the grass made me proud to show it to her.

"What time's Stephen getting here?" Claire asked as we got out of the car.

"About eleven. We're a bit early I'm afraid."

"That's perfect, Robin. We can go to the fairy tree."

She turned to walk down the drive but I called her back.

"No, Claire. There's a quicker way."

I led her past the house and into the back garden.

"So this is where you lived, Robin?" she asked.

"Yes. We kept chickens and they used to get everywhere. It all seems very empty without them."

"Do you think Mum would allow chickens in our

garden? Your omelettes would be even better with our own eggs."

"Maybe one day."

Claire followed me through the gap in the hedge and along the edge of the field. A flock of seagulls took off from the ploughed earth on our approach, feathers glinting in the sunshine. We watched them land further away then climbed over the fence. The ground was slippery underfoot so I held Claire's hand as we made our way down the slope.

I expected her to let go when we reached the bottom. "You've got big hands, Robin," she told me. "It reminds me of being a little girl when Dad used to bring me here."

"Is that why you wanted to come? To remember him?"

She shook her head. "No. I've got something to ask the fairies."

I watched as Claire walked around the tree, trailing her fingers on its trunk. There were quite a few coins studding the surface – I made a mental note to pop down in the week and bag them up for Barnardo's. After three circuits, Claire stopped by the fairies' post box, delved into her anorak pocket, and pulled out a piece of paper which she'd folded until it was about an inch square.

"Aren't you a bit old for that?" I asked.

"You sound just like Mum," she scoffed. "But the fairies always answer. They won't know if I'm sixteen or six."

"Your handwriting might give it away and anyway, how many six-year-olds want to go to Newquay surfing?"

"Oh Robin," she chided me, "you mustn't say it out loud. It won't happen now."

I looked on helplessly as she poked the letter into the

box. There was no way on God's earth she was going to get a reply.

"It probably won't anyway if you keep going on about it to your mother."

I reached for her hand to help her up the slope but she refused, slipping and sliding after me in silence. I waited at the fence, barring her way.

"Look, Claire, Izzie's exhausted. Just give it a rest until you've got all the information she needs. Then you can have a sensible conversation about it."

"I've told her everything I know."

"Then you don't know enough."

"You just don't understand, do you?"

I thought about it. "I can see this means an awful lot to you, Claire, but what I'm not sure of is why."

She kicked at the fence post with her wellington. "I just want to go like everyone else. It's only a week, after all."

I sighed. "Look, just tell your mother who else is going, who'll be in charge, how you're going to get there, and all that stuff. Then she can decide."

"What's the point? She'll say no anyway."

"She'll certainly say no if you don't find out. What have you got to lose?" I turned away and hopped over the fence, striding out towards the house. I had nothing else to say on the matter.

I was halfway across the garden when Stephen appeared through the French windows.

"There you are, Robin. I wondered where you'd got to."

We embraced in the middle of the lawn. "I took Claire down to the fairy tree," I explained.

"Oh, this must be Claire. Hello there."

I turned to see a smiling teenager approach us, cheeks pink from exertion and blonde hair flying behind her.

"Hello Stephen," she said, grasping his outstretched hand. "I've heard so much about you from Robin."

I was beginning a crash course on adolescence – just at the stage in my life when I could barely remember my own.

When we got home I rushed up the stairs two at a time to see how Izzie was. But instead of being tucked up in bed I found her in the study, staring at her computer screen.

"You're not working, are you?"

She turned to me and beamed. "No. I've being doing something I'm sure both you and Claire will approve of. Where is she?"

"Washing the mud off her wellies."

"Fetch her, will you?"

I called down the stairs. "Claire, have you got a minute?"

Back in the study, Izzie had a picture of a staggered terrace of modern apartments on her screen. There were balconies on the first floor and a parched scrap of grass in front. An azure sky stretched into the distance beyond their flat roofs.

"What do you think?"

I leant over and peered at the computer. "They look OK."

"I've booked one. For later this week."

I frowned. "Where are they?"

"Newquay."

"Mum, oh Mum, that's amazing." Claire folded her arms around Izzie and gave her a huge kiss.

"Well I thought we could all go and check it out together. It would be a lovely break and as Robin's lived there he can show us the sights."

I tried to laugh. "It's nineteen years since I've even been there." It was pointless saying I didn't want to go back.

Chapter Thirty-Six

Izzie

The patio door of the rented apartment sticks in its metal runners. I grip the handle more firmly and tug until it rasps open to let the salty air flood in. Below me, Robin is lifting a box from the car, tucking it under one arm before slamming the boot and striding across the lawn. He doesn't look around him, or up at me.

The balcony rail sends a chill through the sleeves of my jumper but the view is magnificent. Beyond the narrow road is the sea, churning and green. Dark clouds loom over the distant headland but Fistral Beach stretches towards it like a strip of pale gold, dotted with walkers. There are even a few surfers and I call to Claire to come and see.

The breeze flicks the hair from her face as she hugs me. "Oh, Mum, this is just so perfect. Thank you." For once, it seems I have done the right thing.

Somewhere in the apartment a door slams.

"Robin, come and look. There are people surfing," Claire squeals.

It takes a moment for him to appear. "There always are in Newquay," he shrugs.

"Can we go, Robin? Will you start to teach me?"

He shakes his head. "No, it's much too cold."

"But they're out in it."

"They're experienced surfers, Claire, and they probably have top-of-the-range drysuits. There's an awful lot of hanging around in the water waiting for a wave when you're learning. We'd be frozen within minutes."

There is a moment when childish petulance crosses Claire's face but then the young adult re-asserts itself. "It just seems a shame to come all this way and do nothing towards it."

"We're not doing nothing, Claire," I remind her. "We're going to check out that hostel and the courses they offer for a start."

"And I can show you the different types of wave, and tell you about the tides and currents." Robin offers. "That's the trickiest bit, knowing which waves you can catch and which to leave."

"Shall we go for a walk along the beach now?" Claire is practically jumping up and down like she used to when she was tiny.

"Why don't you and Izzie go? I'll unpack then see what I can cobble together for tea."

"Please come with us, Robin." I don't want to leave him on his own. It's a family holiday and he's part of the family now. But he has already gone back into the apartment.

While Claire and I find our coats and scarves, the clouds above the headland lift. But the wind still whips in from the sea and white horses glisten in the distance. My walking shoes sink into the sand and I wish I was barefoot so I could feel the softness between my toes.

"So when did Robin live in Newquay, Mum? Was it before or after you met him?"

I consider. "I think it must have been after, because he never mentioned it back then."

"He told me his mum died and that's why he went away."

"Kind of, yes."

"So what happened?"

I stop and look at her. "On the very day Robin took me home to meet his mother, she died. It was one of the best and worst days of my life. There I was with this wonderful new boyfriend and we were so happy, and it was all shattered the moment we walked into the house. She was slumped across the kitchen table. It was just awful. Robin screaming at her to wake up and trying to revive her, then the ambulance men turning up and then a neighbour… just one terrible blur."

"What had happened to her?"

"We… we never really found out for sure. The inquest was inconclusive. But she'd been in a wheelchair for a couple of years and Robin had cared for her, as well as finishing his degree, as well as working. He never talked about it though. I guess he thought it would put me off and he'd only told me that afternoon, but Jean, who lived opposite, filled in the gaps. It… it hit him so hard."

Even at this distance in time the memory punches a hole in my happiness. I turn my face into the wind so my eyes smart from the salt and the sand. "I suppose... when you lost your dad... that was why I was so scared for you."

Claire's arms wrap around me. "It was different for me, Mum."

"Different? In what way?"

"Well I've still got you, haven't I? Robin didn't have anyone once his mum was gone."

"But he did. He had me, he had Jean, he had friends..."

Her grip tightens. "It's not the same, Mum. It's not family."

So here is my sixteen-year-old daughter telling me about grief.

"You wise old thing, Claire," I tease.

She bites her lip. "It's not wise; it's having been through it, I think. I still miss Dad terribly but..."

"I miss him too." I am saying it to comfort her and it makes me feel guilty as hell. Yes, Connor is often around the corners of my mind but if he were actually here... "You know, Claire, just because I'm with Robin now doesn't mean I've forgotten your dad."

"I know that. You're not a forgetter, Mum. You never forgot Robin, did you? I mean, you knew him the moment you saw him."

"Yes."

"I'm glad you did, you know. You needn't feel bad about Dad. He'd have wanted you to be happy and I can see that with Robin you are."

I link my arm with hers. "And I'm happy you're happy.

Come on, let's go back. We mustn't abuse his good nature by letting him do all the chores. It's meant to be a holiday for him too."

As we approach the apartment Robin is on the balcony, silhouetted in the light from the living room. I wave at him and he raises his hand. In it is a glass of wine and I see him mouth the word 'cheers'.

"Pour one for me," I call when we get close enough. He nods and disappears, the patio door grating shut behind him.

Chapter Thirty-Seven

The sand at Watergate Bay is different – wet and shiny from the outgoing tide. I press the toe of my shoe down and water oozes into the hole. Music from the bar drifts across the emptiness and out over the waves.

Robin is different too, thank goodness. Last night – I don't know what it was – but he wasn't himself. Yes, he cooked us a lovely tea, had a few glasses of wine, but he watched TV from the sofa with half-closed eyes. When Claire wanted to talk to him about surfing he feigned sleep. And then he was awake most of the night, grumbling about the bed. He hasn't been like that since… well, just since.

But the sun is shining this morning and he suggested Watergate rather than the town. Over breakfast in the beachfront café, he came to life, teaching Claire surfer slang; 'beached' is apparently more to do with eating too many sausage muffins than ending up in a heap on the sand, and once Claire starts to surf – and Robin gets back on his board

– we will both be honeys. I'm not quite sure how I feel about that.

Now they are a few yards beyond me and snatches of Robin's voice drift on the wind as he points at the sea and explains about waves. Claire pushes her hair out of her eyes with a practised sweep of her hand and I feel sick in my stomach. She is growing away from me. I turn back towards the café, calling over my shoulder that I'm going to get another coffee. Robin puts up his thumb in acknowledgement.

I stand at the counter and order my americano – and a brandy. The girl serving doesn't bat an eyelid. She has braids in her hair which she tosses at the unshaven young man who is polishing glasses. She asks me if I enjoyed my walk on the beach but she doesn't care about my answer. Why should she? I am middle-aged and irrelevant.

I look for a place to sit well away from the bar. Beyond it is another room with picture windows overlooking the bay. Robin and Claire are closer to the edge of the water now and the sun sparkles on the sea beyond them. Even if the window wasn't there I'd be looking at them through scratched glass.

I grip the edges of the bench to steady myself.

A wet nose nuzzles my fingers and I snatch them away.

"Megsy! Behave." The voice is male, with a Cornish burr and I turn to look behind me.

"It's OK, she just surprised me." I fondle the dog's wiry, little ears.

"You did look miles away."

I suppose the man is in his sixties, with a shock of silver

hair and a face like a walnut. He is smiling at me and I warm to him.

"No, not miles – perhaps years."

"Years?"

"Wondering where they went." I indicate the window. "That's my daughter on the beach; she's almost a woman and I can't work out how that happened."

The man laughs, his teeth disappointingly yellow. "I would say you don't look old enough to have a teenage daughter but that would be corny."

I nod. "It would. But the flattery's nice all the same."

"We could all do with a bit of it now and then." He tugs at the dog's collar and sits down at the table next to mine. "You down for half-term?"

"Yes. Claire wants to come here to learn to surf in the summer, so I thought it would be wise to check out the hostel."

"And have you?"

"No. We only arrived yesterday and my partner said it was too nice a day to waste in Newquay."

"That's what I decided too. I should really be at work but when you're self-employed you've only yourself to tick off if you decide to pull a sickie."

I swing my legs over the bench to face him properly. "What do you do?"

"I run a surf school and board-hire operation from Towan Beach, so I probably know the hostel you want to see. It's quite popular, you know – lots of kids do it after their exams. They have quite a party down here."

I try to laugh. "I think that's what I'm worried about."

"I have a daughter too," he tells me. "But I didn't see much of the growing up of her. When she was seventeen her mother was phoning me all the time telling me to do something – she went wild. But then she settled down all of her own accord; she's an estate agent in Truro now, married, two kids. All normal – nobody died."

I turn the brandy glass in my hand. "I think I worry too much because I only lost my husband last year."

"It does make you think. I lost a very good friend about six months ago. Not a wife, or a partner, but someone I had known for a very long time." Suddenly he smiles again. "But I got the dog from the rescue and she filled the gap." He points to the beach. "Have you filled the gap too?"

"Robin filled a gap all of his own."

"Robin?" The man frowns. "When I passed them on the beach I thought there was something familiar about him... A guy that tall... Did he by any chance live in Newquay years back?"

My hand shakes as I put my glass down. "Yes, yes he did."

"I knew it. He hasn't really changed that much but when I saw him it seemed too much of a coincidence."

"That's what I thought when I bumped into him just before Christmas. He hadn't changed at all, apart from the beard. And I hadn't seen him for twenty years."

"Oh, he had the beard when he was here; I used to tease Meg that she liked it because it made him look a bit older. But he was a nice lad – reliable, conscientious. He worked for me, you know, driving my trailer over here every day and then going back to help Meg in the shop. She always did wonder what happened to him."

The last of the brandy trickling down my throat fails to warm me. "Did he just up and leave her as well?"

"He went home to see the damage the hurricane had done, but I think it was just an excuse. Him and Meg – they wouldn't have lasted anyway. She didn't dwell on it over much; it wasn't her way."

The hurricane. 1987.

"Anyway," he carries on. "They weren't together that long. From what I remember he only turned up in the spring. Newquay's full of migratory birds. Always has been."

I stand up. "It's time I hauled them off the beach. We're meant to be going to Padstow for some of Rick Stein's famous fish and chips. Nice to meet you, er..."

"Ed. My name's Ed." He stretches too. "I'll come with you. I'd like to say hello to Robin again."

The sun is bright but the wind cuts through me the moment we step outside. Robin and Claire are walking towards us so we wait on the slipway, Megsy straining her lead towards an overflowing bin.

When they get close enough, Ed steps forward. "Robin! Do you remember me?"

I study Robin's face. He does not smile, not immediately anyway. A muscle twitches somewhere under his beard. "Ed?" he asks.

They grip hands but the wind takes away their words. Then Claire is brought into their circle and I am outside it.

After a moment, Robin reaches his arm towards me. It is stiff like his voice.

"Izzie, this is Ed. I worked for him when I lived down here."

"I know. We've been talking about you in the bar. Your ears must have been burning."

He laughs. "And I thought that was the wind. Come on, it's too chilly to stand here."

I turn and walk towards the car park. They are only just behind me and snatches of their conversation drift past me but I am not listening. The only word I hear is *Meg*.

Chapter Thirty-Eight

We eat in Stein's Café next to the harbour car park. Pine tables, hot oil and vinegar. Up-market chips with everything. I want a glass of wine but Robin orders tea. He says it will warm me; he is feigning concern because I am shivering, even though the car heater has been turned up all the way from Watergate. But I'm not ill, I'm angry: I worried about him for years when all the time he'd just jumped into bed with someone else.

Claire is excited because Ed knows everyone and has offered to show us the hostel tomorrow. He says he'll take Claire and her friends under his wing when she comes down so there's no need for me to worry – or at least that's what Claire tells me. I don't remember him saying that. I don't remember saying she could come back at all. Robin offers nothing; he is silent. Reliving old dreams of Meg, no doubt.

I hear my own voice. "Robin, is this Ed reliable?"

He looks up from his plate, a chip balanced on his fork,

halfway to his mouth. "He always seemed that way to me. But it was a long time ago."

"Oh, Mum, he's being so kind."

"That doesn't mean he's reliable."

"But he's an old man and he's been here nearly forever."

"That's no guarantee of anything. He could be a raving paedophile for all I know."

"Well that wouldn't be a problem for me, would it? I'm almost seventeen – well past the age of consent, if you hadn't noticed." I try to ignore the fact that she is pointing her knife at me.

"I hadn't actually. Mainly because you're acting like a ten-year-old over this."

I look to Robin for some support but he is pretending to seek out bones in his fish.

Claire's cutlery clatters onto the table. "You just don't want me to go this summer. I don't know why you wanted to come here if you were never going to change your mind. What's the point? You never let me do anything."

Robin opens his mouth to speak but I can't let him in case he takes her side.

"Claire, that's quite enough. This holiday is not all about you."

But Robin does chip in. "Your mother's right; she needs a decent break. You know that if you think about it – she's had a tough half-term."

"It's not fair. One moment you're hardly talking to each other and the next you're ganging up on me."

Robin's hand stretches across the table and envelopes

mine. I didn't want it to but his warmth creeping up my arm feels welcome all the same.

"I'm sorry if I've been a bit distant." I don't know if he's talking to me, to Claire, or to both of us. His voice sounds heavy. "Let's not talk about this again until you've seen the hostel tomorrow," he continues. "Let's just finish our lunch and have a nice walk around the town, OK?"

Claire rolls her eyes but she agrees and if she keeps to her word we will have almost twenty-four hours of peace. Robin is looking at me, waiting for my consent. I nod and he squeezes my hand before picking up his fork and spearing another chip.

It's only when we're in the shops that Claire becomes animated again. She points out funny slogans on sweatshirts and fingers her way through trays of shells. She buys a starfish for her dressing table, something reassuringly childish. Robin gazes into the windows of a gallery but won't go in because the pictures are too expensive.

"It doesn't stop us looking," I say, but he shakes his head.

I follow Claire into a jewellery shop. Racks of bead necklaces jostle for space with baskets of earrings. On shelves around the walls silver items are displayed on black velvet cushions, dazzling under brilliant white spotlights.

"Mum," Claire tugs my arm. "Shall I get this for Sasha?" She has a strap of leather in her hand, with three turquoise beads in its centre.

"Sasha? Who's Sasha?"

She looks at me aghast. "Sasha, Mum. You know who Sasha is."

I do, of course I do. My brain is struggling, working through a file of people... And then I have it. No wonder there is panic in her eyes.

"Sorry, darling," I say. "It's the music in here and I'm getting a headache. I didn't hear you properly. Yes, I think Sasha'd like that. I'll wait outside while you pay for it."

The afternoon has turned grey. I lean against a whitewashed wall, the cold shapes of the stones lumpy through my coat.

"What's up?" Robin looms over me.

"I've got a terrible headache. Do you think we could go home?"

"Where's Claire?"

"In the jewellery shop. Just buying a present for S... Sasha. She won't be long."

Robin nods, then pulls me away from the wall and into the softness of his anorak.

Robin and Claire are whispering because they think I'm asleep. I curl under the duvet. It warms me, but I am wrapped so tightly that the ache in my head cascades through my neck and shoulders. So I stretch onto my back, pointing my toes at the wardrobe while my fingers scrabble up the headboard. One slow, deep breath after another.

I have pushed the panic into the corner of the room. I know it's there, somewhere between the curtains and the dressing table. I thought, I hoped, I prayed, even – and really believed – that Robin had driven it away. But now I know it is still there, hiding, ready to surprise me, at the supermarket checkout, outside my classroom, sitting at the traffic lights in my car.

The bedroom door brushes along the carpet and Robin fills the frame, silhouetted by the light from the hall.

"It's OK, I'm awake." I don't know why I'm whispering.

"Can I get you anything? How do you feel?" He hovers in the doorway.

I prop myself up on one elbow. "How about a cup of tea?" It will buy me time to compose myself while he makes it.

He leaves the door ajar, the strip of light falling across the bed. In my mind's eye I follow its path and there, in the living area, I see Claire stretched on the sofa flicking the pages of a magazine and Robin, shoulders hunched, arms folded, leaning against the kitchen unit waiting for the kettle to boil.

I swing my legs over the side of the bed and pull on my cardigan. I feel a bit wobbly when I first stand and my eyes are drawn to the corner between the dressing table and the curtain. When I pull the door open fully, the shadow there disappears.

Claire gets up from the sofa and gives me a hug. "How you feeling, Mum?"

"Much better thanks and I don't want to spoil our evening. What would you like to do? Go for a pub meal or something?"

She shakes her head. "I'm still full after those fish and chips. Robin was saying he might do some jacket potatoes later and I've found a DVD of *Breakfast at Tiffany's* in the bookcase. I've never seen it. Perhaps we could all watch that?"

I smile at her, stiff-cheeked. "That's a lovely idea. Robin?"

"*Breakfast at Tiffany's* was one of Jennifer's favourite films. I'd love to watch it again. I'll just make your cuppa then I'll pop down to the corner shop for some cheese for the potatoes."

"And a bottle of red – it always goes well with cheese."

He turns away as the kettle boils. I assume he agrees.

Chapter Thirty-Nine

S urprisingly – and thankfully – the hostel looks like a converted office block, hidden down a side street near the railway station. Most uninviting, despite Ed's cheery wave as we clamber from the car. Megsy leaps up in greeting, little terrier ears pricked. I crouch to stroke her and she snuggles into me, making snuffling noises.

Ed laughs. "She's well taken with you, Izzie. Now don't you go luring her home. I'd miss her too much."

"She is adorable, but no, I won't steal her. If I took her home she'd only be in an empty house all day." I stroke the top of her head.

"Robin could take her to work with him, Mum."

"Now that'd be a turn up, Robin and Megsy after all these years," Ed winks.

Robin doesn't laugh. He clears his throat. "I meant to ask you about Meg. How is she?"

Ed puts his hand on Robin's arm. "Not with us

anymore. Breast cancer. About six months ago. That's when I got the dog."

Robin is hiding behind his beard again. "I'm sorry, Ed," he says, without a hint of emotion. "That must have been tough."

"Well, when you've been in and out of someone's life since your first day at school it leaves a gap. But you know Meg, she wouldn't want me to waste too much time grieving. I've still got her board in the shop, up on the wall. It's the best reminder – that and the dog. I needed something to shout at."

Robin nods. "Come on," he says, "let's take a look at this hostel."

It does nothing to reassure me when the receptionist has long braided hair and is wearing a hoodie. But he stands to greet us pleasantly enough, although I am conscious of him eyeing Claire up and down. She is beautiful as she smiles at him, and for the first time I wonder why she doesn't have a boyfriend. Perhaps she does. Perhaps she is hiding someone from me because she thinks I won't approve. Perhaps she is hiding someone like him.

My head starts to thump again but I have to get through this. I have to send the panic back to the corner of the bedroom in the rented apartment where it belongs. I reach for Robin's hand. His fingers brush mine then he seems to sense how I am feeling so he wraps an arm around me, saying nothing.

Ed disappears into an office and comes back with a woman in a long, brightly coloured skirt. I cannot decide if her generous proportions are due to pregnancy or simply the way she is. I search her face for clues but there are none. She is of indeterminate age, although a few wisps of grey run through her hair.

"Hello," she says, her slow voice like clotted cream. "I'm Martha. Ed says you want to look around."

"Yes please. Claire would like to come here with some friends in the summer, but I have my reservations." I sound so uptight I hate myself. Robin squeezes my shoulder.

"Most mothers do," says Martha, "only most of them are too afraid to admit it for fear of upsetting their precious offspring. Well done you."

We follow her up the stairs and down a corridor, off which are rooms each containing three pairs of bunk beds. Everything is spotlessly clean; even the lino on the bathroom floors sparkles. It feels cold and clinical and I pray Claire won't like it.

Downstairs is a huge common room with sofas and a TV one end and a dining area the other.

"We take thirty students at a time," Martha explains. "And everyone chips in with the chores." She turns to Claire. "Can you cook, my dear?"

"Yes. I'm not too bad at the basic stuff."

"Then you'll be in demand. There's too many youngsters come here haven't a clue but if you know what you're doing in the kitchen I can promise you won't be cleaning the lavs."

Claire looks a bit shocked, but she smiles politely. I can't tell what she's thinking.

We return to the reception area.

"Now, when are you looking to come down? We get very busy, you know."

"There's a provisional booking already," Claire stammers. She can't look at me.

Martha lifts an enormous diary from the counter. "When for? What's the name?"

"Seventh of July… Jack Granger."

"Who's Jack Granger?" I shoot.

"Oh, no one, Mum. Just one of the lads in Sasha's geography group. His brother came down two years ago so he's organising it."

I turn to Martha. "What about adult supervision – they'll only be seventeen."

"There are rules, and there's always someone on duty but, to be honest, it can be a bit like herding cats. On the other hand, if they've been surfing all day they're normally too knackered to get up to much mischief. But we organise quiz nights and there's a games room we share with the hostel over the road; it's got table tennis, pool, that sort of stuff."

"What about the surfing?" Robin asks.

Martha consults her diary again. "Well, at that time of year we're really busy so we do offload work to other surf schools. How about I book Claire's group in with Ed so you know they're being looked after?"

Robin nods. He's taken over. "I guess that would be helpful. What happens on days when conditions aren't right?"

Ed laughs. "We load up that old trailer and the minibus and go somewhere they are. And if it's flat we bodyboard instead, or if it's completely hopeless we play water polo. If it pisses down we get more into the theory than we would otherwise, so there's plenty to do. They're not allowed to roam the streets and pubs, don't you worry. Noses to the grindstone." He winks at Claire. "You don't think this is going to be a holiday, do you?"

Claire looks up at him, her face glowing with expectation. "It sounds wonderful," she says.

"Come down to my surf shack, little girl, and we'll take a look." He winks at me over the top of her head.

These people are so kind, so welcoming – and so sensible. It's becoming harder for me to say no. As we cross the main road and head down towards the sea I battle with myself to find the reason for my reluctance.

Newquay may be grubby and grotty but on the beach the sunlight reflects off the damp sand, making everything below the tide line seem washed and new. A few surfers are riding the waves and Claire can't take her eyes off them.

Ed struggles with the padlock on the front of what appears to be several garden sheds tacked onto an ageing cricket pavilion. The white paint has been weathered away in places and a huge wooden board creaks in the breeze. The windows are shuttered – against the wind and waves or vandals I can't decide.

The lock finally clicks open and Ed inspects it. "Needs some WD40. Bit like me, really. Don't look at this mess, Izzie. It hasn't had its spring spruce up yet – no point until the last of the storms have passed. It'll just get sand-blasted again."

We troop in and Ed flings open the shutters. The room is

bigger than I expected, with racks of wetsuits on one side and surfboards stacked on the other. In the middle is an old wooden desk and behind it an enormous longboard is fixed diagonally across the wall. I know whose it is before I even read the inscription – 'Megan Tregea 1945 – 2006' – and then a list of surf competition honours spanning the 60s and 70s.

Robin shakes his head. "She never told me."

"She never told anyone anything very much. She liked to be a bit of an enigma. Come on, young Rob, you know that."

"Yeah… I guess I do."

Robin's voice falters and he suddenly sounds very much like 'young Rob', as Ed called him. It takes me back somewhere, to a moment, but although I search my mind for it I can't connect.

Claire is walking along the rows of wetsuits, fingering them. "Are these the sorts of suits the guys out there now will be wearing?"

She is so transparent.

Ed laughs. "You'd like to have a go, wouldn't you?"

"Robin's promised to teach me but he says we don't have the right gear for this time of year."

"We don't have any gear, Claire," Robin corrects her.

"Well, there's plenty here. Winter weight too, if you fancy taking her in. There's a nice little wave at the moment, I have to say."

"Oh, please, Robin, can we?" She's a child again, asking Connor for an ice cream because she knows I'll say no.

Robin looks at me, across what seems like miles of wooden floor, asking the question. I put on my best smile.

"Well if Ed doesn't mind and those wetsuits really are that thick, then I don't see the harm."

"Thanks, Mum." Claire rushes across and hugs me. Already she smells vaguely of rubber.

"We can watch them from the shoreline, Izzie."

I shake my head. "It's a bit cold for me. I'll wait here."

"Why don't you take Megsy up to the café?" Ed suggests. "You'll have a great view of the beach and they make a mean hot chocolate. No brandy though," he adds with a wink.

I can't look at Claire. I pick up Megsy's lead and with a quick "have fun" over my shoulder I'm gone.

I climb the concrete slope. Ed's shack is dwarfed by the aquarium, its sloping glass roofs dominating the beach. I wonder what was there before, when Robin first came here. Was it where Meg had her shop? Meg who won so many trophies, Meg who was an enigma, Meg who was so alluring that Robin leapt into bed with her so very few weeks after leaving me.

From a table by the window I watch them emerge and troop down the beach while Megsy licks my fingers for traces of shortbread. Claire and Robin are dragging boards across the sand and Ed has changed into a pair of fisherman's waders. They pause as he points to something out at sea but I can tell Claire is impatient to be in the water.

She has a long wait. They put their boards down and lie on them, then make swimming actions with their arms while Ed instructs. Robin is much too long for his board, his legs hanging off the end. He looks ridiculous.

All these years I believed he left me a broken man. A

213

shadow cast over my life. That note he left saying he wasn't worthy of me, it was a lie. He just wanted to move on. Released from caring for his mother, he didn't want to be tied down by me. He wanted sunshine and freedom and a casual fling with a woman like Meg. He lied to her too, when he left her; he told her he'd be back.

Robin has abandoned his board on the beach and is helping Claire point hers out to sea and lift it over the surf. He holds it steady as she climbs on, clinging to it for dear life, and when she's ready he looks behind him, waiting for the right wave. Then she's paddling with all her might; he lets go and she is whooshing towards the shore, skewing to a halt in the shallows next to Ed's feet. She leaps up and already Robin is almost beside her, ready to start the process again.

I stir my hot chocolate round and round in a figure of eight. *The past can't hurt you. Wipe it from your brain.* I frown. The words sound familiar – a mantra, almost – but I cannot place them. The more I stir, the harder it becomes.

Chapter Forty

Half-hidden behind the living room curtain, I watch as Robin carries our cases to the car. A thick fisherman's jumper guards him against the chill of the morning. I bought it for him yesterday and he seems to like it. He puts the bags down on the tarmac and stretches. His fingers almost touch the sky.

I didn't want to go to bed last night so I finished the bottle of red on my own. I heard the timer on the heating click off and afterwards just the waves, pounding the beach. I closed my eyes and listened until a car came past and then I picked up the wine and filled my glass with the dregs. There was no point hunting in the cupboard for more.

Robin's hands were gentle on my shoulders. "Come on, Izzie, it's late and we've got a long journey tomorrow."

In the bathroom there was toothpaste freshly squeezed onto my brush and I wanted to weep. Slowly I scrubbed, right into the corners of my mouth. I scrubbed again, and spat, and rinsed. I had no energy to wash my face so I

215

shrugged off my clothes and climbed in next to Robin, squeezing onto the side nearest the door.

He didn't ask why. Perhaps he knew about the demons in the corner next to the dressing table in the same way he knew how I was feeling at the hostel. He wrapped his arms around me, his body a solid wall of comfort. In just a few moments, before I could think anymore, I was asleep.

"One last walk on the beach?" Claire makes me jump.

"Last? It won't be the last, Claire."

"Then I can come back in July? You've decided?" Her voice is breathless.

I turn to face her. "Darling, I'm terrified of letting you go but in truth I have no reason not to."

She hugs me so tight. "I'll be fine, Mum, really I will. I'll be sensible and Ed'll look after me. I won't let you down."

"You never have, Claire." I kiss the top of her head and her hair smells like a woman's, sickly sweet with styling mousse.

Chapter Forty-One

The white van is parked so close to my driveway that I have to angle my car in extra slowly. The wing mirror misses the gatepost by no more than a layer of paint. That's all I need. What the hell's it doing outside my house anyway?

I pull my briefcase and a carrier bag full of workbooks off the back seat. The hall light is on. Robin must be home, but why wouldn't he be? I ignore his greeting and haul my evening's work up to the study and drop it on the floor. The handles of the carrier have cut into my fingers and as I flex them I notice they are shaking.

"Izzie?" Robin's voice drifts from the bottom of the stairs.

"I'll be down once I've changed."

But I don't know if I can be bothered. I want to wrap myself in my dressing gown and watch trash TV – or even better, take a huge glass of red into the bath and lock the door.

I sit on the edge of the bed and massage my toes, looking around me: the photo of Claire as a baby on the wall; Rive Gauche and Angel bottles on the dressing table; Robin's watch on the pillow, claiming it as his own. The black leather strap is soft with wear, and the glass scratched across the middle.

Downstairs, its owner is sitting at the kitchen table and to my absolute astonishment there is a shiny new Blackberry in his hand. He puts it down to hug me, kissing me on the cheek.

"How was your day?"

"I see you've been spending some money." I wriggle free and sit down.

"You noticed the van, then?"

"It's yours?"

He nods.

"I couldn't help but notice it, could I? It's parked halfway across the drive."

"Oh, Izzie, it isn't. It—"

"Well it's completely blocking my view for getting out tomorrow morning."

He puts his hand on my arm. "Well if I don't go first I'll see you out. But I don't really know where else to leave it. I mean, once I've loaded up my tools I'll want to be able to keep an eye on it."

I fold my arms. "I don't want some bloody great white van parked outside my house all the time."

"But you said I should use some of Jennifer's money to get a van and so I have. Where did you think I was going to keep it?"

"That's not all you've been buying, is it?" I flash.

"No, and I'm beginning to regret the Blackberry." He tries to smile. "A normal phone would have been much simpler and I'm not sure how many of my customers are going to email me anyway." He puts it down. "Come on, let's eat."

I shake my head from side to side, trying to shift the dull ache starting behind my eyes. As Robin opens the oven door, mince and tomato and cheese and all homely things rush out.

"I thought I'd make a cottage pie so it's easy to warm Claire's when she comes in. Comfort food. She sounded a bit nervous about this evening, I thought."

"Nervous? I thought she'd gone swimming."

He shakes his head. "Not about that. About Sasha's mum bringing her home so you can talk about Cornwall."

"Well I've said she can go. What's to be nervous about? Does she think I'll go back on my word?"

From the look on Robin's face I can tell she does. "Why doesn't she talk to me?" I burst out. "She's my daughter."

Robin puts down his fork. "I think it's because she's worried about you. In Cornwall, sometimes, it was almost like you weren't with us and she thought you were drinking quite a lot."

"That old chestnut. I was on holiday. I wanted to unwind. What's wrong with the odd glass of wine?"

"Claire doesn't see it like that. She's—"

I push my plate away and gravy slops onto the table. "If my daughter has something to tell me she can say it to my face and not – I repeat *not* – through you."

Robin spins his knife slowly around on the table. It reminds me… of something. His face is pale, contrasting with his eyes which seem to have disappeared back into his head. I expect an outburst but all he says is, "You put me in a difficult position, Izzie. Am I to live here and not listen to Claire? Or listen to her and not tell you about it?" He looks down. "Or do you want me not to be living here? Have you changed your mind?"

"Hah! The get-out clause. Make it my fault when you disappear again. Because it's a habit, isn't it? It wasn't just me, it was Meg as well – and goodness knows who else I don't know about, because you hopped out of my bed and into hers pretty quickly."

A muscle under his beard twitches. "I don't know what you mean."

"It's no good coming Mr Innocent with me. Ed spilt the beans. He told me about Meg. He said she died not knowing what had happened to you. Just like I could have done. Just like I wish I'd done right at this moment. No wonder I was drinking on holiday, with Claire manking on about surfing all the time and your past coming back to slap me in the face. No wonder—"

But I don't have an audience anymore because Robin grabs his keys and slams the kitchen door behind him. His knife spins towards the edge of the table.

I think he would have slammed the front door too but I hear voices outside. Robin's, gruff and deep, drifts over our abandoned meals. "I'm off to B&Q before it closes… need something for a job tomorrow… yes… Izzie's just finishing her tea." I stare at the wooden pepper grinder, gazing right into its grain. I know I have to move; one, two, three... I put my palms on the edge of the table and lever myself up, brush imaginary crumbs from my jeans and waltz into the lounge, shutting the kitchen door behind me.

"Angie, lovely to see you. Glass of wine?"

She gives me a tiny hug and air kisses my cheek. "Great idea. I've got the L-plates on the car – Sasha can drive me home."

The evening has started all over again.

Two long glasses later they leave. Claire rushes into the kitchen, claiming she's starving, so I put the shepherd's pie into the microwave to warm for her. I look at my own plate, orange-coloured fat congealing around the edges.

"I'll heat mine too... Finish it off."

She picks up Robin's knife from the floor. "Why didn't—"

"So are you pleased now the whole Cornwall thing's settled? Perhaps you could invite everyone who's going to supper one Saturday, then I could meet them all. I wouldn't embarrass you, I promise."

She gives me a hug. "Oh, Mum, you never do."

I take another glass of wine to the study with me. I check the clock on my phone. B&Q will have closed ages ago. Every time I hear an engine in the road I prick up my ears, wondering if it could be Robin's van.

In the end there are footsteps, echoing down the pavement. A long stride, but a slow one. There's the click of the latch on the gate and a key in the door. I didn't know I had been holding my breath. I put the cap back on my pen and I'm waiting for him at the top of the stairs. He looks at me, silent, uncertain.

I take his hand and lead him into the bedroom.

We sit down on the bed together. "Where have you been?" I ask.

"To B&Q."

"That's what you told Angie."

"Yes. It's where I went."

"Why?"

He shrugs. "It was open. I looked at power tools until they closed. I picked up some leaflets, read them over a pint in the pub. I'm going to need a new hedge trimmer."

"Where's the van?"

"Outside the pub."

"Because you've had a pint?"

"Because you don't want it here."

Tears spring into my eyes. "Oh, Robin, I'm so sorry. I just feel so... so..."

He pulls me to him, rocking me back and forth. "That's it, Izzie, have a good cry. You'll be better for it, I'm sure."

Will I? Will the tears wash away the terrifying momentary blankness of memory which means I don't know which classroom to go to? Will they soothe the rising panic that lurks in unexpected corners, waiting to catch me out? Can I even tell Robin these things when it's fear of losing him again that's causing them?

But here I am, my face squashed against his jumper, in a grip so vice-like it seems he will never let me go.

"Robin, promise me. Promise me you won't just disappear again."

"I won't," he murmurs. "Last time... last time I was ill. For years really, after I lost Mum. I wanted to contact you but I just couldn't do it, and then, when I did try, they told me you'd moved on. I couldn't stay with Megan either – not when I still loved you. And there was no one else, Izzie. Not ever."

And I cry some more. Because I so, so, want to believe him.

Chapter Forty-Two

Robin

The earth turned beneath my spade, releasing its loamy scent as my namesake bird hopped next to me, looking for worms. Under the trees the daffodils I had planted – what, five, six, years ago? – shone yellow in the pale sunlight. The freshness of it all, the sense of beginnings, stirred my spirit and my mood was improved even further when Maria, the major's Cypriot wife, came out with a mug of coffee and a plate of her homemade biscuits.

I knew it would be ten past eleven exactly and it was my cue to put down my spade. The major – I always thought of him as that, although he insisted I call him George – would have taken his at eleven o'clock then Maria would bring me mine. But today she was not alone; the old man limped down the garden after her, coffee mug in one hand, the other grasping his stick.

"Beautiful morning, Robin," he called.

I nodded. "It really feels like spring. Even the blackbirds think so." I indicated the hedge. "I'll have to give it a good trim later before they start nesting."

"You're nesting too, I hear," said Maria, her black eyes sparkling behind her glasses.

"Don't be so nosey," her husband scolded, but I knew that wouldn't stop her.

I smiled. "If you mean I have a lady friend, well you're right."

"I'm so pleased for you, Robin," she said. "After all those years looking after dear Jennifer you deserve some life."

"I was very happy with Jennifer, you know. She was like a mother to me after I lost my own."

The major snorted. "You were more than a son to her. Look at our boys: here we are, old and decrepit, and we never see them."

"Oh, George, you know that's not true." Maria leapt to the defence of her beloved sons.

It was an argument I had witnessed several times before. I sipped my coffee, nibbled my biscuit, and let my shoulders relax in the sunshine.

"Well, Robin, what do you think?"

I jumped. "I'm so sorry, I was miles away, I—"

Maria laughed heartily. "Thinking thoughts of your lady, no doubt. She is beautiful, Robin?"

"Yes, very. I… I knew Izzie years ago and we met again just before Christmas. She's a widow now so…"

"Ah, that is so romantic, Robin. She is lucky lady."

"Well I don't know about that, but I do my best." I picked up my spade.

"Before you get going again, Robin, we wanted to plant something new to remember Jennifer and we wondered if you had any ideas as to what would be best," asked the major.

"She loved her roses. Perhaps if I took a cutting from one of them? It's time I gave them a short back and sides anyway."

"Take a few cuttings, my boy. They're notoriously fickle plants to get going."

"Do you know, it would be lovely to think of them growing somewhere else. It sounds silly, but I do worry about her plants. If Stephen decides to sell the house, whoever buys it might dig them all up."

"You should take some for yourself, too."

"I will, when I have somewhere permanent to plant them."

Maria stepped forward and gave me a hug. "One day, with your lady…"

"I hope so." But last night I had realised just how fragile my happiness was.

I watched them return to the house, Maria walking two steps behind her husband and carrying the mugs. I crouched close to the earth and held out my hand, the last of the biscuit crumbs stuck to my fingers. I stayed very still, but today the robin wasn't brave enough to take them so I tipped them into the soil where he would find them later.

After I finished at the major's I made my way to

Jennifer's house, grating the van's gears as I reversed into the drive. The damn thing was hard to park anywhere – I needed to practise. I was also reconsidering putting my name on the side after the way Izzie had been last night. Perhaps she didn't want the neighbours to know I was a gardener and handyman.

She'd been better this morning though. She had cried herself to sleep, so exhausted that she lay motionless in my arms all night. But her breathing was steady and shallow and when she woke she said she felt totally different – refreshed and ready to face the day. I didn't know how long she'd been holding those tears inside but it must have done her good for them to all come out.

Rather than unlock the house, I made my way across the lawn and through the gap in the hedge onto the field. The turned earth was fuzzy with the tiny stalks of corn and the sky was a clear, pale blue. To my right, in the woods, every leaf seemed to be a different shade of green. As I slid down the bank to the fairy tree I noticed the first signs of bluebells pushing through. The wheel of the year was turning, the winter of loss relaxing its grip. Everyone was better off when they were in tune with nature so the timing of Izzie's tears had been nigh on perfect. I looked through the branches to the sky and whispered some words of thanks.

Closer to the tree I stopped and listened. I could see no one, but people give their presence away first through sound. A dog barked, but that was some little distance away so I opened the box on the side of the tree and crammed the letters into my pocket before scrambling back to the hedge. I knew Claire's was one of them, but now her wish had been granted I didn't feel so bad about not being able to reply.

Back in Jennifer's kitchen I set the kettle to boil and pulled my pad and pen out of the drawer in the table. I loved opening the children's letters, freeing myself to sink into their world of innocence where the fairies came properly to life. For Jennifer I think the hidden folk always had been real; for me, well, it was different.

Of course there was the occasional child who didn't believe but was after material gain; Xboxes had been the thing last year and I had been able to fob most of them off by explaining the fairies didn't know what an Xbox (or a Wii) was. Children like that didn't tend to have the patience for a long conversation with the hidden folk.

Another popular desire was for a puppy or a kitten and there was one of those today. Samantha, with very wobbly handwriting. The fairies explained that you could love all animals without having a pet of your own and all the rabbits and mice in the wood would be her special friends. It was a fairly standard reply, to be honest. Jennifer had been much more creative. I often wondered what the parents would think if they knew the fairies' letter-writer was a forty-four-year-old childless man. Probably that I was some sort of pervert.

I hadn't planned to read Claire's letter but curiosity got the better of me. I thought I might find out just why she was so set on going to Newquay but to my absolute amazement it wasn't even mentioned.

The letter was about Izzie.

How Claire was worried about her drinking because it

was making her act funny and forget things. About how scared she was that her mother was falling ill again. And how she was afraid that if Izzie did get ill then she would push me away and I was so good for her. And because she was afraid I might go, she couldn't ask me what to do, and anyway I didn't take the drinking thing seriously at all.

It wasn't so much a wish as a desperate outpouring.

The sun still shone as I took the major's cuttings from Jennifer's roses but I worked with an extra jumper on. The spring cut had been an important ritual in Jennifer's year, only recently entrusted to me, and last March she had been out here too, wandering away then coming back to tell me I'd missed a bit. She took a trug full of cuttings to the compost heap and when she returned asked me whose garden it was, because it was going to be beautiful in the summer. Even the memory of it broke my heart.

I sat on my haunches. Already I'd cut back far more than I should. I put my secateurs in my pocket; I'd finish tomorrow. Although why it should matter, when the house would probably be sold by the time the roses bloomed, was beyond me.

As I washed my hands, my thoughts returned to Claire. That Izzie was stressed was obvious but it wasn't surprising with her demanding job, losing Connor, and now a new man on the scene. I had my history of mental wobbles too and she seemed to be coping far better than I did. I had trouble holding down a normal life when disaster struck. If Izzie got a bit forgetful and ratty and needed the odd glass of wine to help her to relax then it wasn't an issue as far as I could see.

But how to get this across to Claire was a puzzle. The words of the fairies' reply formed in my head but I could never put them down on paper. My handwriting would give me away the moment she opened it.

I stood for a long time staring out of the window, soap twisting in my hands, but inspiration didn't come.

Chapter Forty-Three

Blonde hair on the white pillowcase and morning sunshine creeping around the curtains. Warm skin beneath me, her rhythm matching my own. It was Saturday – and I was being offered perfection.

Afterwards, the soft hairs on her arm caught the light and I ran my fingers over them.

"Let's go to Kimmeridge."

"Oh, Robin," she breathed, "I love you so very much."

The sun continued to shine. Leaving Claire to go shopping with Sasha, we ate up the miles to Dorset. Near the coast the grassland undulated into pasture, the sheep white dots on the hillside. Izzie rolled the car to a stop as we crested a hill at the top of the Kimmeridge Estate and the sea came into view.

"How long since you've been here?" she asked.

I put my hand over hers on the gearstick. "You know how long."

"Me too. I couldn't ever... not with anyone else..."

"Me neither." I punched her arm. "No handstands in the sea today though."

"Chicken." She laughed as she took her foot off the brake and we started our descent to the beach.

The tide was in so we climbed the bank to the monument. White horses bobbed in the distance and tumbled over the rock ledges below us, breaking the gunmetal green which stretched to the sky. Behind us the sheep grazed on the hillside, their bleating mixed with the calls of the gulls and the drag of the swell on the pebbles. A fishing boat inched across the horizon.

"Sometimes," Izzie faltered, "when you remember a place from a long time ago, your memory distorts it. But not here; it's all spread out exactly as it should be."

"We didn't come up here last time."

"I know. But I suppose my brain kind of helicoptered out to take in the whole view. Does that make sense?"

"And was the sun always shining too?"

"Of course." She squeezed my hand.

"That's because you bring the sunshine."

"No, we do."

And she took off down the slope, windmilling her arms, her laughter mixed with the gulls and the sea.

I picked up her abandoned handbag and followed. She was waiting for me on the edge of the low cliffs, hands on hips.

"Slowcoach," she chided me.

"I'm just enjoying myself – enjoying you – being so happy."

She started to walk towards the circle of the bay.

"Wednesday night... it made all the difference. But at the time I thought, I'm never going to be able to get into work, face a normal day, after all that emotion. Only I did. It was like my mind was suddenly clear. I'd been struggling, Robin."

"I know. Even though you didn't say."

She twisted a strand of hair between her fingers. "It's odd. You're alive to my moods, somehow, in a way Connor never was. I've wanted that, over the years, without even knowing it. But now I have it, it feels strange."

"Intrusive?"

"See, that's exactly what I mean. You just know."

I was non-committal. "Well... of course. What I can't know, unless you tell me, is why."

"Take a stab at it."

"Losing Connor hit you harder than you wanted to admit. Then there wasn't enough time to grieve before I came back into your life. And I'm here, all the time. It's not like the start of a normal relationship. You've had no space to feel what you've needed to feel. And the stress came pouring in on top of you."

She put her fingers to my lips. "You're putting words into my mouth." She traced the edges of my beard around my mouth. "Do you need space?"

"No. But I'll step back a little if that's what you want."

"Right at this moment I never want to let you out of my sight. But sometimes, when I come home from work and the food's on the table, and the house is clean, and you've picked Claire up from somewhere I feel so... so... guilty that you're having to do all this."

"I don't have to do it, Izzie. And at the moment I'm the one with the time. You wait until summer when – I hope – I'll be working until nine o'clock at night. You'll have to remember where the oven gloves are and how to use the washing machine then."

She shook her head. "I over complicate things, don't I?"

"No. We're just finding our way, that's all."

I took her hand and we climbed down onto the rocks, slippery with seaweed from the receding tide. As we rounded the corner into the bay, a boat chugged towards the open sea, a man preparing mackerel lines on deck. The spray blew up and I could taste the salt in my beard.

We both knew when we had reached the spot. "It's been concreted over," Izzie exclaimed.

"Yes, but it hasn't changed the view." I spread my anorak and we sat down and I pulled her close to me and kissed her. "I wanted to do that last time we were here but I didn't dare."

"I'd started to like you before then, but when we were here... there was a magic to us, and I've never forgotten it. We only had those two really happy days: when we came here and when we went to the fairy tree, and of course that ended so badly..."

"It's funny but for me the fairy-tree day is sort of split into two distinct parts. There's this golden memory of our time together and then this sense of everything shattering. It almost seems like that happened another time, although I know it didn't."

Izzie snuggled closer, the wind blowing her hair across

my face. "That's close to what I told Claire," she said. "The best day and the worst day of my life rolled into one."

"And you didn't even know Mum."

"No, but even though I didn't realise it at the time, it was the day I lost you, and we'd only just started."

"Mum would have loved you. You would have been everything she'd have wanted for me. And you would have had some right old giggles together. But it would have been tough, too. Caring for her... That could have ended us before we'd really begun as well. Sometimes, Izzie, things are meant to be and maybe that wasn't our time. And anyway, there needed to be Claire, and being Connor's daughter makes her who she is."

"Yes," she smiled up at me, "there needed to be Claire."

Chapter Forty-Four

I t really did seem to be our day. We even managed to get a cancellation at Regginas so I was finally able to treat Izzie to a special meal out. We had a taxi so we shared a bottle of wine. And a brandy afterwards – but nothing over the top. When Izzie refused a second glass I thought of Claire's letter and I was pleased.

Izzie wore a green shift dress and she looked so beautiful I didn't even take it off her when we made love. She lay in it afterwards, crumpled and creased, her eyes shining as she said to me, "That reminded me of the first time, under the willow in the fairy tree woods."

I repeated the words to myself but they made no sense. I pretended I hadn't heard, but when she said them again, they hadn't changed. Was she thinking of Connor? She was looking at me, waiting for my response.

"Izzie, I don't remember."

The softness disappeared from her face and her hands twitched to tug her dress down.

"I don't understand…" I faltered. "How I could forget… something so… important…"

"At least you've been honest with me, Robin. At least you didn't pretend."

She had to have meant me. My chest tightened.

"Tell me, Izzie, help me remember what happened."

"It was after we left Jennifer's and we went back to the fairy tree. We held hands and made wishes…"

"Yes." The feel of her fingertips in mine, the heaviness of the air around us, the silence in the woods before the storm. Still real; still with me.

"You remember that?"

I nodded.

"Then it thundered, and started to rain, so we sheltered under a big willow next to the river and you kissed me and we couldn't stop. I had my back to the trunk but I was shaking so much, the way you were touching me… So we lay down and the ground was completely dry. I was wearing a dress… that's what reminded me."

"I remember the dress – it was yellow. And you had plimsolls on. I remember everything, except the most important thing. Izzie, why?"

She could see I was distraught and she pulled me to her, her reply muffled by my hair. "Perhaps, Robin, perhaps because within an hour your mother was dead. You were beside yourself with grief. I guess that's what blotted it out."

That night I heard the swish of wet tyres every time a car passed. I counted the drips from the cracked drainpipe above Izzie's study. A cat fight broke the silence of the smallest hours. But at least I didn't see the light crawl around the curtains. Somehow I slept and dreamt of Kimmeridge.

Chapter Forty-Five

Spring sunshine warmed Jennifer's house and I walked from room to room opening windows to let the air flood in. In my old bedroom the wood had warped so I collected my tools from the van, jimmied the window, and took my plane to the uneven surface. I looked at my watch – it was just before noon. I had time for a coat of primer to dry as well.

I was bending down to stir the paint when I heard a car in the drive. I raised my head and watched as the metallic blue cabriolet pulled to a halt behind my van. Stephen. And he looked every bit as puzzled as I felt to see another vehicle on the drive. I poked my head out of the window.

"Morning," I called.

He grinned up at me. "Oh, it *is* you, Rob. Got yourself a van?"

I nodded. "I'll just finish this then I'll come down."

"I'll put the kettle on," he replied, disappearing past the porch and along the side of the house.

By the time I joined him in the kitchen he had made two mugs of coffee and was rummaging through the pile of post I'd picked up off the mat. He looked up from his task.

"You got my message then?"

"No."

"But you're here?"

I picked up my coffee. "I came to finish pruning the roses. I just got sidetracked by the window – it's got a bit warped over the winter."

"Oh." Stephen looked away and started flicking through the pile of envelopes again.

"What's up?"

He still didn't look at me. "I've got a couple of estate agents coming around this afternoon, just to try and get a handle on the valuation... for probate, you see."

"There's no need to look so awkward. I know you won't want to keep the house."

His chin jerked up and he reminded me so much of Claire. "I might."

I put my hand on his shoulder. "Whatever you do, Stephen, it's your decision and your decision alone. Nothing to do with me."

"I don't like to think of you not being able to come here. In fact, I don't like to think of not being able to come here myself at the moment."

"Then it's too soon for you to decide." I squeezed his shoulder again.

After a few moments he cleared his throat. "You said you didn't get my message. I thought it was odd you didn't call back. I tried to reach you Friday evening and a couple of times on Saturday."

"I left my phone in the van. It's a new one too – a Blackberry – and I'm buggered if I can work out how to access my voicemail."

"But Robin, that's awful. You're running a business. Give it here and I'll sort it out for you." He held out his hand.

"Would you? Claire's already set up my email and I'd feel such a fool if I had to ask her to do anything else."

He arched his eyebrows. "You are hopeless."

We sat down at the table and I handed him my phone, watching as he clicked a few buttons. Then he dialled a number, punched one key and then another. "OK," he said, "ready to record your personal greeting?"

"My what?"

"The message you want people to hear when you've left your phone in the van."

"Oh, isn't there a standard one?"

"Yes, but it's not very friendly. Just say who you are and ask people to leave a name and number so you can call them back."

I cleared my throat. "All right. Let's do it."

"Just say it to practise," Stephen encouraged, so I did.

"All done," he grinned.

"What do you mean?"

"Well I knew you'd sound more natural if you didn't think I was recording. Do you want to listen to it?"

I shook my head. "It's bad enough other people get to hear it."

Stephen was just handing the phone back to me when it bleeped. "Oh, that's probably telling you about my voicemail. Shall I clear it?"

I nodded and he pressed a key, but immediately coloured up, pushing the phone across the table.

"Robin, I'm sorry. It's a text from Izzie. I shouldn't have seen it."

It was simple enough:

Are you over the shock now? Feeling better? Xxx

Stephen fiddled with the handle of his mug. "You did get my message, didn't you?"

"No, really. This was something else." I stood and walked across the kitchen. The dregs of my coffee fizzed and gurgled down the plughole. Through the window I could see the lawn; it would need cutting soon. Stephen said nothing. "It's just that I forgot something, something really important, and it shook me up."

"We all forget things."

"No, not like this." I turned to face him, my fingers gripping the sink behind my back. "Would you ever forget the first time you and Gareth made love?"

Colour spread up Stephen's neck and I apologised for being so blunt. "But you wouldn't though, would you?" I continued and he shook his head. "Not even in twenty years' time?"

He found his voice. "I'd like to think not but you never know. Is that what you forgot, the first time you and Izzie... um..."

"Worse. I didn't even remember that we had."

"I don't suppose that went down very well."

"No, she was really understanding about it. You see it was just hours before my I found my mum dead and she thinks that's the reason. But everything else about that day is so crystal clear – even the little buggers I had to fish out of the Hamble."

Stephen laughed. "Well maybe you got your reward. But honestly, Rob, Izzie could well be right. Shall I ask Gareth what his professional view would be?"

"If you like." To be honest, the last thing I wanted was a psychologist getting his hands on me. "I think I've stopped kicking against it now, but I can't help wondering how things might have been if I'd remembered. If I'd known we'd crossed that barrier it would have been easier to contact her and tell her what had happened, then everything would have been different."

"Maybe it wasn't meant to be different. You know what Gran would have said: everything happens for a reason in the greater scheme of things."

I left Stephen to the estate agents and wandered into the woods. A willow, Izzie had said, close to the water. But after the hurricane it was unimaginable that the original tree would still be here. I tried to think back to those early days when I first returned but I could remember no more than a tangle of vegetation. But a willow will grow back quickly, even cut almost to the floor, and there were three of them dipping their branches into the water. The tide was up and I squelched down the bank towards the nearest.

The sunlight filtered through the canopy although the

air felt chill. My boots sank into the mud as I closed my eyes and tried to remember. Izzie in her yellow dress, against the trunk, lying on the floor, soft lips, wide eyes. It ought to have been erotic, but nothing came. Nothing except the warmth of her hands in mine around the fairy tree, and my singing heart and the smell of rain-washed cities as I walked towards my mother's front door.

My fingernails bit into my palms. Even now it was hard to relive what happened next. Odd, to remember the nightmare and not the dream. But then... my mother hadn't been cold when I'd found her. Maybe if Izzie and I hadn't got so carried away under the tree, maybe I would have been home in time... then I'd have saved her and I'd have known. One action leading to another, no action for which we should not take responsibility. Ripples pushing out from the willow's branches dipping into the Hamble for years to come.

When Jennifer had shared her belief in a single force that connects everything through space and time it had made perfect sense to me. The action of planting a seed in one place rather than another would make it grow better or worse – whether the soil was good or poor, or if it was in a sunny or a shady spot. And that determined the food we would eat – a carrot pulled from the garden, or one that we went to the shop for. And if we left the garden to go to the shop, who we might meet, and what we might say to them, and how that could change their day... A chain of life, a continuity, Jennifer and me as tiny cogs in an enormous cosmic wheel. A wheel we were duty-bound to respect.

I stood under the willow, head bowed, listening to the

rustle of the leaves. When the moment was right I took my penknife from my pocket and cut the ends off three of the branches, stripped them and plaited them together, finally tying them into a small circle. The sap stuck to my fingers as I worked and I could smell spring all around me.

As I placed the circlet into the Hamble and watched it float downstream, I was at peace.

We were in bed when Izzie asked how I was feeling. She turned off the bedside lamp then rolled over to face me, her hand resting on my shoulder.

"I'm OK about it, Izzie. Stephen thinks you're right and it was the shock of finding Mum like that."

"It changed you, Robin. Changed you so completely. But looking back that's hardly surprising."

Her words slid past me almost unnoticed as I warmed to my theme. "It was meant to be. Jennifer made me understand. That day, well, it was pivotal for all of us and shaped our lives: you and I, and what happened to us; Jennifer being cut off from the boys by Susan; me being there to look after Jennifer in the end. It all stemmed from just those few hours. Connor's life even, and Paul, the guy you were with then… Do you know, Izzie, I think perhaps I wasn't meant to remember us making love, because if I had, if I'd known we'd made that commitment, it would have been so much easier to call you and tell you what had happened."

I sensed her catch her breath. "I'm not sure what you mean."

"Well, as it was, I only had the vaguest idea that you might really care for me and even that got completely washed away in the awfulness of what happened with Mum. I hardly even thought of you those first few weeks. It was only later... and by then I couldn't pluck up the courage to call you."

"Robin, you didn't need to call me. I was there. I hardly left your side until you went back to work."

Even now it is impossible to describe the weight of her words. They crushed the air from my lungs and squeezed my skull until it felt as though it would burst.

I thought: this is what it's like to drown.

Chapter Forty-Six

Izzie

When Robin doesn't respond I turn on the light. His shoulder muscles knot into a ridge beneath my hand and his eyes screw shut. If I am struggling, what the hell is this like for him?

"Robin?"

He speaks through clenched teeth, every word careful and deliberate. "The last time I saw you was outside the shop. I went in to buy some milk and you drove away."

"No, I came with you. But perhaps you aren't ready to hear about that now."

His breath comes in a huge gulp. "No, tell me. Tell me how you remember it."

So I do, just an outline. Following him into the house; finding his mother; Jean and the ambulance arriving; the long night of whisky and tears; the empty days that followed, waiting for the funeral when 'The Green, Green Grass of Home' was played.

"I remember everything," he whispers. "I just don't remember you. It's like those books I used to have when I was a kid, pictures with cut-out shapes for you to put the sticker on. Only, your sticker is missing."

"Your memory's blocked me out. It's… it's like what happened next, really. You blocked me out of your life. Over the next few months…"

"Months?" He jerks into a sitting position.

I try my best to sound calm. "Yes. You went back to work but the council turfed you out of the house so we found a flat in Shirley. It was a horrible little place, but it was all we could afford. And you sank lower and lower but I didn't understand. And because I didn't understand you didn't tell me when you lost your job and when I found out I went mad at you and you left me. I never knew where you went or anything… I guess it was Newquay."

"At least that's real. I remember Newquay."

"We know it's real. Ed said you arrived in the spring and that fits with when you left me."

He doesn't respond, just sits, hugging his knees to his chest. After a long, long while, he tells me to turn off the light and get some sleep.

I do, eventually, but I don't think Robin does. Except, in the morning, when I am pottering around the bedroom, putting on my clothes, hunting down my mascara, he doesn't move.

His long body is curled into a ball, his face buried in the duvet. I tell Claire he isn't well.

I text him at morning break but there's no reply. Once I'm back in class I can't check my phone and the ninety minutes to lunch is endless. Even then there's nothing. I sit in my car, watching the daffodils sway on the grass verge as I phone him. Voicemail. I call the house and it's the same. I leave a message, careful words, in case Claire hears it first. I imagine my disembodied voice floating through the empty hall.

Floating, and meeting what? Is Robin even there? Is he asleep? Is he staring at the ceiling, too numb to move? He could be anywhere, doing anything – or nothing. He doesn't want to tell me. The sweat trickles between my shoulder blades and there is an ominous thud behind my right eye.

I stumble from the car and back to the staffroom. I'm in luck – the head of year is there, an oversized Starbucks mug nestling in her lap as she eats her sandwich.

"Fiona, I'm sorry, I have to go home. I've got a migraine coming on."

She looks up at me. "Goodness, Bella, you do look pale. Who have you got this afternoon?"

"Tutor group, but if someone can give their scripts back then they can rework the ones they got wrong in the library. Then a free, then adult numeracy."

"Don't worry, I'll sort something out for them. Are you sure you'll be OK to drive?"

I nod. "It isn't far." I sweep the papers off my desk into my briefcase.

But today it is a long, long way. Every roundabout, every traffic light. And I decide to go via Curbridge, just to make sure Robin's van isn't on Jennifer's drive. But that's a waste of time. I curse out loud. Why did I bother? He probably hasn't left the house. But what if he has? Where will I start looking this time? My hands slip on the steering wheel as I turn off the main road. There at least is Robin's van, parked opposite the pub.

It was churlish of me to make a fuss about the van but he hasn't forgotten it. If I find him I'll tell him it doesn't matter. I swing the car into the drive and rush for the front door, opening it into a silent house. The red light on the answerphone is flashing.

But Robin is there, in the bedroom. He is blinking and struggling to sit up.

"Izzie, are you all right?"

I want to say, *Yes, are you?* but it comes out as a sob. I drop onto the bed and he holds me as tightly as he can.

"You didn't answer your phone," I sniff.

He strokes my hair. "It's been switched off."

"Not the one in the hall."

"I didn't hear it." His voice is flat but his hands feel strong as they travel rhythmically over my throbbing skull.

"I've been so scared."

"I'm sorry, Izzie."

After a while I break free and sit up. "I need to get a grip." I open the bedside drawer and fish inside for some Nurofen.

"Why are you so frightened? Because you're living with a man with a huge chunk of his memory missing?"

I shake my head. "Because I'm scared you'll shut me out like you did before."

"I didn't shut you out. I ran away, from everything. I…" He pulls himself up. "But that's in my reality, not yours."

I gabble on. "You never talked about it. How you felt. What was going on in your head. Even when you lost your job you didn't say. You drank a lot. I don't know… I don't know how you filled your days in that horrid little flat, because I was at work and you didn't even tell me you weren't."

His eyes snap into life. "Izzie, take me to the flat. You never know, it might just trigger something. I might just remember."

"I… I haven't been back there in years."

"Please, Izzie, take me there. Take me there now."

He jumps out of bed and starts pulling on yesterday's boxer shorts, his eyes scanning the room for his socks.

"Robin, clean ones, in the drawer."

"Yes, OK, sorry."

"Have you eaten?"

"No. It's not important. I'm not hungry." His head pops out from a T-shirt.

I stand up. "I'll make you a sandwich to eat in the car while you clean your teeth and comb your hair."

He nods and hurries into the bathroom.

I can't tell him that time has erased the address from my mind. But I do know that the flat was near St Michael's School, because I used to watch the teachers get out of their cars in the morning, eaten with envy for their lives.

We park in a side road near the school just as it is

emptying of traffic. A last group of mothers fills the pavement, three boys kicking a football ahead of them. A ginger-haired toddler clings to an adult hand as she is dragged along, sucking her thumb.

As soon as they have passed, Robin opens the car door and leaps out, looking around him.

"Was it here, Izzie?" He sounds puzzled. "This looks like a nice road."

"Not here, but this is where I used to leave my car. It's just around the corner."

He tucks his arm into mine to hurry me along.

"Slow down, Robin, my legs are about half the length of yours."

We reach the bend and turn towards the main road, but no bells are ringing although I can see the flat in my mind. Upstairs in a Victorian terrace. Bay window to the living room at the front, dingy glass in the bedroom and kitchen overlooking a walled drying yard with two lines slung across it. If you closed all the doors, the stairs and landing were pitch black. I shudder.

"What's wrong, Izzie?"

I stop and look around me. At the end of a leafy walk, across Shirley Road, I can see the pub. Just like it always was, the downstairs of a 1930s house without an ounce of character or charm. But nothing else is the same – nothing I remember. The flesh on my arms begins to crawl but then I realise why.

"Robin, it's gone."

"Gone?"

"Those new flats, it was there. A whole terrace, and the

path was a proper road then. We were about halfway down it. There was a green front door."

We continue to walk until we reach the main road. Apart from the pub, all that's changed too. The halal meat store, world supermarket, curry lounge – all new. The dry cleaner's is still there though, and the hardware shop.

Robin is looking up and down the street. "Do you remember anything?" I ask.

He shakes his head. "I would tell you I've never been here before in my life. Except, you know that isn't true."

I try to help him to remember. "When we first moved in we painted the bedroom because it was so grim. We bought all the stuff from Clarence Hardware over there. And there used to be a bank opposite. We'd get a tenner out of the cashpoint to go to the pub."

He looks again. "There's nothing, Izzie. Absolutely nothing." He lets go of my hand and turns back the way we came. "Come on, we'd better go."

Chapter Forty-Seven

Claire practically follows us through the door.

"You're home early, Mum," she chirps, giving me a hug.

"My last class was cancelled," I tell her, hoping she won't probe.

Instead she turns to Robin. "Are you feeling better now?"

He is not such a good liar as I am and he looks surprised.

"It must have been something you ate, do you think?" I chip in and he nods.

"I'm fine now, Claire. Quite hungry in fact. I might even start cooking some tea."

"I'll do it," I offer.

He squeezes my hand. "We'll do it together."

"That gets me off the hook," laughs Claire, and she disappears up the stairs to her room.

In the kitchen I pull a bottle of wine out of the rack.

"Fancy a glass?"

"No thanks. I don't want to be damaging any more little grey cells." His joke doesn't really come off.

I put the corkscrew back in the drawer. "Then I won't either. Come on, what are we going to cook?"

We keep it simple. Onions caramelised in olive oil, stirred into hot pasta with a tub of soft cheese I found lurking at the back of the fridge. It's begging for a glass of white to go with it but I resist.

Over supper, talk turns to Claire's seventeenth birthday, only weeks away. She wants to know which one of us is going to teach her to drive.

"Proper lessons first," I tell her. "I'll buy you some for your birthday. You don't want to pick up our bad habits."

"I'm a white van driver now, Claire," says Robin, a smile sliding across his face. "And you know what that means. I'm not safe behind the wheel."

"You're not allowed to park it in front of the house either," adds Claire.

"I meant to say—" I start, but Robin cuts across me.

"Well no, Claire, I wouldn't want to lower the tone of the neighbourhood. Professional people live here, after all, not manual labourers. Not kids who grew up on council estates." He winks.

I thump my hand on the table. "I was going to say you can park your van outside. It's not a problem. You just caught me at an awkward moment the first time."

"Council estate? Ooh, Robin, don't tell anyone. They'll think Mum really does like a bit of rough."

She's curled over herself giggling and Robin joins in.

Quip after quip follows, making me out to be some sort of snob. I'm not. *I'm not like that*, I want to scream. My headache returns with a vengeance. I don't understand what's going on. How can Robin be laughing so easily? How come I can't?

I stand to clear the plates and once they're in the dishwasher I scrabble in the drawer for my strongest painkillers.

"Mum, Mum, what d'you think?"

"Sorry, darling, I didn't hear."

"I saw a handyman's van painted with the slogan 'your second husband'. Should Robin do the same?"

I look at them, Claire's cheeks flushed and her face alive, Robin's head slightly on one side as his eyes meet mine. They drop to the packet in my hand.

"It's very funny, Claire," he says, "but it's not really me, is it? It'd be against trade descriptions or something. I've never even been a husband, let alone a second one." He ruffles her hair and stands up. "Headache, Izzie? Why don't you sit down and I'll get those for you with a nice cup of tea."

He's never been a husband but he should have been. I nod my thanks and wander into the living room. A picture of Connor on the mantelpiece follows me to the armchair at the far end and I close my eyes against the day.

Robin brings my tea and tablets and then I go upstairs to have a soak. I hear him and Claire beneath me in the garage;

they must be checking Connor's car. I turn on the taps to drown them out.

I undress in the bedroom while I run my bath. The full-length mirror mocks my middle-aged body. I am tired beyond belief. I slip under the sickly scented foam and grasp my tea, wet hands sticking to the hot mug.

Claire. Almost seventeen. Next year she'll be gone, flying the nest to some far-flung university. I remember the moment myself, sitting on the bottom stair and opening the envelope, my whoop of joy echoing through an empty house. Bristol had accepted me; get the grades and freedom was possible. For the first time, my future had been in my own hands. I had been desperate to take flight.

I don't want it to be like that for Claire. I don't want her to be running away. I don't want to be the mother-bitch-from-hell. I want her to miss me, text me, phone me. I want to be her friend.

The codeine works its magic on the pain behind my eye and the water soothes the aches in my back. I balance my mug of tea on the corner of the bath. The door clicks open.

"Izzie? Can I come in?"

I twist around and smile. "Of course you can. I heard you in the garage. Were you looking at the car?"

"Yes. I showed Claire how to check the oil and the water in the washer bottles."

"Her father would never have thought of that."

Robin sinks to his haunches next to the bath. "I'm not trying to replace Connor."

"You're finding your own way."

"I'm trying. How are you feeling now?"

"Better. You?"

"Too tired to think about it. The car was a good distraction."

I reach out and stroke his hair, leaving a soapy trail. He hangs his head.

"Why don't you go to bed? I'll just have a chat with Claire then slip in later." I pull the plug out of the bath and stand up. The air feels cool and I shiver, so Robin fetches my towel and wraps it around me. "You're the kindest, most wonderful man I've ever met and I love you very much."

He shakes his head but all the same he smiles. "I love you too, Izzie. You're the centre of my world."

I am still glowing when I cross the hall to Claire's room. As I push the door she closes down a window on her computer screen.

"Am I interrupting something?"

"No, Mum, not at all." She tucks a strand of hair behind her ear and smiles at me.

"It's just... I had an idea. How about you have a little party here for your birthday, and invite the people you're going to Newquay with?"

"Mmm... maybe." She picks at the skin alongside her thumbnail. "Mum, there's something I need to tell you."

"Yes?"

"I've got a boyfriend."

"How long has that been going on behind my back?" The words are out before I can stop them.

"Not… not that long. There's just never been the right moment to say. I didn't want it to be something we had half a conversation about on our way to the school bus."

"There've been plenty of other times."

"No, Mum, there haven't. Not when it's just been you and me."

"Don't start blaming Robin for this. He's very good to you. He's—"

"I not blaming Robin," she yells. "I'm blaming you. You're the one who's never got time for me. No wonder I need a boyfriend of my own."

The truth of what she says hits home and I am able to check myself. "I'm sorry, Claire. We've got time now. Tell me all about him. Is he at sixth form with you?"

"Yes. He's nice, Mum. You'll really, really like him. He's quite tall with green eyes and he makes everyone laugh all the time. He lives in Chandlers Ford and his dad's a dentist. He wants to be a marine geologist. That's how I met him – he's in Sasha's geography group."

"You haven't told me his name."

"It's Jack. Jack Granger."

The name rings a bell so loudly it even strikes the right spot in my befuddled brain. "The boy who's organising the trip to Newquay?"

Claire shifts her weight on her chair. "Yes."

"That explains a lot. So really, Claire, how long has this been going on?"

"Only a few weeks." But her eyes can't meet mine.

"So he wasn't the reason you were so desperate to go to

Newquay? Come on, Claire, I work with kids your age and I'm not stupid."

"It wasn't like that, Mum, honestly—"

"Don't use that word with me, Claire, not unless you mean it," I snap. "You're almost seventeen. Have a boyfriend, why not? But don't start lying to me and hiding things from me or—"

"I'm not. You just won't listen!" she screams.

I watch my hands as they stretch to shake her by the shoulders.

"Don't you dare! Don't you dare touch me! I'm not a child." She shrinks against the wall and I back away through the door.

I am trapped in the funnel of the landing and I grip the radiator for support. It burns my hand but I can't let go. I cannot move – not back into Claire's room, nor can I cross the invisible storm to my own. I close my eyes and fight to control my breath; it's all I can hear, a panting dog chasing me.

The feeling that I am about to die recedes. I raise my hand and flex my throbbing fingers. Claire's muffled sobs squeeze under her bedroom door and I escape to my study.

I have visited this internet page so often that the address springs into my browser when I type just the first few letters. Symptoms of stress: feeling overwhelmed, moodiness, constant worrying, panic attacks, headaches... These are all too familiar. But memory loss, on a huge scale? I search the list again and again but it isn't there.

Chapter Forty-Eight

Robin

I didn't even unlock Jennifer's house but went straight to the garage. There, piled on the workbench, were airtight boxes containing half-empty packets of seeds. I checked the dates; some would do. Carrots, beetroot, a handful of broad beans. It was enough – for this year anyway.

It was how Jennifer and I had always done things at the spring equinox. 'More than a nod to heathenry,' she'd laughed, but it fitted in with the view of the world we'd come to share. In the drawer of the dresser were some candles and I planted one in each corner of the vegetable bed and lit them. There was hardly a breeze and the flames burned low and true as my spade cut into the earth, chopping and turning to release its goodness.

I marked drills for the carrots and beetroot and scattered the seeds before raking the soil over. The beans I planted in pairs. It would be a scant crop compared to previous years and if Stephen was to sell I wondered who would be here to harvest it. It didn't matter; it would be a gift to the house's future from its past. A past that was not as solid as it seemed.

I'd worn myself into a state of exhaustion, gnawing at how Izzie's recollection of events could be so different to mine – and yet I had no answers. I'd watched Jennifer's brain fragment as the Alzheimer's took hold. Was the same happening to me?

The damp from the earth seeped through the knees of my trousers. We had been here, in the garden, when Jennifer told me of her fears. Before that we'd just laughed when she'd forgotten someone's name or couldn't remember where the milk pan was.

It had been spring too, but later, probably April. I was doing the proper planting, burying runner bean seeds in the trench we'd kept open all winter. I hadn't heard her approach.

"Robin?" I looked up. "Robin, I'm scared."

I stood. Jennifer's best grey cardigan was wrapped tightly around her, but she was shivering. "What is it?"

"The doctor's referred me to a consultant. These memory lapses... he thinks... they might be... significant."

"Surely he's just being cautious?"

She shook her head. "Who knows?" There was a chatter of magpies in the distance. "Actually, I think I'd rather not."

"That's silly, Jennifer. It might be something perfectly treatable." I stood up, wiping the earth off my hands on my trousers.

"And if it isn't?" She wasn't a woman who cried, but her

voice was shaking now.

"Then I'll look after you."

"Robin, no. You don't know what you're offering..."

I wrapped my arms around her and she felt frozen to my touch. "No. But if worse comes to worst we'll find out together."

Now I took a handful of earth and crumbled it through my fingers. I had kept my promise but it was the hardest thing I've ever done. I watched as one of the flames guttered. The rite was not complete.

I hauled myself up on my spade and extinguished three of the candles. The other I picked up and, shielding its flame, carried through the gap in the hedge and along the bottom of the field. The air was filled with birdsong and the trees were fuzzy green with new life.

I paused at the top of the bank. Below me a dog was nosing around the fairy tree so I knew people would not be far away. Before long, two women came into view, deep in conversation. They didn't even glance at the tree and soon they were out of sight again. I slid down the slope and placed the candle between the oak's roots.

Jennifer always said the candle was a gift for the hidden folk who guarded the tree. I never thought she meant the words literally until I read that even today a majority of people in her native Iceland don't discount the existence of elves and fairies. But by then it was too late to ask her; she may have understood the question, but I could not have trusted her response. Could I trust my own?

I had no one to turn to, no one who would understand how the yawning gap in my mind was threatening to swallow me. No one. Not anymore. Unless... Of course, I couldn't talk to Jennifer about this, but I could be near her – in a way. I almost sprinted up the slope, gathered the remaining candles from the earth and jumped into my van.

I parked at the top of the woodland burial site and made my way through the trees. I had done this only once before, with Jennifer, when she was well enough to want to come here and choose her final resting place. As we'd emerged into the clearing she had gasped at the Solent set out before us, the Isle of Wight emerging from the hazy sparkle of the sea. She'd turned to me and nodded. "I'll rest well here, Robin," was what she said.

Her grave was to the far left of the clearing. The earth had yet to settle and a flinty mound marked the place, a terracotta pot of tête-à-tête at its centre. Stephen. I should have guessed he'd been coming here. My own visit was long overdue.

I took the candles out of my anorak pocket and set two at her head and one at her feet. The clearing was sheltered so they lit easily and I sat back against a nearby tree to watch them burn.

On the other side of the burial ground was a coppice of firs. I had watched Jennifer's funeral from amongst their shadows. I had come here to wait, suffering days of agony when nothing happened, and I had wondered if Stephen had forgotten her wishes. Or if there were more sinister reasons for the delay. I haunted the little wood by day and at last the grave diggers came.

Across the field was a manor house which was being converted into flats and I had bedded down there after the builders went home. Roses climbed the walls and a few miraculous blooms had evaded the frost. In the quiet of dusk I picked them but they crumbled to petals in my hands. For a moment I had been dismayed, but then I had gathered them up and spread them at the bottom of Jennifer's grave, a scented mattress to help her rest.

I had watched the funeral. Neighbours, clients, people I knew from the village. Farmer Westland helping the major and Maria down the slope. Undertakers carrying a simple wicker coffin and behind them, Stephen and Gareth, a woman in a black coat, and another man.

As the service began I studied the strangers. Too far away to see their faces, I could only assume that the woman was Susan. The man was younger, fair and solid-looking, and I guessed it was Toby. They stood apart from Stephen, who was held upright by nothing more than Gareth's arm. I should have been there, on the other side of him. Thirty paces and I would have been. But my courage failed me and I had slunk away.

"Forgive me, Jennifer," I now whispered.

The sun crept along the edge of the wood, warming my legs as I stretched them across the earth. My fingers dug into the chalk around the tree roots, meeting an acorn, rolling smooth around my hand. And in my mind I travelled with Jennifer, her memory fragmenting, flitting from present to past, from anguish to peace and back again. And then, as I closed my eyes, she came to a place of light and she turned and seemed to say, "Your journey is different".

I sat under the tree and shared her tranquillity until the candles burned themselves out.

Chapter Forty-Nine

Claire's schoolbag corkscrewed across the hall and thudded into the bottom of the stairs.

"Come on," I joked. "It's Friday. You ought to be happy. No more college for a couple of days."

"I'd rather be there than here," she stormed.

"Hey, what's up?" I leant against the doorjamb.

"Don't pretend she hasn't told you."

"I'm assuming 'she' is Izzie?"

"Well who else would it be?" She planted her hands on her hips.

"Could have been the cat's mother, the way you said it..."

"Don't start being the disapproving parent. It doesn't suit you."

"And being a stroppy teenager doesn't suit you. So why don't we just cut to the chase and you tell me what's wrong?"

Claire sank onto the bottom stair. "I can't make her

listen. She doesn't believe me, and I haven't lied to her. Well, not really."

"I'm afraid none of that makes any sense to me at all."

"You mean she really hasn't told you?"

I shook my head.

"We had the worst row we've ever had last night and she didn't tell you? She probably isn't even upset about it. I think that's worse. I think... all day..." Her head fell towards her knees and she started to sob.

I crouched down beside her. "Shh, I'm sure your mum is upset if you've had a falling out but perhaps she wanted to keep it private between the two of you. And anyway, I was fast asleep when she came to bed and there's never any time in the mornings."

"That was my whole point. There isn't time to talk in the mornings so that's why I didn't tell her, but she thought I was hiding it deliberately, but if that was the case then I wouldn't have told her at all, would I?"

"Told her what?"

Claire's chin jutted out. "That I've got a boyfriend."

I considered the news. "And Izzie isn't happy about it?"

"She... she didn't seem to care one way or the other. She just went off on one because she thought I'd hidden it from her."

"What made her think that?"

"Because it was Jack who organised the trip to Newquay, so she thought I was so keen on it because I was going out with him then."

"But you weren't?"

"No." She twisted the ends of her scarf. "I did fancy

him, though. I did, you know, want to impress him. And… and… when we went to Newquay at half-term and you, like, knew everyone and we went in the sea, he thought it was well cool and I think it was then that he started to notice me."

"And your mum didn't believe that?"

"I never got the chance to tell her the full story. She wouldn't listen."

I hauled myself up on the newel post. "Well she is a bit stressed at the moment."

"She's always stressed."

"Claire, she does her best. She's had a bloody awful seven months."

"But she's got you now."

A car slowed outside then turned into the drive. Claire leapt to her feet.

"Go and wash your face," I told her. "I'll try and square it with your mum but I can't promise it'll be straight away. I'll need to find the right moment."

I was still standing in the hall when the front door opened and Izzie appeared.

"Hello, Robin. What have you been up to today?" she asked as she put her briefcase on the bottom step.

"I went to Jennifer's," I told her, "to plant a few vegetables. I hope they grow before Stephen decides to sell."

"You could plant some here, you know."

"Oh, I don't know…"

"Rather plant them at your real home, would you?"

An argument was the last thing any of us needed so I

took Izzie in my arms and held her until I felt her shoulders relax. "Sorry," she murmured.

"It's OK. Claire told me you've had a row so I rather expected you to feel shitty."

Izzie looked up at me. "She's home then?"

I nodded.

"What did she tell you?"

"That you wouldn't listen to the full story. She was crying, Izzie. She's really upset. Just like you," I added as an afterthought.

"I wasn't very fair on her, really."

"Then go and tell her so."

She jerked her head upwards. "I can't do that. Honestly, Robin, you know nothing about parenting."

"I know two people I care about are hurting."

Her eyes dropped away from mine and after a few moments she said. "You are so wise sometimes."

"And so stupid at others." I gave her a little shove. "Up you go and sort it out. I'll walk into town for a swift half and bring us back some fish and chips."

She turned to me from three steps up and smiled. "And a bottle of white to go with them."

It was Friday, after all.

Chapter Fifty

I was glad to be left to myself in the garden. Izzie and Claire were friends again and had headed off to Chandler's Ford for Izzie to meet Jack. I'd been invited but I'd declined; I wanted to start on our new vegetable patch.

Before she left, Izzie and I picked the place. The garden wasn't large and the lawn grew right to the fence on the left hand side. An old Christmas tree had been planted half way along, but if it was removed the area would catch a great deal of afternoon sun so I set to work with my chainsaw.

I have never liked killing healthy trees but sometimes it has to be done. In truth, it was hard to call this woebegone spruce particularly vigorous and once I had resolved to take the logs to Jennifer's for the Aga I felt better about it. Nevertheless, it showered me with evil brown needles which stuck to my hair and jumper.

The noise of the chainsaw meant I didn't hear my phone. It was only when I wandered up the garden to get myself a drink from the outside tap that I noticed the missed call. Stephen. I rang him back.

"Hi, Rob. Learned to use your voicemail?"

"I can even text quicker than a word a minute too."

Stephen laughed. "I'm very glad to hear it. Now, the reason I called was that Gareth and I have come down to Gran's for the weekend. Do you and Izzie fancy supper at The Robin Hood tonight?"

"I'd love to but Izzie isn't here right now. Can I call you back?"

"No, text me. I'll book a table for seven anyway. It'd be lovely to see you both."

Hoisted by my own petard. I lowered myself onto the edge of the patio, found Izzie's number, and fumbled my way across my Blackberry's ridiculously small keyboard.

The paving beneath me had been warmed by the sun. I traced its rough edges with my fingers and looked around me. Beyond next door's fence, an ornamental cherry was bursting into life and daffodils waved in the breeze along the border. A pair of sparrows were picking around in the mess of pine needles surrounding the tree stump; if I went back to my work straight away I would only disturb them. It was a good excuse.

I closed my eyes and let myself drift. My phone buzzed. I jumped. I read the message. I smiled.

Dinner sounds great. So's Jack. Love you loads xxxxxxxxx

After supper we stayed at our table as the restaurant emptied and the bar became louder. I prevaricated over having another beer as we had to collect Claire from the cinema but when Izzie suggested I stayed with the boys I was easily persuaded. She drained the last of her coffee and kissed Stephen and Gareth goodbye before weaving her way through the bar.

Watching her make her way to the pub door, Stephen said, "She's a lovely lady, Rob."

"I know. I'm so lucky. Who'd have thought I'd find her again after all these years."

"Is she still OK about you forgetting, you know…?"

My hand locked around my glass but to my surprise the words ran out freely enough.

"She's been amazing – especially as it's much worse than one incident. It's months. Months of a life with Izzie I've just blotted out."

Gareth leant forward. "What do you mean, blotted out?"

So I told them. Stephen stared into his glass the whole time I was talking. After a while I ground to a halt.

But Gareth kept asking questions, especially what my memories of that time were.

"I walked away from it all. I couldn't be in the house. Mum was everywhere, so I went on a walking trip. I never came back."

"Where did you go?"

"Along the south coast as far as Looe then I cut inland over the moors and ended up in Newquay for the summer. And I know I was there because when we went down at half-term we met someone I used to know. But that would have tied in with the time Izzie and I split up. I could have just gone straight to Newquay." I picked up my beer glass then put it down again.

"So you both knew you were at Jennifer's beforehand because she validated your memory and you both knew you were in Newquay because someone else did."

"Pretty much," I shrugged.

"Robin, how stable would you say Izzie is?"

"What do you mean?"

"Just humour me a moment. It's just... she seems a bit brittle to me." He steepled his fat, little fingers together in a way which seemed calculated to irritate me.

"Of course she's stressed. I mean, she's only been widowed seven months—"

"And how did she cope with that?" Gareth jumped in.

I took a deep breath. "From what I can gather she was strong while Claire needed her to be but then she did fall apart. She had to take a month or so off work but she went back in January. Since then she's had me to cope with – and Claire – and her job's pretty stressful too. But I'm still not sure what you're getting at."

"I'm wondering – and it's just a hunch, mind you – if this is more down to Izzie than you."

I leant forwards. "How do you mean?"

"Well let's just suppose seeing you believe her version of events puts her in a position of power in the relationship and that would make someone who's pretty fragile feel more secure."

"Oh come on, that's just the worst sort of psychobabble shit."

Stephen shifted on his chair. In losing my temper with Gareth I was letting him down all over again. I ran my hand through my hair and muttered an apology.

"No offence taken. It's a big thing to throw at you. I can see it hasn't even occurred to you that your memory could be right and Izzie's wrong."

"No, Gareth. Izzie must be remembering right. There's things she's said that mean she had to have been there, like how I found Mum after she died, and the music that was played at her funeral."

"Things you could have told her."

"Now, look—" I started, leaning over the table towards him.

"Gareth, please stop this." Stephen's voice was firm. "I know it's interesting for you, but it's Rob's life we're talking about, something he's having to live with every waking moment. And I can't imagine what that must be like for him because I'm really struggling just trying to get my head around it."

I stretched my hand across the table and covered his. "Thank you, Stephen."

He pulled his away and stood up. "Come on, let's settle the bill and go home."

Chapter Fifty-One

The house containing Gareth's consulting room was one of a row of Victorian terraced properties, anonymous apart from the wooden plaque by the door: Bognor Therapy Centre. As I stepped into the hall a bell rang so loudly that it made me jump and I was glad no one was there to see me.

The reception area was light and spacious with pale laminate flooring and brightly coloured sofas. The bay window housed a tank in which small orange fish swayed to a gentle undertone of classical music, as though a string quartet was playing next door.

A thin man of about thirty sat behind a desk.

"I'm here to see Gareth... Dr Rhys. He said to come at the end of his clinic."

"Oh, yes, you must be Robin. Go down the corridor and up the stairs. He has his own waiting area at the top."

The music seemed to follow me through the house. The steps opened onto a square landing with a kitchenette on one side and a pair of yellow sofas on the other. I ignored them both and gazed out of the window onto the small yard behind. The terrace was almost back to back with the houses beyond, and next door a couple of tea towels flapped on a rotary dryer. It was how Izzie had described the view from our flat in Shirley, but no ghost of a memory stirred.

It seemed rude to turn around when Gareth showed his client out, and as her heels clipped down the stairs I felt his hand on my shoulder.

"I'm glad you wanted to come."

"I wanted to apologise for Saturday. You were only trying to help and I was rather churlish. I don't want any bad blood between us. It would upset Stephen."

Gareth smiled. "He was noticeably brighter after you phoned."

I nodded. "That's good. I sense... I don't know... he's kind of looking at me with new eyes because of this."

"Maybe. But I think that's only because he feels he's growing in his understanding of you."

"And not in a good way."

Gareth sat down and I lowered myself onto the sofa nearest the window. "Stephen's looking for answers too, Rob. When you went away after Jennifer died it was a double blow to him – a second bereavement, almost. The fact he couldn't reach you, and the worry about what had happened to you... Quite frankly, if it had been me who'd found you in Winchester I'd have punched your lights out."

I stared at the floor as Gareth continued. "However, all along the professional part of me knew you were acting that way because you'd reached the point where you couldn't cope any more. The way you cared for Jennifer was extraordinary – you must have been absolutely exhausted – and I'd seen enough of you to know that you would never hurt anyone deliberately, so don't think I bear any sort of grudge.

"And of course neither does Stephen, but he didn't understand either. He was just so glad when you came back. With his parents and brother having turned their backs on him, you're all the family he has. But this apparent gap in your memory is forcing him to accept that you have some imperfections – he had rather put you on a pedestal, to be honest. And I think he's pretty scared; he asked me if you could have some sort of early onset dementia."

For the first time I met his eyes. "Could I?"

"Not from what I've seen, no."

"I did think perhaps it wasn't. It's so different from what happened to Jennifer. I've... I've been thinking about her a lot. For the first time, really..." From nowhere, a wave of misery threatened to engulf me.

It took me some minutes to pull myself together. Gareth stood up and put the kettle on. "Tea? Coffee?"

"Tea would be nice," I croaked. I tipped my head up, willing the tears to flow back into my eyes.

"If you want to cry then you should," said Gareth.

I tried to smile. "Bloody psychobabble therapist."

He grinned back at me. "It's a job."

As he waited for the kettle to boil he asked me how Izzie was.

"Is that a polite or a professional enquiry?"

He popped a tea bag into each mug. "Bit of both, really. Depends how much psychobabble shit you want to hear."

"I just can't believe she'd do what you say."

"I'm not saying it's necessarily deliberate."

"Then what is it, Ga? I don't understand."

He handed me my tea and sat back on the sofa.

"Now, this is just my theory, remember, but let's suppose initially that the broken memory was yours, that you did forget making love with her when you knew each other before. Revealing that showed Izzie a vulnerability in you where maybe she hadn't seen one before."

"That's not right. I mean, how vulnerable would you want me to be? When she first saw me I was a down-and-out, and then she found me in hospital, sick as a dog."

"And she took you in – rescued you, if you like. She didn't flinch from your weakness, or perhaps even want you to be strong. But think, Robin, emotionally speaking, who wears the trousers in your relationship?" He held up his hand. "I don't expect you to answer that, but think about it. My hunch is, however tough Izzie wants to be, it's you. Not being 'in charge' could make her feel insecure. Then suddenly, bang, you're on the back foot again and she senses the power balance tip in her favour."

"I'm sorry, Gareth, it sounds so Machiavellian and Izzie's not like that."

"I did say this isn't a deliberate or conscious thing."

"I'm afraid it's completely beyond my understanding."

"It's only a theory, remember. It's just that, in my experience, it seems the most likely answer."

I balanced my mug on the arm of the sofa. "You mean you've come across this before?"

"Not in quite such an extreme way, not the recreation of months and months, but I have seen it in my clinics, yes."

I felt myself clutching at straws. "But surely that isn't the only answer?"

He put his mug down on the table. "There are several recognised psychological conditions that affect memory but I think we can rule most of them out. Bipolar does it, and that might fit with Izzie's depression, but in those cases the memories are more obviously delusional and Izzie's version of events is completely plausible.

"Then there's something called false memory syndrome, and although at one time many psychologists didn't believe it existed, there is now some conclusive laboratory evidence that it does. Researchers actually managed to plant false memories alongside real ones and about a quarter of the participants ended up believing them. That's a significant minority."

"So who would have planted this memory in Izzie... well, in either of us?"

"It doesn't have to have been anyone else, Robin. You could have very easily done it yourselves. I'll send some links to that Blackberry of yours, if you like."

I stared at the dregs of tea in the bottom of my mug. "I'd rather... you know... that Izzie was right. One way or another, her story or mine, I was a total shit back then – a shit and a coward. I feel like I owe her this one."

Gareth leant forwards. "Hair shirts don't sit happily in relationships, Robin. You'd do well to remember that."

Chapter Fifty-Two

Claire had chosen a trip to Bournemouth as her birthday treat but the weather gods were far from smiling. Even so, the stiff breeze cutting along Bournemouth seafront wasn't enough to keep the hardened surfers out of the water and Claire and Jack watched them ride the waves with envy.

"You are going to teach me, aren't you?" she asked.

"Sure," I answered, although in truth I was regretting the offer, if only because the sea looked far too cold.

"So can we start over Easter?"

"If the conditions are right."

She gazed towards the sea. "Like today?"

"Yes, but not today. Although we'd better get your rash vest sorted and check out what gear we can hire."

As we walked along the promenade to the shop, Jack asked me where I had learned to surf. He was a polite young man, opening doors for Izzie, but there was something about him I felt uncomfortable with. Perhaps I was just unsure of my role in Claire's birthday-treat-cum-meet-the-parents day. I didn't feel any better when I overheard Izzie whispering to Claire, telling her not to pick too expensive a present.

I was standing beside a display of longboards and it took me right back to Megan's shop and her remark about waiting for a handout from her. My fingers closed around a roll of twenty pound notes in my pocket and I wandered over to Claire and peeled three off.

"That's your budget, birthday girl. I want you to get a decent rash vest then spend every last penny of it before we leave this shop."

"Robin, that's too much," Izzie interjected. Claire looked uncertain for a moment but I winked at her and she threw her arms around me.

"Oh, Robin, thank you. Come on, help me choose the best one; I don't know what to look for."

Inevitably, Jack was far more switched on about cool surf wear but at least I made sure she found a vest which was good quality as well as bearing the right logo. With the rest of the money she bought herself a pair of pink flip-flops and left the shop bubbling with excitement.

Izzie held me back as we walked towards Harry Ramsden's. "It was too much, Robin. You should have bought her the rash vest and been done with it."

"Not a cheap one, though."

She looked away. "You heard me then?"

"Yes, and you made me feel about an inch tall."

She buried her chin in the collar of her jacket. "I didn't mean to."

I took her hand and gave it a squeeze. "I know. And anyway, you're kind of half-right – I won't be able to make much of a contribution towards lunch now."

"You make all the contribution I need just by being here. Today would have been so hard on my own."

"You must both be thinking of Connor."

"He was a very hands-on father, very committed. I'm sure Claire misses him much more than she shows me."

"Maybe Jack's come along at just the right time."

She looked up at me, the breeze snatching her hair away from her face. "Maybe. I hope so, anyway."

After we had lunch we wandered into the Winter Gardens and watched as Jack took Claire in the static balloon as a birthday treat. She didn't look down at us, only at the sea and the sky, and as Izzie held my hand, my mind flicked back to walking through this very park before my first night sleeping under the stars on the beach. As I had passed the pier 'I Will Survive' had drifted out over the sand and I had even managed a wry smile. How could that sort of detail be a figment of my imagination?

I lay awake that night and retraced my steps: Bournemouth, Sandbanks, Swanage, Anvil Rock, West Lulworth, Weymouth… then other trips to these places mixed themselves in and I wondered if perhaps I had become confused. Maybe I had lived in a dream world where I was travelling, away from the nightmare my life had become, as I trashed my job and let Izzie down so badly.

But through the wreckage of memory a coherent thought began to emerge. Was there somewhere I had visited for the first and only time on my trip? Was there a place where my recollections might be pure? Could I think of a place, sketch it out, draw a plan, write down as much as I could about it, then go, go and find out if it was real?

Gareth had planted a noxious seed and the way Izzie'd made me feel in the surf shop had given it light and air. I wanted to be able to destroy it just as soon as I could. I didn't want to be thinking constantly about who was in control. I wanted to enjoy my life with Izzie. I wanted our love to be pure and natural and good.

I rolled over and wrapped my arm around her. She stirred just enough to wriggle a little closer and I brushed her hair with my lips, drinking in her scent. Perhaps I was the one who was overcomplicating things now.

Chapter Fifty-Three

West Bay was the place I'd only ever been to on my journey west. And it was just close enough for a day trip during the Easter holidays. Izzie was keen; she'd never been there and when Claire said we should take some time for ourselves I was glad. I reasoned she'd rather be with Jack anyway.

Jack. I hadn't expected to bump into him first thing one morning in Netley, especially with a bedraggled brunette in impossibly high heels and no skirt I could see clinging to his arm. He was going to walk straight past me but I barred his way.

"Good party, Jack?" I enquired.

"Oh—Morning, Mr Vail. Yes… it was OK." His eyes seemed glued to the pavement.

"Did you not invite Claire or did she not want to go?"

Colour rose in his cheeks and before he could reply the girl butted in. "Who's Claire?"

I was happy to supply the information. "Claire's his girlfriend."

The girl's face seemed to collapse in on itself, but to her credit she had spirit. "You fucking, lying bastard," she spat, before disentangling herself from his grasp and tottering up the road. After four or five steps she stopped and yelled, "And don't try to text me – you were a fucking useless lay anyway."

I didn't wait to hear his response, but carried on into the Co-op to get myself a pasty for lunch.

When I came out, to my surprise Jack was waiting.

"Mr Vail?"

I stopped. "Yes."

"Are you going to tell Claire?"

I considered. "I think I'll probably tell her mother."

He shifted his weight from one foot to the other. "Could I... I mean... is there anything I could do to change your mind?"

I shook my head. "Claire's precious to me. If she's going to get hurt then best get it over with."

"Claire's precious to me as well."

The strange thing was that I believed him. Looking into his eyes, man to man, there was an honesty I hadn't seen before.

"Then why did you screw around?"

He shuffled and looked down. "You know how it is... I was drunk, it was offered..."

"Weakness isn't an excuse, Jack."

"I know. I don't deserve Claire."

"No, you don't. Not at the moment anyway."

"I'm so sorry. Please don't tell Mrs O'Briain. Claire's so different – she's really amazing and I don't want to lose her," he mumbled.

And there I was, not seventeen, but twenty-three, feeling exactly the same way about Izzie. But I wasn't going to let him off the hook completely. "I'll think about it," I said and walked past him to unlock my van.

Chapter Fifty-Four

Izzie

I am looking at Claire and Robin through glass. I can see them move but I can't hear them speak. It feels as though I'm still dreaming, but I can't be because I'm standing at the spare room window gazing down on the garden. I pick up a smoked-glass rabbit from the windowsill and it feels cool and heavy in my hand.

They are marking out a square for the vegetable patch with string. The hole where the fir tree was gapes black and empty. Claire walks backwards with the tape then stops where Robin indicates and puts a peg in the lawn, an expanse of flesh yawning between her skin-tight jeans and the back of her sweatshirt. It disappears when she looks up and speaks to Robin and there is a twitch somewhere under his beard that indicates his smile.

I'm getting fed up with that beard. It's tidy now, just one shade lighter than his chestnut hair and just as neatly trimmed, but it hides his face. If I asked him, would he shave it off?

The glass is cold against my forehead. I'm torn between going back to bed and running across the lawn in my bare feet to join them. The sun is shining and it's the Easter holidays but exhaustion wins and I stumble back to my room and sleep for another couple of hours.

Later, we go to the garden centre to buy seeds. Robin hasn't finished digging the bed but he needs compost and loads two huge bags into the boot of my car before we have a late lunch in the outdoor café. The warmth seeps through my fleece and Robin stretches in his chair, his legs blocking the gravel path. We list the vegetables we want to grow while Claire texts Sasha and makes a bid for some mushrooms to put in Robin's omelettes.

He laughs at the idea that they can be planted in a vegetable bed and draws pictures of spores on a paper napkin. If Claire is feigning interest she does it well enough to persuade him to buy a mushroom starter kit for her to try to grow some in what looks like an enormous paper bag. It is to be her special project.

"What's mine?" I ask him.

"Sitting in a deckchair looking beautiful," he grins.

"No, come on, I don't want to be a bystander in this family."

He flicks his pen between his fingers. "Well, you're going to have more time than me over the summer, so you can be in charge of the salad section: lettuce, radish, that sort of thing. You can plant them at half-term and harvest them in the long holidays. How does that sound?"

A reluctant concession – that's how. "Oh, so you're committing yourself to the things that take longer to grow? That's good."

"Izzie," he falters, "I don't understand."

Claire jumps up. "Oh she's just stressed, Robin, as per usual. Take no notice. I'm off to see the pygmy goats. Are you coming?"

"In a minute," he murmurs.

Once she goes his eyes meet mine. "Is it me? Have I said something or…"

I shake my head. "I'm sorry. I'm just so tired."

"It's been a long term, what with… everything."

"Yes. Come on, let's go see those goats." I stand and wrap my arm around his waist. Instantly his is across my shoulder, his fingers digging into the top of my arm as he pulls me into him. I whisper my thanks but I'm not sure he hears.

Chapter Fifty-Five

I sleep most of Monday. Claire must have crept around the house and when I finally surface I thank her. She makes me tea and gives me a hug, telling me I look better for it.

On Tuesday, Robin and I go to West Bay. The moment we step out of the car the sea air zings into my lungs and through my veins. Robin strides towards the ticket machine – rangy, taut buttocks, broad shoulders. I wish we had booked into a hotel.

It's almost lunchtime. The harbour is a disappointing concrete-lined rectangle with a row of takeaway kiosks behind it. Fish and burgers and ice cream. But on their landward side is a square with a pub in one corner. There are a few tables outside and hooks just begging for hanging baskets. Two wooden tubs of tulips flank the door. The river runs close by and I am drawn to it – or more precisely, to the island in the middle.

It isn't really an island. There's a footbridge over the water to an enormous boathouse facing downstream. Except it's not a boathouse – it's a fish restaurant. We study the menu on the landward end of the bridge. It's not too pricey, either. I tell Robin it's my treat, instead of an Easter egg. To my relief, he agrees.

We sit by the window, the river flowing around us, families of ducks bobbing by. Robin's mood is as reflective as the water. When the waitress comes he breaks his silence to order fish pie while I opt for a crayfish salad. We have a chilled chablis each. His fingers are damp from the glass as he traces the outline of my hand on the tablecloth, lingering for a moment on my wedding ring.

"A year," I tell him. "I'll wear it for a year for Connor, but that's all."

He pulls away. "I didn't mean anything by touching it, Izzie. You wear it for as long as you like. I don't mind. It's… it's nothing to do with me." There's that hint of impermanence again. "I can love you whether or not you have that ring on your finger," he continues. "It's a symbol – and symbols are important – but it represents something that's gone. I don't feel challenged by your memories. They're precious. Keep them safe."

After lunch we explore. We stand for a long while by the charmless harbour, watching a fishing ketch unload its haul. Next to us a man is nailing a sign to the rails, advertising boat trips along the Jurassic coast.

"Wouldn't it be nice to come back and do one of those?" I ask.

"It would be interesting to see it from the sea looking up. After all, I've wa—" Robin stops and turns away from me along the harbour.

"What did you say?"

"It would be interesting, that's all."

We stroll over cobbles to the old village, dwarfed by the development around it. Many of the cottages have holiday let signs next to their doors. I guess the remaining fishermen prefer the modern houses further from the water. We scrunch along the beach and Robin kicks over pebbles, searching for fossils. He finds a small section of trilobite and it is the most animated I have seen him all day.

We go into a café for a cup of tea. I make a beeline for the ladies then join Robin at the counter just as he is being served.

"… About then, I think. There was a right old kerfuffle because the design was so modern. It's odd, because they blend in quite well now."

"What blends in?" I ask.

"Those flats. Your fella here remembers them being built."

Robin puts his arm around my shoulder and points out of one of the windows. "Those, Izzie, the ones on an angle to the beach, with all that plate glass."

I wait until we're sitting down before I shoot at him. "You didn't say you'd been here before."

He looks at his hands. "Didn't I? It's not important. I just brought Jennifer here once to visit a friend and I wandered around while they had a natter."

"Oh, OK."

He picks up the teapot and starts to pour. "I couldn't quite remember when it was. That's why I asked the lady at the counter if she knew when the flats went up. It was something to say to her anyway."

"You're not bothering to make much conversation with me today." My finger starts on a figure of eight on the plastic tablecloth. Robin's eyes follow it.

"I'm sorry, Izzie."

"Is it because coming here's made you think of Jennifer?"

He shrugs.

"Robin, why did you want to come here?"

"Because I remembered it as a nice place and I thought we'd enjoy a day out together. Only, clearly you're not enjoying it." There is no rancour in his voice, only sadness.

"No, Robin. That's not the case. I've had a lovely time but I'm just a bit worried about you, that's all. You're so quiet."

"I guess even a chatterbox like me shuts up sometimes."

But then he talks and talks, all the long miles to Chandler's Ford to collect Claire.

It's a surprise when Jack's mother invites me in for a drink. Robin has stayed in the car so I fetch him. He rolls his eyes.

"I know," I tell him. "I feel rather underdressed for the

occasion too. Jack's mum looks like she's just stepped out of a beauty parlour."

Robin smiles. "She still won't hold a candle to you."

"Come on, let's get this over with then we can go home and be scruffy in peace."

We're ushered down a narrow hall into a room overlooking the garden. Pale-blue curtains in a quiet floral pattern frame an enormous expanse of glass and the cushions on the cream leather sofas match them. I wish I had taken off my deck shoes at the front door; I'm sure I'm trailing sand and shingle through the house. Robin's trainers look huge and grubby.

"Colin's just home from work – he's freshening up. We thought it would be a nice opportunity to meet you, if you're not in a rush." The comment sounds barbed. The few times I've collected Claire I haven't even crossed the threshold.

"Term time's just so hectic," I offer by way of excuse.

"Oh, but those lovely long holidays you have. I do so envy you."

"It has its advantages." Teaching has its disadvantages too, but I want to be polite.

Louise pours me a gin and tonic and fetches a Coke for Robin from the fridge. Jack and Claire tumble down the stairs, making me wonder what they've been up to in his bedroom. A chat about something closer to home than the birds and bees seems somewhat overdue.

Claire hugs me and then Robin. "Did you have a good day?" she asks.

"Lovely thanks. We had a gorgeous lunch in the fish

restaurant and then just wandered around. Robin found part of a trilobite on the beach."

"Super cool, Mr Vail," says Jack, but he doesn't look at Robin. Or at me.

The silence is broken by a stocky man in chinos and a Ralf Lauren polo shirt breezing in. He shakes our hands and introduces himself. When Robin stands to greet him he towers over him. Colin bustles away to the granite slab in front of the fireplace and remains there until Robin folds himself back onto the sofa. Claire bounces into the empty seat next to him.

"So nice to meet Claire's parents at last," Colin says as Louise hands him his drink. "Isn't it, darling?"

At last? Once again I ask myself how long this relationship has been going on.

"Oh, but Isobel was saying how busy she is in term time, darling. She's a teacher."

Colin looks at Robin. "And what's your line of business?"

"Gardening."

"Design or contracting?"

Robin's beard twitches. "Just gardening. And handyman work, decorating, putting up shelves – you know the sort of thing. You probably pay someone to do those jobs yourself."

He says it so pleasantly that I wonder why I feel embarrassed. Louise laughs. "I wish we did but Colin loves having a go and it's not his forte at all." I look around the immaculate room. "You're so lucky, Isobel, having a man who's good with his hands."

"Yes, and I suppose gardening follows logically if you have a degree in botany."

Colin and Louise look suitably surprised. That'll teach them to be so frigging judgmental. I squeeze Robin's hand and sneak him a triumphant glance. He's isn't looking at me though. He's studying the carpet.

Chapter Fifty-Six

The conversation I know I have to have with Claire looms over my week. It's not that there's no opportunity – Robin is working long days painting the cricket pavilion at Burridge – it's just that I'm too much of a coward to take it.

In my mind we talk a hundred times and it never turns out well: Claire laughs at me because she slept with Jack weeks ago; Claire goes off in a huff; Claire lies to me again... I am sure other mothers don't make such a hash of things. I wish I had kept up with some of my girlfriends, then I would have someone to ask. But somehow, over the years, I've not been good at keeping in touch with people. On Easter Saturday afternoon I have a few glasses of wine – Dutch courage – but all that happens is I fall asleep on the sofa and only wake when Robin comes home.

On Easter Sunday Robin gets up first and is already in the kitchen with Claire by the time I come down. I give her

her chocolate egg but instead of saying thank you she asks why I haven't bought one for Robin.

He turns from making the toast. "Your mum and I had a deal, Claire. She bought me lunch on Tuesday instead. Fish pie, it was. Lovely."

"Fish pie isn't very traditional," Claire grumbles, breaking into the cardboard wrapping to free her Maltesers.

"Neither is chocolate," Robin replies.

"Yes, but eggs are." Claire pops a sweet into her mouth. "Like hot cross buns."

"The stone in front of the tomb and the crucifixion," I join in.

Robin puts the toast down on the table. "Fertility and Eostre."

He says it in a strange way, not like Easter at all.

"Eostre?" Claire mimics him.

"Yes, the goddess of spring in the old calendar."

"The old calendar?"

"Pre-Christian. Before they came and nicked our beliefs," he laughs.

"So the word Easter comes from before Christ?" Claire is clearly enthralled.

"It's possible. She was an Anglo Saxon goddess associated with the spring equinox but her name could be much older. In heathenry, many rites are celebrated by baking and her symbol is a cross. And to pagans a cross means giving in all its forms, so a fish pie definitely counts."

"You know a lot about it."

Robins nods. "It comes from Jennifer. Her knowledge,

her beliefs – I kind of absorbed them over the years. They made more sense to me than any organised religion."

"So you mean you're a pagan? Wow." Claire is looking at him with something close to awe.

He shrugs. "I suppose. If you must label it."

"What, druids and stuff, and dancing naked under the trees at dawn?" She leans forwards but I am pinned to the back of my chair, the wooden bars eating into my back.

Robin's laugh ricochets around my head. "Not on your life! For us it was more about respect for the natural world. Yes, we have rites and celebrations…"

Tea slops over the table as I put my mug down. "You really believe in all that mumbo jumbo?"

He frowns. "It depends what you mean by 'all', Izzie."

"All of it? Any of it! Worshipping rocks and trees? Are you completely stupid?" My voice has risen to a scream.

Robin shoots back in his chair. "Izzie, please, calm down."

"But it's what you believe. It's important."

"Yes, it is. But only to me. I'm not asking you to buy into it. Or insult me because of it either."

I ignore the warning note in his voice. "But it's not normal. Paganism… it's some kind of warped freak show—"

He flings his knife from his hand and it spins across the table, his face a sudden storm of anger.

"Yeah, a freak, that's exactly what you think I am, isn't it? Dodgy memory, dodgy bank balance, dodgy job and now I'm stupid as well. Well on that count at least you're right." Three strides and he's at the kitchen door. He twists around to face me. "You can forget it, Izzie, just forget it, OK?"

Claire and I sit in silence. Upstairs doors slam and drawers open and close. Butter congeals on Robin's abandoned toast. Finally she touches my arm.

"Stop him, Mum."

"No."

She stands up.

"Claire, no. He must do what he feels is right."

"But Mum… don't you love him?"

"This… this isn't about me."

Heavy footsteps run down the stairs. The front door opens, but it doesn't close. Not immediately. We listen as an enormous anorak rustles from its hook and wellingtons and walking boots are gathered up, scraping across the floor. Then, finally, there is a gentle click and a few minutes later the sound of Robin's van starting.

Then Claire does move. "Mum, what have you done?" she yells before she rushes from the room. But she is enough of my daughter not to try to follow him. Instead she throws herself howling onto the sofa.

One thought and one alone comes into my mind. I whisper it out loud. "How the hell did that happen?" One minute we were having a slightly fractious but entirely normal family breakfast and the next Robin has gone. There must have been warning signs. How have I missed them?

My numbness is pierced by Claire's sobs. I edge onto the sofa and stroke her hair.

"Shh, darling. He'll come back."

"But he packed. He took everything."

"Perhaps not everything."

"Oh, Mum, you know what I mean."

I have no answer. My hand runs over and over her head. The rhythm soothes me.

Claire rolls onto her back and wipes her nose on the sleeve of her sweatshirt. "Why, Mum?"

I screw up my face. "I... I don't know. It was such a small thing, after all."

She sits up. "I don't mean why did he leave, I meant why did you go for him like that?"

"Like what?"

"Like you're always doing when he's so lovely to us. You're a week into the holidays. You shouldn't be stressed by now."

"Like I always do?" Do I?

"You know you do. Every little thing and you're on his case. You were never like that with Dad."

I can't remember. I stand up and wander into the hall. Robin has left his keys on the table; he really does mean this. Claire hears me pick them up and starts to cry again.

I crouch beside the sofa. "What would you like me to do?" I ask.

She looks up and sniffs. "Tell me, do you want Robin back?"

"Of course I do."

"Then phone him. Say you're sorry. He'll come back if you do, I know he will."

I wish I could share her confidence. "All right. But best give him time to calm down first, don't you think?"

Claire nods. "I've never seen him angry before."

While we wait we decide to plant the vegetable patch. Claire texts Jack to postpone their date and I'm glad.

The packets of seeds are in a shoebox in the garage. Robin had a plan where everything should go and Claire makes a better fist of remembering than I do. I keep thinking about being relegated to planting the salad at half-term. Now I'm following the instructions on the packs, raking over the earth, making little drills and watching as Claire counts the seeds in. The soil smells damp and comforting and the sun starts to warm my back.

In the distance the doorbell rings.

"You go," says Claire. "It might be Robin."

It's the longest walk across the lawn and my boots stick to my feet as I heel them off on the sill of the patio doors. I all but run across the living room and skid onto the tiles in the hall. There is a tall shape through the glass but I know it isn't Robin. It's Jack.

"I'm sorry to disturb you, Mrs O'Briain, but I was worried about Claire. I won't stay long and I won't be any trouble. Mum dropped me over with my bike so I can cycle back."

I'm clutching the doorframe.

"Mrs O'Briain?"

"Sorry, Jack, I was miles away. Thanks so much for coming though. Claire's in the garden. I'll show you."

At first I watch them through the kitchen window. I see the sheer delight on Claire's face when she sees who it is. He spins her around and wraps her into him and she just comes up to his chin. Robin holding me. I can't think that; it isn't. This is Claire. Jack kisses the tip of her nose and she burrows her face into his sweatshirt.

After a while she pulls away. I can't see her face but Jack's is tense, anxious. He is talking very fast and holding both her hands. If he glances towards the house he will see me for the peeping Tom I am. I turn away and make myself a cup of tea I don't want and open a newspaper I am incapable of reading.

I hear them come through the patio door.

"I'll be off then, Mrs O'Briain."

I offer him a drink before he goes and he gulps down a can of Coke, one hand holding Claire's all the time. "Thanks for coming," I say. "It really is nice of you."

He smiles. "I so wanted to."

Claire sees him to the front door. I suspect she waves him off down the street as well. She looks thoughtful when she comes back into the kitchen.

"Good choice, Claire," I tell her. "Unusually considerate for a teenager."

"Yes, he was worried about us – but also feeling a bit guilty."

"Guilty? Why on earth would he feel guilty?"

Some Coke has spilt onto the table and Claire starts to make shapes in it with her index finger. "When I texted him I said I couldn't understand how something so small had blown up so quickly and there must be something else behind it. He came over to tell me he knew what it might be. Was it, Mum? Did you and Robin argue over Jack?"

"Why would we do that? And Claire, look at me while we're talking."

Her head jerks up. "Robin caught Jack out. He... he went with another girl after a party and... and they bumped into Robin. Of course he asked him not to say anything but Robin said he was going to tell you. Jack wondered if perhaps that had sparked something off."

Why is it teenagers always think they're the centre of the universe? "So Jack came around here to unburden his own guilt when you're hurting so badly anyway?"

"No, Mum. It wasn't like that. He said he'd wanted to tell me on Tuesday but he wasn't brave enough. He said he wanted it out in the open and that I was different and he'd never do it again, and he didn't want any lies between us."

I wonder if he would have said the same if he hadn't been caught. I wonder if by 'went with' he meant he'd had sex with the other girl. I wonder what Claire took it to mean. I wonder if sex means anything at all to these kids. I wonder why Robin didn't tell me, when it was my daughter's welfare at stake.

"Mum?"

My fury gathers pace but it is unformed, swirling circles of emotion. Purples, blacks, deep, deep reds.

"Mum? Are you OK?"

Colours inside my head and bursting in front of my eyes...

I stand up and grope for the sink, finding it just in time. Acrid tea and yellow bile splatter on the stainless steel. I cling to the taps as Claire supports me, her child's body all that holds me upright.

Chapter Fifty-Seven

Robin

On Easter Monday it rained. Great torrents whipped through the gaps in Jennifer's window frames and smashed the early blossom from the trees. I hurried from the woodstore, arms full of logs, and managed to light the Aga. Apart from laying old towels on the windowsills I couldn't think of anything else to do.

As soon as I arrived the day before, I'd left a voicemail for Stephen telling him I was back – it was his house, after all. I was relieved he hadn't picked up; I would've struggled to tell him about what had happened, so I just said I hoped me being back here wouldn't change his plans. Even if he put the house on the market tomorrow and someone snapped it up I'd have at least a couple of months to find a new home.

I tried to see the kitchen through a buyer's eyes. The

vases in the corner next to the sink, the wooden chopping boards, the kettle with the chipped enamel spout, the piles of recipes cut from magazines; it was all so achingly familiar to me but a total mess to anyone else. In Izzie's kitchen I'd kept the worktops clear and sparkling. But I couldn't think about Izzie or her kitchen right now.

Sorting out some of the crap seemed like a sensible occupation and I decided to start with the attic. Jennifer's bedroom was the largest and I pushed her bed back against the wardrobe to make the most of the floor space. Caught in the patina of fluff on the carpet was a hairgrip. As I picked it up and tucked it into the pocket of my jeans, I was almost defeated before I had begun.

Dampness filled my nostrils as I opened the loft hatch. I reached up and pulled on the ladder, releasing a cascade of dust. I climbed a few steps, groped for the nearest black plastic bag, and hauled it down and along the landing.

I don't think Jennifer ever threw anything out. The bag was full of threadbare curtains and cushion covers which had been in the living room. Patterned with small birds, they had seemed alive to her when she became ill and I had changed them for plain green ones. It made no difference; she still saw sparrows flying around the room and even put out seeds for them in her best china dishes. I wondered if every bag and box would hold such cruel memories.

Some held no memories for me at all: crates of Susan's school books, a suitcase of toy dolls, years' worth of *Reader's Digest* from the 50s and 60s. Some of this might have a saleable value and I set it to one side to show to Stephen. To this pile I added two pictures in ornate frames, so mildewed

I could only just make out that they were landscapes, and went back to the attic to fetch the next box.

This one was mine – I knew the moment I opened the lid – and it was full of papers from the early years of my business. I'd known nothing about bookkeeping but Jennifer had made me list all the money I earned and keep all the receipts for things I'd bought. Yellow and faded as they were, I could still make some of them out: 59p for a packet of broad bean seeds in 1993, a handwritten garage bill for a service from the same year for £45. This lot was destined to light my next bonfire.

"Rob? Where are you?"

I was so taken aback by the sound of Stephen's voice I didn't reply. I shoved the papers into the box and unfolded myself from the floor.

"Ga, the loft hatch is open."

The catch in his voice brought me back to reality. "It's OK, I'm here, in your gran's bedroom. I'm sorting out stuff from the attic."

Stephen picked his way through the mess to hug me while Gareth hovered at the door. "Are you OK?" Stephen asked.

"I'll live."

"What happened?"

What had indeed? "Come on, let's make a cuppa. What are you guys doing here anyway?"

"We were staying in the New Forest so when I got your message we thought we'd drop by on the way home to see how you were."

"I didn't mean to put you out. I just thought I should let

you know I was back. It is your house, after all." I started down the stairs but Stephen put his hand on my arm.

"And it's your home, Rob, for however long you want it to be."

"Now that's downright sentimental. I mean, if you put it on the market now I'd still have at least a couple of months to sort myself out. I'm making a start, as you can see."

"We'll talk about it later." The angle of his chin told me it would be futile to argue.

It was Gareth who asked what had gone wrong with Izzie and I found I couldn't answer.

"Is the damage repairable? Do you want to repair it?" he persisted.

"I miss her so much I feel raw inside," I confessed. "That's why I'm not really thinking about it. And you, Mr Psychobabble, are about to tell me I need to."

He shook his head. "In your own time. Just shout if you feel yourself getting low."

"Well of course I'll get low. I've just walked out on the best thing I ever had or am likely to have. How low is low, for God's sake?"

"You know the difference, Robin."

I nodded. I suppose I did.

After they left I hopped into my van and drove to the petrol station for a few supplies, including a four-pack of lager. It tasted horrible, all sugar and tin cans, but on an empty stomach it did the trick and blunted the pain just enough for the cogs to start to whir.

I now knew what people meant by the phrase seeing red. Anger was a relative stranger to me but the morning before in Izzie's kitchen it had burst from nowhere and caused irreparable damage. Why?

I tried to trace it to its beginning, but I couldn't. Like water running off a field, forming into streams, merging into a river, it had built unnoticed. Had Gareth started it, with his assertion that Izzie felt she needed to control me? Had he made me notice that perhaps it was true? Or was it Izzie's obvious embarrassment in front of Jack's parents when I told them I was a gardener? Did she really believe it made me not good enough, or did she just want me to feel like the underdog? Did it even matter now?

Tuesday had been a strange day anyway. I knew, the moment we drove down the road into West Bay and I saw the cliffs rising over the sea, that I had been there before. The memory of the bay spread out below me was so vivid, so strong. The shingle beach, the little harbour – I just remembered it, that was all.

The block of flats had clinched it. In my mind's eye I saw them half-built, surrounded by scaffolding. They had stuck out like a sore thumb but now they were just the first of a line. It was a lie that I'd been to West Bay with Jennifer in the early 90s; I had travelled through myself in the autumn of 1986. I was certain of it. Well, as certain as I could be.

And there I faltered. The ring pull on the fourth can of lager fizzed back and I poured the insipid liquid into my glass. The rain was still beating against the kitchen window, fluorescent light illuminating the forsythia gyrating in the wind outside. Just like Izzie and me: twisted and tangled beyond all recognition.

Chapter Fifty-Eight

I t rained for a week, then the weather turned clear. I struggled to work through the downpour. The major was kind, insisting I clear his garage, but other clients kept me outside, battling to mend fences and scrubbing down patios. Inevitably I caught a cold which dragged me down.

But sunshine always helps. I forked the lawn behind Jennifer's house to help it drain and tied the climbing roses back to their wires. I edged the grass to make it look tidier and my annoying cough started to ease. In the woods the trees were bursting with the brightest green leaves and I knew without looking at the calendar that it was almost Beltane.

It had always been Jennifer's favourite festival and over the last few years we had celebrated it any number of times. Whenever she had asked me if it was Beltane I had answered yes. I don't know if that was right or wrong, but our simple ritual of making a bonfire and carrying a lighted torch from it around the edges of her land had filled her with so much delight that it had never been in my heart to refuse.

This year I would be doing it alone. And now I knew it was something I could never have shared with Izzie anyway. I tried to use the thought to miss her less but it was futile.

I built the bonfire before I went to work on the Saturday morning. Seasonal clients had crawled out of the woodwork now that lawns and hedges needed cutting on a regular basis and thankfully I had hardly a daylight hour to myself. I pulled the fallen logs from the orchard and stacked them into a pyramid before starting my search for kindling. It didn't take me long to remember the box of papers languishing in Jennifer's bedroom. I carried it into the garden and started to scrunch the receipts and lists into balls.

I almost had enough to light the fire when I saw it: an edge of blue plastic squashed against the cardboard on one side. For a moment I wondered what it was but then I realised it was my Post Office book. I sat back on my knees and opened a page at random: Weymouth 14th October 1986, Seaton 29th October 1986, Exeter 4th November. I closed my eyes. When I opened them again the stamps were still there – a little smudged in places but official. Proof that I had made my journey.

I felt no jubilation. How low was low? I took the book upstairs and put it in the chest of drawers in my bedroom, alongside my driving licence, under a pile of T-shirts.

My Beltane celebrations did not go according to plan. When I came back from work Stephen's car was in the drive and there was a note on the kitchen table saying he and Gareth were in the Horse & Jockey. I had a quick wash and changed my clothes before strolling down the road to join them.

As far as I can remember we did a lot of drinking, played darts increasingly badly, and it was pretty late when we finally got around to eating. They had obviously decided I needed taking out of myself, but by the time we wove our way home it was far too late to light the bonfire and I would have been far too drunk to strike a match anyway. It was all I could do to fall into bed.

I paid a heavy price for those few hours of oblivion, waking at four in the morning with a raging hangover. My head thumped, my stomach churned, and Izzie filled my head. I failed to stagger to the bathroom and was sick in my wastepaper bin. I lay on the floor and clung to it as dawn crept into the sky.

The last thing I wanted was for Stephen to see me like this. I pulled on an old pair of jeans and a sweatshirt before padding downstairs and dowsing my face in cold water at the kitchen sink. The dew from the grass soaked into my trousers as I crossed the lawn. I averted my eyes from the untouched bonfire. Beltane had passed – there was little point in lighting it now. I had failed Jennifer's memory and the year would be a poor one for me and for the garden.

The woods were full of bluebells and their soft shimmer glowed between the trunks as the rising birdsong surrounded me. I slid to the floor under the fairy tree and its roots embraced me, the knots of its bark burrowing into my back. I closed my eyes, desperate to lose myself in its magic.

The air became warm and heavy with thunder. The chattering of the birds ceased. And there, in the perfect stillness, I heard myself begging, "Please, please let it come right for Izzie and me in the end." The softness of her hands in mine... A flash of lightning... I opened my eyes to catch glimpses of her yellow dress running away from me between the trees. I leapt to my feet, heart pounding, but when I looked again there was no one there.

Stephen all but ran across the lawn to meet me.

"Rob, what's wrong?"

"Just hungover. I went for a walk—"

"But you're crying."

"No I'm not."

He reached up and touched my cheek and I realised it was wet and I could taste salt in my beard. My head felt as though it was made of cotton wool.

"How odd," I marvelled. "I didn't even know."

He took me by the hand and led me into the kitchen where Gareth was making a pot of tea.

"Hey, Mr Psychobabble," I told him, "looks like I need your help. I've been crying and I didn't even know it."

"Denial, Rob. You're a master of it."

"It's nice to be good at something."

He shook his head as he sat down next to me. "Self-esteem issues, too. You'll have to watch yourself."

"I bet I tick all of your boxes. I'm a freak. Izzie thinks I'm a freak so I must be."

"Bullshit."

"What did you say?" I moved my head from side to side to try to clear the fuzz.

"Bullshit. You're not a freak. You're just an ordinary bloke struggling to deal with a relationship breakdown and a massive hangover."

"Of course I'm a freak. I'm a gardener with a degree in botany, for God's sake. If I have any belief at all it's heathen and I'm piss poor at that. And you don't want to know what's wrong with my memory… except… except…" I felt the tears start again.

"Except what?"

"Except it's not my memory. It's Izzie's. I have proof. My Post Office book – I found it in the attic. Like a passport, it's stamped with the places I went." The torrent of emotion sweeping over me was unbearable but somehow I caught a foothold in it. "Look," I told them, "I'm babbling like a madman. I'm probably still drunk. I'd best go and sleep it off, OK?"

Stephen forced a mug of tea into my shaking hands. "Take this up with you and drink it first."

His kindness almost killed me.

The sound of Stephen's car starting outside woke me and I listened as the engine receded up the drive, surprised at how alone I felt. I groped for my watch, finding someone had put a glass of water beside my bed, and I sipped it gratefully. As I came to, I realised I didn't feel anywhere near as bad as I should have done, which gave me a choice: I could lie here and wallow in my misery or get up and do something useful.

I swung my legs out of bed and pulled on a pair of old work trousers. There was a light drizzle misting the roses but that didn't matter. I'd dismantle my Beltane bonfire then put the whole sorry weekend behind me.

As I stepped onto the landing I almost jumped out of my skin when Stephen called, "You awake then, Rob?"

I followed the sound of his voice to Jennifer's bedroom where he was sitting on the floor going through the boxes I'd left for him. I leant against the door jamb. "Why are you still here? I heard the car…"

"That was Gareth. He needs to get back to work tomorrow."

"And what about you?"

"I decided to take an extra couple of days."

"What, to sort out your gran's things?"

He slotted a stack of *Reader's Digests* back into their box. "No. To make sure you're OK."

"That's very kind of you, Stephen, but I'm only hungover."

He was still fiddling with the magazines. "I'm worried it's more than that. This morning, when we couldn't find you, I was so scared you'd gone off again."

I walked into the room and sank down onto the bed. Jennifer's bed. I'd sat here so many times when it was two in the morning and she wanted her lunch, or to get up and walk in the woods. My hand ran over the counterpane, my palm following the contours of the sculpted silk flowers.

"I won't do that to you again, Stephen, I promise." But could I? At the time I had hardly known what I was doing myself, but somehow now, deep inside – and even without Izzie – I knew I'd moved on.

I heard Stephen's footsteps cross the carpet and I looked up at him. There was the small, frightened boy I'd fished out of the Hamble all those years ago, still trying to put a brave face on things.

"I owe you an explanation," I told him. "But not here, not where I found her. Sometimes I can almost see her lying on the floor and that's when I did something... something maybe I shouldn't have."

"What?"

I stood up. "Let's go downstairs."

In the kitchen Stephen made tea while I nibbled on a cracker. My stomach was still churning but I was so lightheaded I knew I needed something. I didn't want to have this conversation but it was long overdue. I couldn't have Stephen living his life wondering if I'd do another runner and nor could I push him away so he didn't have to worry.

He sat down opposite me, acres distant across the square table. "OK, so what did you do?"

"I picked her up and put her on the bed."

"And then?"

"Then I phoned you, then the doctor. Then there's a blank until you all actually arrived."

"But you said you'd done something wrong?"

I sat back, cradling my mug in my hands. "It seems a small, insignificant thing now but back then it took on huge proportions. It was the act of putting her back to bed. I couldn't leave her on the floor, Stephen, I just couldn't. But I told the doctor that the bed was where I found her and when Gareth said there'd be a post-mortem I knew they'd discover that I'd lied."

"But it wouldn't have mattered."

"I know that now but I wasn't thinking. I probably wasn't capable of rational thought. I just remembered what happened after my mother died. She was chronically disabled following an accident and she took too many painkillers. The police came and asked all sorts of questions. It was unbearable and I knew I couldn't go through that again."

"But Robin, that wouldn't have happened. It didn't happen…"

"I didn't leave the house with the intention of leaving for good. I just kept walking and then I found I couldn't come back."

The Aga hissed as the drizzle formed patterns on the window behind his head. In the fading light it was hard to read his expression. "I don't understand," he said. "This was your home. Even without Gran you had your home and you had me."

"I didn't see it like that. I didn't see… anything… at the time. I wasn't even seeing in colour – quite literally. I suppose it was the shock, but also the deep-down exhaustion of caring for someone twenty-four hours a day. She didn't even know who I was half the time. Sometimes she thought I was you but towards the end, more and more, she called me *faðir*. It took me ages to work out it was Icelandic for father."

"Gareth and I... we should have helped you more."

"You offered no end of times, Stephen, you know you did, but I wouldn't let you. You had jobs to hold down and, I suppose, I didn't want your memories of your grandmother to be clouded by what she was like in the end. You did your bit, sorting out the shares and things so we had enough money. I'm only telling you about this now so you know it was everything coming together that tipped me over the edge. It won't happen again."

He nodded, and whispered "Thank you."

The emotion of the moment was almost too much so I stood up. "There are a few jobs I should be doing in the garden and, to be honest, I need the fresh air."

I gazed at the dampened bonfire for a long time but somehow couldn't begin to dismantle it. My failure to mark Beltane made me feel rootless and I walked from one corner of the garden to the other as Jennifer and I had done so many times over the years. Nearest the wood, the shimmer of bluebells seemed to glow in the pale light, but while I let their beauty flood through me my mind was well and truly elsewhere – back in another wood, watching Jennifer's funeral, my self-loathing increasing with every minute I stood there, unable to take the few short steps to support Stephen. I watched the mourning party trudge from the

EVA GLYN

graveside and then the diggers returned to shovel over the earth. And I turned and walked in the opposite direction.

That night I had slept in a copse just off the South Downs Way, curled into the damp loaminess beneath a naked ash tree, the hood of my coat my only pillow. I was just too tired to go on, but I had woken before dawn and by early morning I was in Winchester, cold and thirsty. I don't remember feeling hungry at all. Behind the cathedral were the wooden huts of the Christmas market and I hunkered down under the broad eaves of one of them, out of the wind.

When the stallholders arrived I moved on. I suppose I drifted around the market – I don't really know – until the Christmas songs and carols drove me away. Somehow I ended up in a cheap café with a mug of coffee in front of me, but there was hardly any money in my pocket so I couldn't buy another and eventually I was told I'd outstayed my welcome.

It was a member of the Salvation Army band who rescued me. Maybe that day, maybe the next. All I knew was the constant merging of grey and cold. I didn't feel anything. I don't remember thinking anything. Then this kind gentleman in his peaked cap, carrying a trumpet case under his arm, led me to a hostel where at least I had a meal and a bed.

I recognised the grey as depression but I wouldn't be helped. Only Jennifer could help me and now she had gone. I had no thought at all of returning to her empty house, but now, standing in the garden in the soft dampness of an early May afternoon, I wondered at it. The place was my sanctuary, my home.

The light came on in the kitchen and Stephen waved through the window. I pointed to the path to the woods and signalled I'd be ten minutes. Over the stile, and slipping down the slope, I slid to a halt in front of the fairy tree and put my hand on its trunk. Tall, strong – a survivor. Up, up into its canopy I gazed, with the rough bark imprinting itself into my outstretched palm, and I knew I was a survivor too.

Chapter Fifty-Nine

Despite my piss-poor performance at Beltane, my vegetable patch was growing nicely. I crouched over a row of beetroot, teasing out the smallest plants to give the others a better chance. A cabbage butterfly fluttered onto the purple sprouting. I watched it a little guiltily; if I wanted a decent crop I'd have to spray them but I hated to harm even the most destructive of my winged visitors.

"You didn't reply to my letter."

I leapt up and spun around, almost losing my balance in the process. "Claire!"

"The one I wrote to the fairies. You answered the others but you never replied to me..." Her voice was breaking, taking my heart crashing down with it.

I held out my arms. "Because you'd have known my writing."

For one dreadful moment I thought she was going to ignore my invitation, but then she barrelled into me, burrowing her face in my fleece as I held her as tightly as I possibly could. Over the top of her head I noticed Jack.

"Hello, Mr Vail."

"Thanks for coming. It means a lot to me."

"It does to Claire too."

It took Claire and me a few moments to compose ourselves then I led them into the kitchen. There were two questions at the top of my mind but I was only brave enough to ask one of them.

"So how did you know it was me who writes the fairies' letters?"

"Like you said, I recognised your writing. I was looking in the folder for one addressed to me and I knew straight away it must be you. Then… then I read some of the others and I realised, you know, well, I remembered more than realised. You're kind of special, Robin, and I wanted to see you again."

"I'm glad you did. I was watching a learner driver the other day and wondered how you were getting on."

"I… I haven't started yet." We both looked at the table.

It was Jack who spoke. "If you don't mind me asking, Mr Vail, how did you end up writing those letters?"

"It was Jennifer, the lady who owned this house. I don't think she began the whole fairy tree thing. She told me it just happened over time – a ribbon here, a necklace there – human nature, she said it was. Then the wishes started to arrive. At first they were just tiny pieces of paper pinned to the tree and Jennifer liked to read them. Then one day a child had written quite a long letter to the fairies so she decided to reply.

"It was a long time after I came to live here that she told me what she was doing, although I had already guessed. I saw her going to the wood one night and I followed her. As I watched her kneel by the tree I thought it was some sort of ritual, but even if it was she was collecting the letters as well."

Claire was hesitant. "You said... at Easter... Jennifer was pagan too."

"Pagan." Jack sounded thoughtful. "Does that mean she believed the fairies existed and she was doing their work?"

I shook my head. "Not in the sense of little people with wings living in holes in trees, no. But in the sense that nature is full of spirits, something ephemeral we can never quite touch but need to respect, then yes, I think she did."

"And do you?"

I chose my words carefully. "When I take something from the trees, like my Yule log for example, I stop to ask first, but I couldn't tell you who or what I think I'm asking. It's about respect, really. The natural world is so incredible, there has to be some greater force behind it. I mean, when you think that a tiny seed can turn into a tree which gives you fruit for generations, it's pretty awe inspiring. I guess for me it's finding a way to make a connection with something bigger and better."

"That is just so cool," enthused Jack. "I'm going to look it up on the internet when I get home."

"Well I wouldn't tell your parents. They'll think I'm a weirdo as well as a lowlife gardener. Not that it matters now, I guess."

Claire's eyes met mine. "Robin, do you miss Mum?"

"Of course I do. I've tried to text her loads of times…"

"She never said."

"That's because I never press send. I can't get the words right. Then one of my clients told me I should send her a card instead but I can't seem to find the right one."

"Robin, that's really lame. There are hundreds of cards out there."

"There's about a dozen in here too." I pulled a bundle from the drawer under the worktop. "I keep buying them but none of them seems right."

"You are useless," Claire told me as Jack started to laugh. She turned on him. "This might be funny to you but you know how down Mum is and all the time she's suffering because Robin can't decide which card to send. It's pathetic."

I pushed them across the table. "Well, you choose then."

She spread them out in front of her. One was a line drawing of a heron, another had the words *I'm sorry* embossed on it in foil letters, but most of them were glossy landscape photographs – Old Harry rocks, the beach huts at Hengistbury Head, Golden Cap. For one reason or another I had discounted them all.

Claire held them as though they were playing cards, the pictures facing away from me. She discarded four of them immediately and was left with seven fanned out in her hands.

"Close your eyes and pick."

"That's a cop-out, Claire. You said you'd choose one," Jack interrupted.

"No I didn't. Robin just asked me to, and how could I

tell Mum if I had? No, any of these will do and this is the quickest way."

"OK." My hand shot out and picked the one furthest to the left – a gnarled oak tree in the New Forest, its autumnal colours set dramatically against the blue of the sky.

"No, Claire, not that one. Let me pick another."

She shook her head. "No , and what's more, you're going to write it now."

"Oh come on, give the guy a break…" Jack interceded on my behalf.

But Claire was adamant. "We'll go and finish our walk and when we come back I expect it to be done."

Their chatter receded across the garden and I shifted in my chair. Not only had Claire forced my hand but the clues she'd given to Izzie's state of mind spurred me on. I opened the card flat on the table and picked up a pen.

Dear Izzie,

That was the easy bit.

Maria had asked me what I wanted to say but there were a million things running around my head and I couldn't possibly fit them all onto one little card. Most of them I'd never write down anyway. Finding the words was impossible. I spun the pen slowly around on the table with my index finger.

Dear Izzie,

How are you?

It sounded like a polite enquiry but I was desperate to know. But if I was that desperate, why had I left it so long to ask? Tell the truth.

I have tried to text or write so many times but have never found the right words. I'm glad Claire turned up here this afternoon and made me sit down and do it.

Was that the right thing to say? Would Izzie think I was only getting in touch because of Claire? Perhaps I should pick another card and start again? I thumbed through them: Old Harry Rocks looked appealing. No, I would finish this one first, and when I was absolutely happy with what I'd written I could copy it onto Old Harry and be done. I reread my few lines and realised I had said absolutely nothing. I looked at my watch. Thirty-five minutes had passed.

The ceiling offered no inspiration, but I allowed my eyes to wander along the crack that extended from the light fitting to just above the door. What did I want to happen when Izzie read the card? That was easy: I wanted to see her. Like I'd said to Maria, just to have the chance to talk to her, to see if there was any way...

I would really like to see you. Just so we can talk properly about us.

Yes, that was all right. But what I hadn't done was apologise for running away again, for disappearing from her life when I'd promised I wouldn't. But I hadn't really disappeared, not this time. It wouldn't have taken much thought on her part to work out where I was. Maybe all this was futile anyway. Maybe she wanted me out of her life and she'd just laugh at my attempts at reconciliation.

I heard Jack's voice across the lawn. There was nothing for it: do or die. I scrawled:

Love, Robin

And sealed the card into its envelope. I was just writing Izzie's name on the front when they burst through the door.

"You cut that fine," Claire chided me.

"It's still not right," I grumbled. "Wouldn't it just be easier if you told her I'd love to see her?"

She rolled her eyes. "No it wouldn't. Honestly, Robin, how old are you? Forty-five or something? Have you learned nothing about women?"

I stood up and handed her the envelope. "Obviously not. Now run along. It'll be your bedtime soon."

Claire laughed. "You know nothing about teenagers, either."

Jack reached out to shake my hand. "That's not true though, is it Mr Vail? In the end I... I told Claire about when we met that morning, but you never let on, did you? That was pretty awesome."

I nodded. "I had a bet with myself that you cared

enough about Claire to do the right thing. Now bugger off the two of you. I need to get back to my vegetable patch."

Claire gave me a rib-crushing hug. "Whatever... whatever happens between you and Mum, can I come to see you again?"

"Claire, I would absolutely love that. But you must be honest with Izzie about where you're going, that's all I ask."

"I will. I promise."

She tucked the card into her pocket and they set off down the drive, clasped hands swinging between them. A thought struck me.

"Jack," I called. "It's Robin, not Mr Vail."

He turned and grinned at me, raising his thumb.

Chapter Sixty

Twenty minutes for Claire to get home, then perhaps another five while she said goodbye to Jack. Then maybe five or ten to give the card to Izzie. My index finger marked each segment of time on my watch. I went back into the house to fetch my phone.

I finished thinning the beetroot and started to rake a patch of earth for some radish seeds. An hour had gone by. Perhaps Jack had stayed for a while. Maybe Izzie had gone out. Maybe she'd ripped the envelope to shreds and thrown it in the bin. More than likely I would never know.

I worked in the garden until the light faded, my phone obstinately silent. I wasn't hungry but I made myself a ham sandwich and a mug of tea, sweeping the abandoned cards back into the drawer before I sat down. I flicked through the TV pages of the local freebie paper but nothing grabbed my interest.

I picked up my phone, searching for a flashing red light.

I turned it off and on again. Silence. There was nothing for it but to go to bed.

I was too hot with my duvet and too cold without it. Lying in the tangled sheets a part of me travelled with my card, back into Izzie's room. I could see her wriggling out of her jeans and pulling her T-shirt over her head. The curve of her breast as she turned towards the bathroom was so real I could touch her, the warmth of her flesh beneath my fingers. The pain of loss had never been so intense.

I must have slept a little because I dreamt about the fairy tree – and it was calling me. I stumbled along the landing and knocked a picture off the wall in my attempt to steady myself. My head was full of oak leaves catching the wind, coloured ribbons whispering the faintest suggestion of my name.

I stepped into the shower and drenched myself with icy water but the tree held me back from wakefulness. When I opened the window the dawn air was still, but all the same the branches stirred in my mind, more insistent with every moment that passed. There was nothing for it – I had to go to the woods.

Even from the top of the slope the damage was obvious; every offering within reach had been stripped away and was lying on the floor, a muddle of broken toys and beads and seashells. The box for the children's letters was smashed against a nearby stone and the plastic pocket for the fairies' replies nowhere to be seen. I was filled with rage as I flung myself into the centre of the carnage.

I was not alone in my anger. Kneeling on the other side

of the tree was a woman, digging between the roots with her bare hands, her invectives mingled with sobs.

"You bastard, bastard tree. It's your fault. You started it."

Izzie.

I must have said it out loud. She glanced up, her hair a mass of rats' tails, her eyes sunken holes.

"Bastard tree, oh, you bastard tree." Her fingers returned to gouging the earth.

"Izzie, stop." But my words were useless. I dropped to my knees beside her and pulled her hands away, pinioning them at her sides.

"Let. Me. Go." The bitterness of alcohol was hot on my face.

"Why are you doing this?"

"Bastard tree… started all this… Split our lives in two… It was here… the storm… Bastard, bastard, bastard…"

She was fighting to escape my grasp but I was stronger.

"Izzie, slow down. I don't understand."

"But it's your tree. Your bastard, bastard tree… It took you from me, made you forget… made you lie… Made you come back here and not to me… Oh, Robin…"

"Izzie, it's just a tree. It can't make anyone do anything." Yet I had felt it calling me this morning, and she was right. All those years ago it had made me come back.

She must have sensed the shiver run through my body because she twisted away and a hand came free. Her fist headed for my jaw but I caught her wrist again. She cried out.

"Izzie, please, just stop. I don't want to hurt you. It's the last thing I want. Please, just calm down and come to the house so we can talk."

"You don't want to talk. You just want to save your precious tree." Her voice was more slurred than angry now.

"No, I want to save us." I let go of her wrists and wrapped my arm around her shoulder, pulling her to me.

"Robin, it's not fair. I know you're lying but I feel so... so... safe like this." She was barely coherent through her sobs.

So we knelt under the tree and I held her until I heard an early dog walker moving through the woods. I stood up and hauled her to her feet. "Come on, time we weren't here."

I resisted the temptation to lock the kitchen door behind us. Instead, I pulled out a chair and Izzie sank into it.

"First things first," I told her. "Where's Claire?"

Her brow furrowed. "At home. Asleep."

I looked at the clock. "She won't be for much longer. Give her a call and let her know you're safe with me."

Izzie's eyes were blank. "Where's my handbag?"

"It wasn't by the tree."

She fished in her jacket pockets but pulled out nothing but her keys and a crumpled tissue. "No phone."

"Use mine, then."

I put it into her hand and she looked at it for a moment. "No, you do it. I'm... well, I've had a bit to drink and she doesn't like that." It was the first thing she'd said that made any sense.

Claire sounded as though she'd been asleep and I

apologised for waking her. "I needed to tell you that your mum's with me."

"Why? What happened?"

"Er... I don't know. Perhaps once you gave her my card..."

"I didn't. I told her we'd seen you, but when I said it was you writing the letters for the fairies she went off on one so I didn't think it was the right moment. But whatever I said worked if she's there now."

"Well... yes. We're going to spend some time together, see what we can work out. You'll be OK getting into college on your own today?"

"No problem. I can catch the bus from the village."

"Good girl. If you need us call on my phone. You'll probably trip over your mum's handbag in the hall."

"She must have left in a hurry. Is she OK?"

I looked at Izzie trying to disentangle the tissue from her keys. "Yes. Bit emotional, but then, we both are."

"Sounds promising. Give her my love – and you, too, Robin."

"Thanks, Claire."

I turned to Izzie. "Now, black coffee, hot bath, or both? Or would you just like to go to sleep?"

"Are you emotional, Robin? You're hiding it well if you are."

"Of course I am." I spread my hands on the table. "Churned up, scared... full of love for you, really. It's hard to put it all into words."

"You'll... you'll make me cry again."

"No, I don't want to do that."

"I'll have that bath then."

"Come on, I'll find you a towel."

I took Izzie upstairs to the bathroom I thought of as Jennifer's. It was clean but not very warm so I turned on the heater and went to hunt in the airing cupboard for a towel. Yellow and white stripes to match the curtains. Yellow and white tiles too. Jennifer had loved it – said it was a slice of spring even in the winter.

Izzie was sitting on the edge of the bath. "So this must be where Jennifer put the boys after their dip in the river."

"Yes."

"That was really when I started to love you, the way you were that day. And I did peep when you were in the shower – and I wasn't disappointed."

I sank down next to her. "Whatever happened, huh?"

I meant it in a self-deprecating way but she carried on, her face serious. "We're going to find out, Robin. As soon as I've had this bath we're going to retrace our steps. First your version of events and then mine. It's got to jog some memory, stir something in one of us at the very least. I can't go on like this." She looked up at me, her pupils huge. "Or do you think I've lost the plot completely?"

"But I thought... I thought we'd established that mine was wrong?"

"Not really, Robin, and it's been playing on my mind. We need to find out, otherwise not knowing will always haunt us."

"Well, if you put it like that." I stood up. "Right. I'll get us some breakfast."

But in reality I stood on the landing for a long while,

listening to the pipes creak and groan as the water gushed into the bath and the gentle sloosh as Izzie slid into it. Comforting as the sounds were I felt sick inside.

If the moment of reckoning had finally come, how would Izzie cope with the truth?

Chapter Sixty-One

We retraced our steps across the garden, along the bottom of the field and into the woods.

At the top of the slope Izzie paused. "This was it, wasn't it? We were OK until we reached the tree. Everything was the same."

"As far as we can tell."

"Yes, it must have been. And then... then we walked down the slope and held hands and made our wishes. And it thundered. But there's no thunder today."

"We'll have to pretend."

The fairy tree looked strange, stripped of its finery. A necklace of brightly coloured wooden beads and some ribbons remained in the higher branches but I had never seen the trunk so bare. We held hands around it.

"Will you wish for the same thing?" she asked and I nodded.

"I thought we had to."

"I don't want to. It... it might all happen again."

"What do you mean?"

She shook her head. "Come on, let's get on with it."

The tingle of her fingers stretching out to mine felt the same, but this morning there was no drumbeat of thunder, just a backdrop of birdsong as we made our wishes.

Afterwards, we held hands as we took the path towards the pub.

"Is this then, or now?" I said.

"Both. Don't you remember?" Izzie replied.

"In my memory we walked down to the river."

At the car park Izzie asked, "What happened next?"

"You gave me a lift home."

She looked puzzled. "But that's right – I remember that."

"Well that's good, isn't it?" I held out my hand for her keys. "Only this time, I'd better drive, I think."

She nodded. "I do feel a bit... lightheaded."

Through Botley and over the motorway. So far so good. But my hands slipped on the steering wheel as we turned towards Swaythling. *It's only a place*, I told myself, *a place like any other*. Even so, my stomach was churning as I parked outside the Tesco Express where the corner shop used to be.

"Why are you stopping here?"

"Because it's where you dropped me. I... I had to get some milk or something." I undid my seatbelt. "No, Izzie, that's a lie. I didn't need any milk. I was ashamed I lived on a council estate and I didn't want you to know."

She put her hand on my knee. "Shh, Robin. Don't get angry at yourself. It was a long time ago."

"It was a web of lies." I thumped the steering wheel.

"No one knew. No one... about my mum, where I lived... I was so ashamed. I thought... I thought for a long time... that my selfishness had killed her, and I loved her so much."

"I know. Jean told me how close you were."

All I could taste was bile. "How did you meet Auntie Jean?"

She shook her head. "In my version of events I met her that day."

The car shuddered as a van sped past. "Izzie, I'm not sure we should do this."

"We have to, Robin. I need to know who's right and who's wrong."

Her hands were trembling as they rested on her lap; I recognised the hell she was going through. I thought about my Post Office book. I could end it by showing her that. I didn't have to go back at all. But what then? How would her broken soul deal with proof in black and white? Perhaps, if we went through with this, I could find a way to save her from that.

So I went into the shop, bought nothing, then walked up the hill with Izzie following a few steps behind. There were traffic lights now at my turn off the main road, and low walls in front of houses where there had once been hedges. I crossed to the other side and followed the pavement into a street which now boasted speed humps. Everything had changed; everything was the same.

The cul-de-sac dipped down a slope: four houses each side with another six around the bowl at the end. Ours had been the last on the right before the road began its curve. I stopped a few yards away on the opposite side. It was so changed I hardly knew it. If it wasn't my reality anymore then perhaps I could make it Izzie's.

Clearly number four wasn't a council house these days. It had been extended with a glass-enclosed porch and an enormous bay which must have almost doubled the size of the living room. The attic now had a dormer window facing south and the garage had been completely rebuilt. A child's bicycle lay on the front lawn.

I sat down on the wall of the nearest garden, feeling less guilty than I should have because it was overgrown and boasted a for-sale sign. Izzie joined me.

"It's so different," I told her. "It didn't have that porch or the bay at the front."

"They've converted the attic too."

It could have been a guess, or…

"Mm."

I must have sounded too non-committal.

"If I tell you I know the house with the privet hedge and the red front door was Jean's, then will you believe me?"

"I don't… I don't disbelieve you. Not at all. It's just…"

Her hand covered mine on the wall. "I know."

But she didn't. My brain was struggling to cope with the fact that Izzie knew where Auntie Jean lived. It changed everything, and nothing. I thought again about the Post Office book but bringing the two together made no sense. There was proof for both of our realities and that could not be.

I stretched my legs across the pavement. Weeds sprouted through the cracks in the concrete, florets of yellow groundsel breaking up the grey. I closed my eyes and let the distant hum of traffic wash over me while Izzie sat silently beside me.

"What do we do now?" I asked her eventually. "We can't go into the house."

"I know. Just tell me, tell me what you remember."

"I was whistling. I remember that. Because I was so happy. Because for the first time I really believed you'd choose me over Paul." I looked up. "What happened to Paul?"

"It was messy. It was late before I had the chance to phone him and I wouldn't leave you, so it all came out…"

"Excuse me. You're blocking the pavement."

I leapt up and started to apologise but the sight of the dumpy pensioner with unlikely jet-black hair stopped me in my tracks. "Auntie Jean!"

Never before had I seen anyone's jaw drop. "Robin! Oh my God! After all these years…" She gripped me so tightly that the air was knocked out of my lungs. I hugged her back and the tears that had been threatening for what seemed like hours escaped.

She stood back and looked up at me. "Oh, you great big softie."

I smiled at her. "You remember me."

"Of course I remember you, you daft idiot. I've known you since you were in nappies."

Izzie spoke softly. "Do you remember me?"

Auntie Jean peered at her, but there was no flicker of recognition.

"I'm Izzie." There was a tremor in her voice and my hand reached out and found hers.

"Izzie... yes, of course. Sentimental old fool that I am I've still got your letter somewhere."

"My letter?"

Auntie Jean beamed at us. "Well, there's no point standing around on the pavement. Let's go in and have a cup of tea. We've got so much to catch up on." She hugged me again. "Oh, Robin, I just can't believe you've come back."

The living room was not as I remembered, but that was hardly surprising after twenty years. A brown three-seater sofa was pushed against the back wall with a matching recliner positioned to have an equally good view of the road and of an impressive flat-screen television. One wall was filled with shelving and I studied the photographs displayed along it: a family Christmas, Uncle Len sitting in a deckchair, and numerous pictures of what I took to be grandchildren.

Auntie Jean put the tray down on the coffee table then came to stand next to me.

"That was the last Christmas before Len was taken. He had a heart attack, bless him – very quick. There's our Sonia next to him, and her partner Mark, and Joel and Kelly. Her oldest, Michael, was with his dad – you remember, Phil? You and your mum went to the wedding just after she came out of hospital."

I nodded. "Yes, I do. And I'm sorry to hear about Uncle Len."

"Oh, I do miss him. But Sonia only lives in Woolston so she pops round every so often and Michael sometimes stays when he wants to get away from the other kids. He's an apprentice at Hamble boatyard – thinks he's very grown up." Her laugh was the same raucous cackle and my mother's echoed alongside it.

"So where's life taken you, Robin?" She turned to Izzie. "You found him before I did. Perhaps I should have given you a letter and not the other way around."

"It was only at Christmas," I jumped in. "I hadn't seen Izzie for years but we… we bumped into each other in Winchester."

"Don't tell me you've been living in Winchester and you never came to see me?"

I looked at my feet. "No, it's worse than that. I've been in Curbridge most of the time."

"And you never came until now? Oh, Robin, why not? Didn't you know I'd be worried sick about you?"

"I couldn't face coming back. I was ill for a long time, only I didn't know it then. Depression they'd call it these days. I landed on my feet though; I lodged with a lovely lady until she died last year."

"You could have come to me, Robin. You knew I had a spare room. I'd have looked after you."

"I'm sorry, Auntie Jean." I still couldn't look at her.

"Two postcards, Robin, and then you disappeared. That was harsh. And I didn't know what to do when they came to clear your poor mother's house."

I shook my head. "I did mean to come back but somehow I just kept on going."

"And it wasn't only me you abandoned. It was this poor scrap of a girl here too. I'd never seen anyone so thin and pale when I went over to see who was knocking on your mother's door."

Izzie was looking fairly pale now. The dark circles under her eyes were almost clown-like and her hands were shaking again as she clasped her teacup.

"You didn't remember me?" she asked.

"Not at first, but I do now. Of course I do. You were the only one of Robin's friends who ever came looking for him, miserable lot."

"No, I mean you didn't remember me then?"

Auntie Jean frowned. "I don't think we'd met. You told me you'd had to track down his address through the register of deaths."

Izzie struggled to raise her head. "Robin, I'm so sorry... I don't... feel very well."

I sat down next to her and held both her hands. "That's OK. I'll run back and get the car and I'll take you home."

"Thank you. I'm sorry Mrs—"

"It's Jean. Everyone calls me Jean – or Auntie Jean. But you're not going to walk out on me again, Robin, are you?"

I fished in my wallet and gave her a card. "You know how to reach me now."

She stared at it for a moment.

"Gardener and handyman. Robin, your mother would have been... surprised."

Chapter Sixty-Two

As soon as we reached her house Izzie made for the stairs.

I hovered at the bottom. "Can I get you anything? A hot drink, perhaps."

She stopped long enough to shake her head but she didn't turn, not until she was almost at the top. "Maybe... maybe in a couple of hours..."

"OK."

I wandered into the living room and sank onto the sofa. Izzie was only yards away, upstairs, but she'd dismissed me. I could be no comfort. I could—

The telephone shrieked in the hall. I rushed to answer it, dragging the offending object into the living room with me and closing the door, sending it clattering to the floor in the process.

"S-Sorry about that."

The voice at the other end sounded hesitant. "Can I speak to Bella O'Briain please?"

I almost didn't recognise the name. "Who's calling?"

"It's Fiona, her head of year."

"I'm afraid she isn't well. I'd rather not disturb her."

The voice asserted itself. "Who am I talking to?"

"I'm Robin."

There was a short silence. "I thought you'd split up."

"I'm here looking after her. I'm so sorry, I didn't think to phone her work."

"What's wrong with her?"

I arched my back against the door. "I'm not a doctor."

"Robin, if I phoned back and said it was her friend Fiona, would you answer me then? I know she's had her problems since Connor died – and I also know she has terrible migraines."

This was news to me, but I pounced on it. "I think it's much more likely to be the latter, friend Fiona. Whatever it is she just wants to sleep it off."

"Can I phone this evening then, to find out how she is?"

"Of course. I'll let her know when she wakes up."

I balanced the phone on the arm of the sofa and ventured into the kitchen. Beside the inevitable empty wine bottle, the table boasted two half-eaten packets of crisps, two crumpled cans of tonic and the gin abandoned with its lid off. Not that there was much left anyway. Plates from a meal I assumed to be Sunday tea were pushed to one side and I packed them into the dishwasher. When I opened the fridge to put away the butter I started to peruse the contents, wondering what to make for tea. But would I be cooking it? I looked around the familiar room and found myself in no man's land.

Bottles in the recycling, plates and glasses in the dishwasher, I turned to scrubbing the wine rings and bits of stale crisp off the kitchen table. Wringing out the cloth over the sink, I glanced into the garden; the vegetable patch had not only been planted but was flourishing.

I slipped out of the patio doors to take a closer look. The glossy-leaved perpetual spinach was almost six inches high and the runner beans along the fence would soon be ready for a net to climb. Fronds of carrot rippled in the breeze and the beetroot was every bit as advanced as my own. The lawn could have done with a cut and the shrubs were growing with gay abandon, but the vegetables were a paragon of garden virtue. It gave me hope.

I left it a full two hours before disturbing Izzie. With a mug of tea in each hand and a packet of biscuits under my arm, I eased her door open. She was sitting up in bed staring into space.

"How are you feeling?"

"I took some Nurofen when I woke."

"I've brought you some tea."

Her voice sounded dead as she thanked me.

"Fiona called. She assumed you had a migraine so I let her."

She nodded.

I put her mug down on the bedside table. "Shall I stay?"

"Yes. I want you to read something."

"What's that?"

"The letter I wrote you twenty and a half years ago. Jean gave it to me when you went to fetch the car."

347

I perched on the end of the bed and she handed me a piece of paper. I unfolded it carefully.

"The address… is that the flat in Shirley?"

"Yes. I'm glad… I did live there, Robin. I knew I had."

Like I knew I hadn't. I started to read.

Dear Robin,

I am leaving this letter with Jean in the hope you will at least contact her if you don't come back. I have been to see her a few times and at first it helped being able to talk about you with someone who knows you well, but now I'm not so sure and I don't think I'll go again.

I am hurt beyond belief by the fact you are not here but then I tell myself it's nothing compared to what you must be feeling about your mum. At least I have the tiniest hope of seeing you again, even if sometimes I wonder if you are dead as well. I wish you had told me what happened so I could have comforted you. I'm sure you would have if I had committed sooner.

In the end I told Paul we were finished part way through our holiday and got a flight home so I could be out of our flat before he returned. I think he had been half expecting it; he said he had sensed me moving away and had just hoped I would come back. But I can't and he understood.

As soon as I went back to work I phoned your office and they told me you were on compassionate leave. I asked for your address so I could send a card but they wouldn't give it to me. They said you were expected back soon, but you never came. I went in to see Felicity when they needed some stationery but it was so hard I cried and she took pity on me. She said she'd seen us together in the wine bar. Later she phoned me to say that the partners had announced you weren't coming back and she'd seen the letters they'd sent you returned 'not known'.

I found your address through the register of deaths and came straight away but I was too late. You had gone and the house was empty. Jean saw me and told me everything that had happened so then I knew. She showed me your postcards and she had high hopes you'd come home. But now it's nearly Christmas and if you don't come then, I'm not sure you ever will.

But just in case I wanted to write and let you know where I am. Robin, I am desperate to see you again. I didn't know I could miss anyone like this. Please, please, if you read this get in touch. Just so I know you are alive and don't have to keep wondering. Just so we can talk.

All my love (and I mean that)

Izzie xx

My eyes were burning and my throat rasped when I spoke. "So now we know."

"Yes."

"What you wrote… about missing me… when I could, I don't know, feel again I suppose… it's how I felt about you.

I couldn't believe the pain." I looked up. "I can't believe it now."

"Now it's my turn to feel numb."

The front gate creaked and there were footsteps on the drive, culminating in a clatter of envelopes through the letterbox. A passing car drowned the postman's retreat but he whistled as he made his way up the road. A bird sang in reply. In the distance a radio played.

"I'm here for you, Izzie. This time I'm not running away."

"I'm not sure I'm ready to... resume... I'm scared, Robin, scared for me and for Claire that one way or another I'm a very sick woman. Although I think... we both need you. But perhaps that's not fair."

"Don't worry, you'll get through this. I know what it's like, remember, to have part of your past ripped away and I'm here. I'm still standing."

"Perhaps your roots are stronger than mine." She gazed beyond me, out of the window.

"I didn't have any roots – but I made them all the same. Jennifer helped me to grow them and now I'm going to help you."

She was a long time in replying. "Why?"

"Because our time wasn't then, Izzie. It was never meant to be then. What I need you to believe is that our time is now."

Chapter Sixty-Three

Izzie

There is certainty in mathematics; it is solid, reliable. Teaching calculus to my A-level group, coaching my adult class towards their numeracy certificates, I know the answers and it grounds me. Right and wrong, black and white. Real.

It gets me through the day. And part of the evening too, when I'm marking. I'm exhausted but all the same I wish I had a thousand scripts in front of me, because once I put down my red pen my grasp on the world around me slithers and slides away.

The house is quiet. Claire's staying over at Sasha's to prepare for a sociology presentation they have to give tomorrow. Last week she wouldn't have gone. Now she thinks Robin is back in my life and everything's fine.

I stand and stretch, carry the bag of books down the stairs and place it next to the back door so I don't forget it in the morning. Is there anything on television? I wonder. Anything to distract me? Oh yes, it's all factual: *Chelsea Flower Show*, the news, *The Apprentice*... I wander into the kitchen to fetch the gin and a bottle of tonic from the fridge.

I'm halfway through Alan Titchmarsh dissecting a show garden when I remember I haven't eaten. Or at least, I don't think I have. I hug my knees to me, trying to stop the trembling deep inside. I can't remember twenty years ago, I can't remember tonight... What the hell can I be sure of in between?

Don't go there. I mustn't go there. But the thought follows me into the kitchen. There is no dirty plate on the table and everything in the dishwasher is clean. My heart thuds a little less as I make some toast and spread it with Marmite. As an afterthought I take a banana back to the sofa as well.

The toast sticks to the roof of my mouth, claggy and dry. I am about to pour myself another gin but wine goes better with food so I get up again, return to the kitchen and open a bottle of red. It's the last one so I'll need to go to the supermarket on my way home tomorrow.

Practicalities are good. I make a list on the back of an envelope and it soothes me. I'll buy some lasagne for the weekend, one of Claire's favourites. Wine, bread, salad, maybe some steak for when Robin comes over tomorrow, tonic water. We probably need loo roll as well.

My tumbler is empty so I fill it with wine. The television burbles. Connor's photograph glares at me so I look away. What would he make of this? I don't know. I don't know anything anymore.

I have a strange sensation of insects crawling up my

neck and over the back of my skull. How much of our marriage was as I remember it? When did the wrong memories end and the right ones begin? Some of them have to be right, I'm almost sure of it. A holiday in Rhodes when Claire was ten; staying in a house in the old town; cool, dark, tucked under the massive walls. We visited a valley full of butterflies and one rested on Claire's arm.

But what about Connor and my whirlwind romance? How could I have been on the rebound from Robin if I never even went out with him? And later, through all the years... Every argument I backed down on, every time I held my tongue... All built on the premise of wanting to make it up to Connor because he was second best.

I look at his photograph again. He was a good man. At least, I remember him as one. I reach for the wine bottle but it's empty. The kitchen is too far to fetch the gin. I curl myself into a tight ball on the sofa and try to will my whirling thoughts away.

———————

Fiona's invitation to grab lunch at the café on Hill Head beach is unusual but it sounds innocuous enough, and after all, it is the Friday before half-term, we both have a free period last thing in the morning, and the weather is glorious. But as we settle at an outside table with our coffee and paninis she launches her assault.

"Bella, I'm worried about you. You haven't been yourself since you had that migraine. It's as though you've been in some sort of daze."

"Sometimes they're hard to shake off, that's all."

"Have you seen anyone about them?"

I falter. "The pharmacist gave me some pills and they work most of the time. Monday was a total aberration."

"What happened?"

"I woke up with it and it wouldn't go away."

She flaps her hand at a seagull trying to land on the edge of the table. "Do you think... anything to do with seeing Robin again triggered it?"

"Why should it? And anyway, I'm not really seeing him." The seagull attempts a return and I channel my annoyance into brushing it away.

"But I thought... He answered the phone when I rang for about the third time and said he was looking after you."

"Claire called him. They kept in touch. When she couldn't reach me she panicked and she thought he still had a key." There, that was easy enough. But it's another falsehood, even if this time I created it deliberately. Does that mean I created the others?

"She's a sensible girl."

I smile. "I'm very proud of her." And I prattle on about how well she's doing at school and how brilliantly she's coped with losing Connor. But I've fallen into a trap.

"And how are you coping? Deep down."

"I'm fine." My panini tastes like cardboard.

"Do you think Robin came along a bit too soon? Is that why you're holding back now?"

I put it down and fold my arms. "You think he did, don't you?"

"It's not my place to judge, Bella, I'm just trying to help."

"I'm fine."

She shifts in her chair. "Look, there's no easy way to say this but are you drinking too much? Some mornings… well, you do smell just a little tiny bit of alcohol when you come into school. I mean, not enough for me to stop you teaching… I'm not saying you turn up drunk or anything…"

Not enough for her to stop me teaching. The words drop through me like ice, even on this sweltering day. I gaze out over the sparkling sea towards the Isle of Wight. "Perhaps… it's a side effect of the migraine tablets. I mean, I do have a glass or two of wine with my supper, but nothing… I'll check with the pharmacist tomorrow."

"Why don't you book an appointment with your GP? Explain. They might be able to give you something different." She picks up her panini and puts it down again. "I mean, I think you should anyway. What if there's something serious underlying these headaches?"

Somehow I manage to look her in the eye. "It won't happen again."

———

Our conversation haunts me, though, as I drift around Sainsbury's after work. During the afternoon I've been able to focus on teaching: black and white, right and wrong. Numbers. But now that's been ripped away from me for a whole week and I honestly don't know how I'm going to get through it.

Maybe Fiona was right. I should see my GP. Maybe it is an illness – a tumour, or dementia even. I'm rooted to the spot in front of the pasta, gazing blindly at the rows of spaghetti, penne, and tagliatelle until a woman nudges me with her trolley and I grab the nearest packet and flee.

The aisle closes in on me, shelves toppling as it narrows, people ghostly as they back away. My hand is over my mouth as I cannon towards the light streaming in from the windows, swerving past queues of shoppers and finally into the fresh air and back to my car, where I promptly throw up.

"Are you all right, love?" There's a man in front of me in a store uniform and hi-vis jacket.

I unfurl my fingers from the spaghetti. "I'm sorry... I didn't pay... Can you take it back for me?"

"Of course I will, but are you all right? We have first aiders..."

"No really, I'm fine. It must be something I ate..."

"Well, as long as you're sure."

I watch him walk away, then I open the car door, perching sideways on the seat while I clean myself down with a tissue and some water from my drinking bottle. I have nothing for tea and Robin's coming over. I can't go back in there. I can't cancel either, because if I do I'll have to explain to Claire and she's really looking forward to seeing him.

Giving my hands a final wipe I pick up my phone and text him.

Can you bring fish & chips? I'll pay. Running late at school.

It's my second lie today. Or maybe my third… or maybe my whole frigging life's a lie. I swing my legs into the car and turn on the engine, the aircon cooling my forehead as it rests on the steering wheel. *Don't think, Izzie. Drive. Just drive.*

After a shower and a gin and tonic I feel better. There's no wine in the house but I convince myself that doesn't matter. I'll be dropping Claire at Jack's tomorrow so I can go to Waitrose in Chandler's Ford to stock up. I really don't think I can face Sainsbury's again.

The doorbell rings and I hear Claire rush to answer it. I'm pulling on my jeans when she calls, "Mum, Robin's here."

"Lovely. I won't be a tic." I don't want them talking about me behind my back.

Of course, they're not. When I arrive in the kitchen Robin is laying the table while Claire pulls the warm plates from the oven. It's like I've gone back in time to when Robin was living here. Even the warm oil and vinegar smell emanating from the neatly wrapped packages on the table summons up Friday nights before everything went wrong.

Robin beams at me. "Cod for us and scampi for Claire. I hope that's still right."

He's remembered. He would.

After supper Claire beats a tactful retreat upstairs saying she wants to make a start on her economics essay because once her homework's done she can enjoy half-term. I decide not to mention the word *revision* because I figure she's old enough to know what needs to be done. She's certainly matured these last few months. Maybe she's had to.

I make Robin a mug of tea and pour myself a gin, but only a small one because I feel as though he's watching me, then we wander through to the sitting room and sit down at either end of the sofa.

There's an uneasy silence.

"So, how are you?"

I glance up into his eyes but they are so full of love that I have to look away. How can I love him back when everything's crumbling around me? How can I not when I've loved him my whole adult life? But how could I have loved him when I blocked him from my memory for years? The memory I can no longer trust.

"Izzie?"

There's a strange buzzing between my ears as the thoughts spin round and round, but then a shaft of light appears. Robin is the one person who really will understand about my memories being wrong.

I shake my head. "You know how it is."

"I know how it was for me, but how is it for you?"

"Like I can't trust myself anymore. Like I don't know what's real. I had a panic attack in the supermarket. That's why there was nothing for tea."

He stretches out his legs. "Then half-term's come at just the right moment."

"No, it hasn't. The only time I feel anywhere near right is when I'm teaching."

I've snapped at him and his eventual reply is cautious. "I found that... the gardening – working – it really helped. Made me feel grounded."

"Numbers do the same for me."

"It's important. You need some sort of foothold. Maybe you could try to teach me a bit of advanced maths? But I warn you, the old grey matter's pretty rusty."

I sink back into the cushions, cradling my glass. "You are just the kindest, kindest man."

A smile flashes under his beard. "But although distraction is important, you need to start to deal with it as well."

I shake my head. "You coped marvellously from what I remember. Always assuming I remember it right. I'm just..." The words are stuck in my throat. "I just feel... broken."

"But you're not and that's important. Your memories may be, but you are still you."

All I can do is shake my head. To fill the silence he tries a different tack.

"Have you told Claire yet?"

"I'm not that stupid. Honestly, think how worried she'd be. She must never, ever know and that's the end of it."

"Then you need to start dealing with it sooner rather than later."

I desperately want another gin but if he tries to stop me we'll argue and I can't face that. Robin is my only ally in this battle.

"The trouble is... I don't know how big a gap I'm dealing with. I... I can't be sure of anything... anytime..."

"Finding proof was important to me and I think it would help you too. I got you to take me to Shirley, remember?"

I nod. I do. And at least I really did live there, even if he didn't.

"And when I didn't find evidence there I got to thinking where else I had been just once in my life, on that trip. The answer was West Bay."

"No wonder you were so... distant that day."

"Before we went I sketched a little map of what I remembered, made some notes. And there it all was. Those flats being the right date clinched it."

"Why didn't you say?"

He fiddles with the handle of his mug. "Because much as I wanted to prove my memory right, I didn't want yours to be wrong. Looking back, I reckon I really screwed up there. I should have been braver. It put a lie between us, a wedge... like when you split a tree trunk into logs. One hammer blow and we were ripped apart."

"We can't be whole until I am." The words come out as a whisper.

"I know. But if you're saying there's hope..." He smiles at me, "And I guess, even if there isn't, I'm here for you Izzie, I really am."

He's solid and strong, and I want so much to creep into his arms but it can't be that way. "So what should I do?"

"Look for that foothold, that truth, then prove it. Old

diaries, photographs, stuff on the web. Even a scrap of evidence and you'll feel a bit more confident."

"And then what?"

"I talked to Gareth…"

"No. I couldn't." My heart thuds at the thought of actually telling anyone. But if I'm really ill… but I can research that too online. Look for evidence. Prove the equation.

Robin's touch on my arm is gentle and brief. "No need to worry about that now. First things first."

"Yes, I suppose so. I need to think. Or at least, try to think straight. Thank you, Robin. This has really helped."

He nods, then we sit in silence until he says. "Right, I'd better make tracks. Let me know how you get on. Anytime. Day or night. I won't switch off my phone."

I look up at him. "I need to do this myself."

I stand to see him out. In the hall he calls to Claire that he's leaving and she bundles down the stairs to give him a hug. "Are you coming over next week? We could all go for a day out."

He glances at me.

"We'll have to see. I've got a lot of work on at the moment, but of course I—"

"Well at least let me cook that meal I promised you. You can come after work one day," I tell him, and he smiles right to the corners of his eyes.

Once the front door has closed Claire turns to me. "So how did you get on?"

I shrug. "We had a nice chat."

"About anything important?"

My heart thuds in my chest. He hasn't said anything to her, has he? "Like what?"

"Like getting back together properly."

"Claire, it's much too soon. We both need time."

She shrugs and turns back towards the staircase.

"All right."

Chapter Sixty-Four

The sulphurous glow of the street-lamps illuminates the empty half of the bed. I've never slept in the middle; it doesn't feel right. Not after Connor, not after Robin. I stretch my arm across and stroke the vacant pillow. My hand looks yellow but my wedding ring glints. There's a yearning inside me that's so unfamiliar that at first it's hard to place.

Robin talked about photographs, and in a box in the bottom of the wardrobe are the albums Connor put together. Every milestone of our lives was recorded. *For when we get old, Izzie. For when we forget.* I've forgotten now, but I haven't been able to look at them since he died.

It feels completely wrong to do so without him, but where is he? Where is the man, even in his own house? Not in this room – the empty half of the bed quickly became Robin's. The gap yawns huge; it's not what I thought it was.

I struggle to carry the box and open my bedroom door at the same time. I listen on the landing, tuning in for Claire's breathing. It is there, light and even, and I creep down the stairs.

Connor's car, sealed into the garage, suits my purpose. I put down the box and find the keys in the hall table. The concrete floor is cold and there's a faint smell of oil. Robin again. Can he really be everywhere? Inside the car I will be safe from his intrusion.

I pad past the bonnet and put the box on the passenger seat. A pipe from the engine... Is that how it's done? The thought, unbidden, rocks me. I shake my head like a dog, making myself dizzy and my ears ring. *Claire. Claire. Claire.* When I'm sensible again, I leave the door between the garage and the hall open. Then I get into the car.

The leather seat is cool beneath my nightshirt. I close my eyes and inhale. He is here – I was right – a half-eaten packet of mints in the cup holder. I pick it up and kiss the paper, just where his beautiful hands tore it. On that last trip to Heathrow, perhaps, juggling the sweets against the steering wheel, singing along to the radio or a CD. Which?

I turn the key one click in the ignition and the interior light comes on. I fumble the buttons on the stereo, making sure the volume is low. Bryan Adams, 'Summer of '69' – one of his favourites. I bought him the greatest hits CD years ago. He still listened to it, right to the end.

I pick a photo album from the top of the box. April 1995. There's Claire, tiny, fair-haired, wearing a bright green sweatshirt with the name of her school on. We lived in Hedge End and she was standing by the front door, trying not to fidget. I remember it now. "One for the grandmas," Connor had said. I see him as clearly as I can see the picture, in faded jeans and a white T-shirt, his fringe falling over his eyes. I was dressed for work, waiting with the car door open, and swooped down on Claire as soon as he had finished, dropping her off in the playground before making my way to my own classroom.

Next is a holiday in Ireland. Paddling in the sea with Connor's sisters, the breeze taking our hair away and carrying our laughter across the beach. Then there was a sudden squall and we went for fish and chips: seven adults, five children, two tables pushed together in the steaming café. Claire spilt vinegar down her dress and cried because it was her favourite.

Memories, one after the other, so crystal clear it isn't in my heart to doubt them, come flooding in. *Connor, oh Connor, where are you?*

It's not fair. There was so much more living you had to do.

When Claire wakes I have been crying for a long time. I found him. I found him in his car, in the middle of the night, with the comfort of our memories. I found him, and we travelled through the years together – a journey that was long overdue.

"Mum, what are you doing?" Panic edges her voice.

"Looking at old photos. I wanted to be somewhere... somewhere your father was. Does that make sense?"

"You're crying."

"It's not fair. It's just so not fair. He was too young..."

We take the photographs to the kitchen and empty the box on the table. The sky lightens over the garden as I make tea and Claire puts the albums in order. We pull our chairs close, wrap our arms around each other, and reconstruct the story of the O'Briain family. We laugh a lot and we cry even more.

And then a picture appears which triggers a string of memories before and after it. In minute detail. It was my fortieth birthday and Claire took the photo: Connor and me, leaning against the rails on Brighton seafront, his arm over my shoulder pulling me close.

I try to sound casual. "Claire, do you remember what happened next?"

She smiles. "Of course I do. There was a man dressed as a clown and he gave you a plastic flower when I said it was your birthday. You were so embarrassed but Dad and I couldn't stop laughing. Then we went into that posh hotel for afternoon tea and Dad made you wear it in your hair. The waitress kept rolling her eyes but even you were creasing up by then."

And that's my foothold. So I cling to it.

All weekend we talk about Connor and I only realise how much we haven't before when Claire hugs me and tells me how brilliant it is to be able to say his name. We're in the garden at the time, crouching to encourage the young runner beans up their poles, and I am so astonished I topple onto the carrots.

"Careful, Mum."

I stand and dust myself off, sticking my hands in my pockets. "I hadn't realised… Have you been not talking about your father deliberately?"

Her fingers wrap around a bean. "I didn't feel I could with you. That's all."

"Well you can. In fact, I'd like you to. I'm missing him so much…" And tears start to roll down my cheeks again.

It's later, when we're making supper, that she drops the bombshell. "I'm not really sure I should be going to Newquay. Not with you this upset."

I had been about to pull some wine from the rack but I turn to face her. "That's over a month away. I hope to goodness I'll stop randomly bursting into tears well before then."

"It's not just the tears though, is it?" She's looking pointedly at the bottles behind me.

"There's no reason at all you can't go. Assuming you still want to?"

"I do, but not if I'm worrying about you all the time."

That is so wrong, just so wrong. It's me who should be worrying about her, not the other way around. My hand hovers over the wine rack but I stop myself. A meal isn't a meal without a drink and an evening isn't an evening… But the last thing I want is a row with Claire. I can have a quick gin later when she's talking to Jack – or sneak one up to the bath and enjoy it there.

I walk over to the hob and prod the potatoes, then give the parsley sauce a stir. Claire is still watching me so I join her next to the draining board and wrap my arm around her shoulders. "I know I wasn't keen on this trip at first and I'll still worry about you every moment you're away, but you're growing up and I have to get used to the fact that you want a life of your own."

"I had hoped, you know, you'd be back with Robin by then so he could, you know, be there for you."

"He is there for me, Claire. Very much so. But at the moment it's as a friend and I couldn't want a better one." It's the truth. The absolute truth. Another foothold.

Claire squeezes me. "Well all right. But let me know if you change your mind."

One thing's for sure, I have to stop crying in front of her. I ponder it in the bath, sipping my gin. It can't happen at work, either. But if I carry on like this I'll have no more tears left anyway. Maybe blocking Connor from my mind was the right thing to do, and after all, it worked with Robin all those years ago. So now Claire's helped me to prove my memories, why can't I just shut him away again?

But they're not proven, are they? Not really. There's a blurred line between what is wrong and what is right. More than a line – blurred years between the day at the fairy tree with Robin and when Claire was old enough to start remembering. How will I ever find out about those? I have my foothold but it isn't enough.

Those missing years are crucial. In many ways they made me who I am. I lost the love of my life. Yes, that happened, because whatever the how and why, I didn't see

Robin again for twenty years. I remember the flat in Shirley. I remember feeling broken. But why did I remember that he was there too?

Did I want him so badly I made it up?

And later, when my mother hauled me up by my bootstraps and bailed me out? That was so like her it probably did happen, and after all I did end up a teacher. She'd have swept down from Watford, given me a good talking to, then gone back to her WRVS work without a further thought. She'd fixed me so I could get on with my life. She's not here to fix me now.

Tears fall again and my head starts to thump. Could Fiona be right? Could there be a physical cause? It's the scariest thought of all, because there's no way I can leave Claire. I remember only too well how Robin was after losing his mother. But then I don't, do I? How much of what I believe is built on untruths?

The water goes cold around me and it's only when Claire calls goodnight that I find it in myself to creep downstairs and sit on the sofa, Connor's picture in one hand and a fresh gin in the other. I press the coolness of the glass against my forehead. Why, oh why, is this happening to me? But there is no answer in Connor's smiling eyes.

It is as I'm washing up my glass that I do remember something. Not Connor, but Robin. When we thought it was his memory at fault. Something about not having any wine because he didn't want any more little grey cells disappearing. My hand shakes. No, it can't be that. It's not as though I drink very much, do I?

Oh come on, Izzie, one moment you're having a breakdown, the next it's a tumour and now it's the booze.

Get a bloody grip.

Tomorrow you need to phone your GP and sort this whole wretched mess out.

Chapter Sixty-Five

I sit in my car and gaze at the roses clambering over Jennifer's front porch as I wait for Robin to come home. Pale pink and deep mauve in a swirling embrace, the leaves rocking gently in the breeze. I am too drained, too defeated, to do anything other than draw figures of eight on the steering wheel with my fingertip while I watch them dance.

There's a scrunch of tyres, an engine behind me. Robin's van. Will he be angry or will he understand? I can't even look in his direction but I hear his footsteps on the gravel and his shadow falls across me. After a moment he opens the car door.

He clears his throat. "How did your appointment go?"

I look up. He's in his work clothes, his sweatshirt grubby with grass stains and a dead leaf in his hair. "I bottled it."

He crouches down, his warm, earthy smell level with my nose, his eyes fixed on mine. His voice is sad, not angry. "Oh, Izzie."

"I know. But I couldn't... I couldn't... Fiona said something this morning – about another child – but I hadn't thought... I hadn't thought... Robin, they could take Claire away."

He holds my hand as I sob. Nothing else. But the way he changes his grip to echo mine, I know he understands. I free myself and reach into my pocket for a tissue to blow my nose. He unfolds his long body and stretches.

"Come on, I'll make us a mug of tea. I've got some lemon cake too. Maria made it – she's always trying to feed me up."

We sit opposite each other on low armchairs in the old dining room, with the French doors open to let in the scent of the honeysuckle surrounding them. The cake sticks to the roof of my mouth and the tea is too hot to wash it away.

"So if you go to the GP, you think there's a risk they would put Claire into care because you're ill?"

"There's no one else to look after her, is there?" I want to add *not since you moved out* but that would sound as though I'm blaming him.

"Well there is. There's me, there's Sasha's mum – maybe Jack's parents too, at a push. But I guess there's no legal basis for any of that."

"No."

He speaks slowly. "The thing is, if there's something physically wrong going undiagnosed..."

"You don't have to say it."

"OK, but what I mean is, I don't really think you have the option to do nothing."

The tea scalds my mouth and I put my mug on the floor.

"To be honest, I've been in such a panic all afternoon I haven't been able to think straight at all."

"Want some help?"

I nod.

"Then take me through the possible reasons."

"I… I don't think I can."

"I know it's hard. When I thought I had a problem, everything just kept swirling around. But you have your foothold, don't you? You know your memories are fine for the last ten, twelve years. Nothing recent is missing. And from what I saw of Jennifer, dementia works the opposite way. The old memories last the longest." He shrugs. "Not that I'm an expert – I just have some practical experience of it. And Gareth said he didn't think it was the case with me either, and what you're going through now is the other side of the same coin."

I run my finger over the braid on the arm of the chair. "Do you think… Gareth would talk to me?"

"In an instant."

"Off the record?"

"I don't know about that. But probably. An initial chat at least. I don't really know how it works but you could always ask him."

"Could you do it for me?"

"Of course." He picks up his phone. He's not going to give me the chance to change my mind.

I stand and wander into the garden. The early evening warmth is reflecting from the walls and the grass feels so soft I can't resist the urge to kick off my sandals and walk barefoot. It takes me back to a moment in time I struggle to place and the peaceful scene around me fractures. I dig my fingernails into my palms. *Think, Izzie, think.* Yes, my first trip to Ireland with Connor. A field so lush I told him I felt as though I'd walked into a butter advert, so he galloped around pretending to be a bull. But more than that I remember a feeling, a tautness inside me, holding something back, not laughing as much as I should have.

Robin is crossing the lawn, holding out his Blackberry. "It's all good. He and Stephen are coming for the weekend. Just have a quick chat with him to sort out a time you can talk."

Then he marches away towards the vegetable patch as I put the phone to my ear and say Gareth's name.

Chapter Sixty-Six

Once Robin and Stephen close the door behind them the kitchen is still, but we can hear them at the front of the house cutting roses to take to Jennifer's grave.

"It's about time they went up there together," Gareth says.

"I wish I'd known Jennifer better."

"So do I. By the time Stephen brought me home she had already lost so much of herself. But the better part of her lives on in Robin. And Stephen too, in some ways."

"Her beliefs?"

He nods. "And her compassion, and kindness, and inherent good sense. I feel I know her from the way they both speak about her."

"She certainly turned Robin's life around."

"Stephen's too. When he came out, his parents didn't want to know him, and his brother, Toby, was always the blue-eyed boy with them anyway. He'd always felt second best, even in his own home, until Jennifer made him believe otherwise."

"Being second best is hard."

Gareth steeples his fingers together. "You say that with some feeling."

"I was never top of my mother's priority list. And when I had Claire... the intensity of that love... I didn't dare have another child in case it wasn't the same."

"You were frightened that the love you had to give was limited in some way because of your relationship with your mother?"

"Not because of that. Because I had given so much to Robin. Connor..." I swallow hard. "Connor was second best, but he made me feel safe and he loved me. I hope to God he never knew. I did everything I could to... to..." Tears threaten. *Bugger.* I've had a good couple of days up until now.

"It must be hard to hide your feelings from someone for twenty years."

I sniff. "The thing is, I was good at hiding them from myself too. For years, really. And now I say it out loud I wonder... perhaps that was where the memory went? But even so, why the hell did I fabricate a completely different one?"

"Tell me about those memories."

And so I do, while he sits back with his head on one side as he listens. Normally, Gareth is full of energy but now he is still, his attention focused completely on me. It encourages me to talk and I go on and on and on, everything I thought had happened spewed into a messy bundle on the table between us.

Eventually I draw breath. "I'm sorry. I've… I've never spoken about it before. I've never been able to. But of course it doesn't matter because it isn't real."

"You said you blocked Robin from your memories for years. How do you think that happened?"

"I don't know. I… You see, he must have been there at first, because otherwise why would Connor have felt like second best? I do remember though – as much as I can be sure of anything – that when Claire was born I knew I had to move on."

"And you succeeded?"

"Up to a point. And anyway, I didn't have the energy for anything other than being a mother and a wife. I was the main breadwinner. I went back to work very quickly. There was no time to dwell on the past."

I close my eyes. The hiss of the Aga fills the silence and away in the woods a pheasant calls. And then there's something…

"Gareth?"

"Yes?"

"How… how do I know anything is real? The gap… it could be huge."

"Trust yourself, Izzie. Tell me what made you say that."

"When Claire was three,"—my mouth is dry so I sip my tea, but it's cold—"Connor wanted to bring her to the fairy tree. Someone must have told him about it. So we had a family outing. W-when we walked up that slope and I saw it, it was like a tidal wave crushing me. It all came back: Robin and me holding hands around the trunk to wish, the storm, and making love under the willow... I was absolutely devastated. Too broken to even try to hide it from Connor.

"Connor was very possessive. And I was OK with that because it made me feel loved, and safe. I couldn't tell him the truth about how much I loved Robin though – he'd have hated it. And he might have guessed I didn't love him as much. So instead I told him the tree brought back such awful memories – of a hateful, moody, drunken man, who lied to me when he lost his job then walked out, leaving me up to my neck in debt. But could I... could I have made that up?"

"Would I be right in thinking that remembering this is something of a revelation?"

"Yes, yes it is." I stand and pace the length of the table and back. "That I could have made it up deliberately... then actually started to believe it... It's not possible, is it?"

"Of course it is."

That stops me in my tracks. "Really? How?"

"Memory is a complex thing, easily distorted and fractured. There has been great debate over the years as to whether false memory syndrome actually exists, but it's been proved under lab conditions so I believe it does."

I sit back down, clutching the edge of my seat. "Tell me."

"The best known experiment reminded people of three genuine childhood memories and threw in a false one. Over time, when they were talked about, almost a quarter of the people believed them all."

"But how?"

"Well, firstly, very few people remember as accurately as they think they do. They might perceive the actual event incorrectly, or perhaps something happens later to compromise memory retrieval once it has faded. The brain associates it with the wrong thing, if you like. And surrounded by the real memories, it becomes a truth all of its own."

I trace a figure of eight on the table. "So I'm not so strange, after all?"

"Well lots of other things affect memory too, like grief, stress, depression – things with which I understand you're familiar. Not to mention other stuff like alcohol abuse, even menopause. But all those tend to damage short-term memory. No, I'd say this is definitely false memory syndrome. It's hard to see it could be anything else."

I put my head on my folded arms on the table and weep.

Chapter Sixty-Seven

I look at the plate of carbonara in front of me, spaghetti twisted and tangled with no conceivable way of winding it onto my fork. I push it away.

"Aren't you hungry, Mum?" Claire asks.

"It's my own fault. A grateful parent brought in a huge box of doughnuts for afternoon break."

It's not a lie. What I don't say is that I didn't eat any of them. In truth, I was too busy watching Fiona watching me. There's something up, I know there is. But I also know damn well it can't be because I smell of alcohol because I hardly drink anything in the week and I've taken to using mouthwash every morning anyway.

I need to distract us both. "It's your statistics paper tomorrow, isn't it? Do you want to go through anything?"

"No, it's all good. I thought I'd cram for an hour after tea, then perhaps we can go for a walk to clear my head? Maybe just up to the copse and back?"

"That's a great idea. I need to check the test for the

numeracy group. It's their last lesson next week and although we don't want to call it an exam, we need some sort of assessment and I have to hand it in to the office tomorrow for printing."

I leave Claire to finish her tea alone, telling her I'll microwave mine if I feel hungry later. I pour a small gin from the bottle in my bathroom cupboard into my toothmug and take it to the study. But I don't look at the assessment. I tip back in my chair and stare at the ceiling.

I still can't make sense of it. Everything's mashed and muddled, when it all seemed so clear on Saturday afternoon talking to Gareth. I should ring him – he said to call any time – but I don't want to disturb his evening. He emailed me some links on false memory syndrome and even though I know he's right, they confused me even more.

I know what happened. I've found a reason. It's years in the past. So why can't I let it go? For the hundredth time I tell myself it shouldn't be this hard, but for some reason it is. It's as if my foundations have been shaken and I don't trust myself anymore.

I want another gin but it can wait until Claire and I get back from our walk. We've had a little evening ramble a few times now and it's good to do something together. Sometimes we work in the garden for half an hour instead. Anything to get us outside, she says. I'm so proud of the young woman she's become.

I look at my watch. I've only been here twenty minutes. Best get my work done. I'm sure if I really try I can concentrate. They're lovely safe numbers after all but I'm pretty tired, to be honest. Another drink would perk me up no end but then Claire calls that she's ready and I tuck my empty toothmug behind the computer and go to join her.

Claire is quiet as we make our way down the footpath to the copse so I ask her if everything's all right.

"Everything's fine. Well, fine-ish. Jack's just a bit exam stressy at the moment."

"And are you?"

"No point. I've put in the work so what else can you do? But I'm lucky, aren't I, because you and Dad always made it clear that exams aren't the be all and end all. Jack's parents heap the pressure on."

"That's sad and unnecessary – counterproductive even. But there's only a few weeks to go and then you'll be off to Newquay and he can forget all about it."

Claire fiddles with the hem of her sweatshirt. It's a sign I know well. I stop and smile at her. "Spit it out."

"I still don't know if I should go."

"Because of Jack?"

"No… because of you."

"I'm all right Claire. I only burst into tears very occasionally now and I promise I'll eat my tea when we get back." I laugh and link my arm through hers. "Honestly, talking to Gareth on Saturday helped me to sort out a few things that were bothering me and I feel so much better."

"What sort of things?"

I've been ready for this. "Mainly to do with why I hadn't grieved for your father sooner. It made me feel very guilty, you know."

"Mum, you mustn't. He'd never have wanted that. He'd

want you to be happy and I know he'd have liked Robin. I mean, how could anyone not?"

"How indeed. He texted today and asked if it was too late to take you for a little surfing practice before your trip. I said he'd have to ask you and he will when he's checked the conditions and tides."

Her face is shining. "Oh wow, that's fabulous."

Robin is so good for her. All I want now is for me to be good for him.

Chapter Sixty-Eight

"**B**ella, can I have a word?"

It's not as though I haven't been expecting it all day, but all the same, Fiona's voice at my shoulder makes me jump. "I'm invigilating next period. How about afterwards?"

"It's OK. I've asked Val to cover for you. Let's find somewhere quiet."

I follow her along corridors and up stairs, focusing on the way her handbag strap digs into the fleshy part of her shoulder. I feel sick to my soul but I have no energy to run and a strange feeling of inevitability settles over me. She takes me to the small office in the first aid suite used for counselling and to my surprise the school nurse is already there.

"What's all this about?" I ask.

"Sit down, Bella, please. It's going to be hard enough without you being aggressive."

"And do I need to be aggressive?"

She draws herself up to her full height. "You're not going to like this any more than I do, but it will be far better if we stay calm."

The nurse intervenes. "Why don't you both sit down?"

I turn to her. "Can I ask what you're doing here?"

"To support you. What Fiona has to say needs a witness and she thought someone sympathetic and not on the teaching staff…"

I sit down with a thud. "Spit it out then. Let's get this over with."

There is deep sorrow in Fiona's eyes and she's clasping and unclasping her fingers. She's my friend and I'm not making this any easier for her. I wish I could but I barely have enough bravado left for myself.

"Your drinking has become a matter of concern."

"My drinking? What drinking?"

"I fully accept you may not realise the extent of the problem, but coming in every morning smelling of alcohol and mouthwash is no different to coming in smelling of alcohol."

"Yes, but I don't come in drunk. I don't drink enough to get drunk."

"How much are you drinking?" asks the nurse.

I am tempted to say *None of your business* but this is serious so I'd best be honest. "A couple of gins most nights. Bottle of wine at the weekend." The look passing between them tells me they don't believe me. "It's the truth."

Fiona carries on. "Apart from the effect on your health, you're making mistakes. It was rumoured that some of the examples you worked through with your revision groups were incorrect and now there's a glaring error in the assessment you set for the numeracy class so I have no choice but to act."

"No, that's not right."

"I'm afraid it is. I should go down the formal disciplinary route but I don't want to. You're a good teacher, Bella, one of the best I've worked with, and you've had a really shit time this year. So instead I'm asking you to apply for sick leave for the rest of the term and to seek treatment. OK?"

"No, of course it's not OK. I... I..." I look at her, and then at the nurse. "I don't have a choice, do I?"

Fiona shakes her head. "I'm so sorry." She pulls an envelope from her bag. "Here's a letter explaining it all. Also some leaflets about alcohol abuse. Please, Bella, read them. For your sake and for Claire's."

Claire. The fear of her being taken away washes over me like ice and with it a moment of clarity, but just as it's within my grasp it snaps away when Fiona asks if she should collect my things from the staffroom.

I pull together what shreds of dignity I have left and stand with shaking legs. "No thank you. I'll do it myself."

I wake up dripping with sweat because I dreamt the false memory. I was with Robin, in the flat in Shirley, everything dark and grey and stinking of stale booze. But it was him screaming at me because I'd drunk myself out of a job and hadn't told him.

Claire's alarm goes off across the landing. I need to get up too, pretend to go to work. Yesterday she went to Sasha's in the morning to prepare for their French oral so I was able to go out then sneak back. Today she's revising at home.

My head is enveloped in the fog of nightmare and I can't look at myself in the bathroom mirror. I clean my teeth then try a cold shower, but after a few moments I'm shivering too much. Mouthwash, makeup, work clothes. How long will I be able to keep this up?

Claire is in the kitchen in her dressing gown, shovelling cereal into her mouth. She waves at the kettle. "I've made your tea."

"Thank you, darling. I'll just grab a yoghurt then I need to get going."

"Busy day?"

"I'm invigilating first lesson so I can't be late."

I drive to the end of the road then pull over. Where to? I tap the steering wheel, frowning, and then… inspiration. Or desperation. I hear my voice saying to Claire, *The last time I saw Robin he was wearing a suit.* I knew then it was a lie but now it's a different one. Either way, Caffè Nero in Winchester was the first time I'd thought of him in ages and it's as good a place as any to have a coffee and to fight off the dream.

Of course, everything is different. It's barely half-full and the Christmas carols have been replaced by a soundtrack of smooth jazz. There are still a couple of homeless men around the Buttercross so before I sit down I buy two coffees and two bars of chocolate and take them across. One already has an open can of cider at his side.

I settle at a table at the back of the café where no one will see me. I think about the false memory; I can see it, hear it, smell it even. Robin, half-in and half-out of the duvet, me yelling at him, the air around us foetid with booze. It's all just so strong. And wrong. I pick up my coffee but the mug almost slides out of my hands. Sweet Jesus... It's me who's trying to hide the fact that I'm about to lose my job because I drink too much, not Robin. What if it wasn't a memory at all but some perverted premonition?

Even in my befuddled state I know that is just so much bullshit. Someone has left a newspaper on the next table so I grab it and start to flick through the pages. It's full of the internal machinations of the labour party as Tony Blair prepares to step down so on I go past the Wimbledon gossip and ads for Pimm's and Gordon's Gin. God, I could murder one now...

My hand freezes. The thought collides with a quote in bold below a picture of Jamie Lee Curtis: *recovery is an acceptance that your life is a shambles and you have to change.* Painkillers, booze, she's done it all, but she quit when she started to worry about the effect it was having on her daughter. Her words, they're speaking directly to me. I know they are. I can't swallow – I can barely breathe. Before I change my mind I whip out my phone and text Gareth.

I have a drink problem. Please, please help me.

Chapter Sixty-Nine

"Nothing worthwhile is ever easy, Izzie."

"Just shut the fuck up and leave me alone!" I watch as Robin shrugs his shoulders then lopes along the landing to the top of the stairs. For good measure, I slam the bedroom door behind him.

Not my bedroom. Jennifer's bedroom. Or rather, the temporary guest room for the temporary guest. Claire refused point blank to go Newquay until Robin cooked up this plan, which basically means he becomes my jailer for a week.

No. That's unfair. I know I'm being unreasonable and unfair. And angry when I should be grateful. And all sorts of other inappropriate emotions. Gareth says that's OK; it's what recovery's like. He also says it's OK if you slide off the wagon sometimes, as long as you recognise it as a mistake. And at first I did, more than once, but now I've been completely clean for six whole days. It feels more like six months.

Telling Claire was the hardest thing I've ever done. I waited until after her last exam then sat her down and showed her the letter from the school and told her I was getting help. I don't deny I had the largest possible gin before I did it but worse than anything was watching the grey pallor of fear grip her features. I shoved my phone across the table.

"Gareth's number is on there. Call him. Ask him anything you like."

She nodded and took it up to her room.

Later that evening she went through every cupboard and drawer in the house and emptied every bottle she found. I stood by mutely, more ashamed than if I'd been dragged naked through the school by my hair. My voice shook when I asked if I was allowed to hug her and she barrelled into my arms and told me how proud she was I was trying to stop drinking and she'd do everything she could to help.

It was only later I heard her sobbing in her room, and that was the moment I properly vowed I really would stop.

In the last ten months my child has experienced more heartache than most youngsters can even conceive. She's lost her father and has had to stand by while her previously reliable and competent mother dissolved into a waste of space incapable of holding down a relationship or a job. But I will beat this, I will. I kept the Jamie Lee Curtis interview from the paper, and when Robin saw it in my handbag he told me she was the only woman on the planet sexier than me.

Robin. Time to eat humble pie. I slink down to the

kitchen where he's scraping new potatoes. He turns and smiles. "Claire says you need regular feeding. She practically gave me a list of times."

"Robin, I'm really sorry I spoke to you like that."

"Wasn't the first time and I'd be very surprised if it's the last. Regard me as your safety valve. And your butler. And your chef, laundry maid, bottlewasher... Well, maybe not bottlewasher."

"How come you're so patient?"

He leans against the sink and dries his hands on a tea towel as he looks at me. "Living with someone with Alzheimer's would do it. At least, underneath it all, you're still you. And more importantly, we'll get you back. I can put up with any amount of shit in the short term if I keep my eye on the prize."

"It's a small miracle you want me back, the way I've treated you. Or do you want the me you knew twenty years ago?"

A smile flashes in the centre of his beard. "For a start, a man of my age going out with a twenty-three-year-old would feel seriously perverted. But honestly, Izzie, there have been plenty of times this year when I've seen the best in you. Plenty. But it isn't just the best I want, it's the whole package. I don't ever want you to feel you have to pretend to be something you're not."

Tears catch in the back of my throat but I swallow them down. "Then I don't have to pretend I'm not gagging for a glass of wine?"

"I'd actually rather you didn't pretend, but either way you're not getting one. You're on day six dry, remember?

Gareth told you it begins to get better after a week and you're so very nearly there."

"He said three to seven days." I fold my arms.

"And is it easier?"

"Not with Claire hundreds of miles away doing goodness knows what."

"On the holiday you insisted she went on because you're such an unselfish mother."

"Go on, make it all my fault…"

Robin turns sharply and starts to run the tap. Have I finally riled him? But when he faces me again he has a glass of water in his hand. "Now, are you going to drink this or throw it over me? The choice is yours, but if it's the latter, would you mind doing it outside? I've already mopped this floor once today."

And in that moment all I want to do is kiss him. But that isn't part of this deal and I need the time to be right. Instead I ask if there's anything I can do towards supper.

"You can pick some broad beans. And if you root around enough you'll probably find a courgette or two as well."

There is a heaviness in the air and grey clouds fill the sky over the river. I pick up the trug from the decking in front of the dilapidated summerhouse then cross the lawn. I might spruce it up this week. It looks so sad and neglected, and it would give me something to do. But then I remember it isn't Robin's to spruce and I start to wonder when Stephen will put the house on the market. And what Robin will do when he does.

It doesn't take much to tip me into feeling I need a drink. At first I despised myself every time I did but Gareth has taught me to roll with the punches by grounding myself in the here and now. I close my eyes and listen to the birds chirping in the hedge, and down in the woods a dog barks. *Don't think, Izzie, just be. Just be.*

The craving fades and I carry on to the vegetable patch. Gareth explained that the here and now is tough because of the way alcohol affects the brain – it actually causes symptoms similar to depression – and we had a long conversation about which came first for me in those long, dark nights last winter. For the first time I really talked about how it felt to suddenly be a lone parent and to know I wasn't coping.

Once I'd sealed losing Robin into a box all those years before, I'd coped with everything. I was the family's coper – the breadwinner, the serious one. In that I'd become very like my own mother, something I swore I would never be. Life came easy to Connor and while it was probably what attracted me to him, I had also envied him for it. Sometimes it felt as though I was on the outside looking in while he and Claire had all the fun. I'd never really looked at it that way before – not consciously. It's strange what you find out about yourself when you know the person listening won't judge. And I'm beginning to realise that the biggest falsehood of all was telling myself I wasn't drinking too much.

I crouch next to the beans and feel for the fattest pods. In just five sessions with Gareth I've found out quite a lot, especially yesterday when the fog really started to clear. First, I judge myself too harshly (I judge others as well, but that's too uncomfortable a thought so I push it away) so I need to cut myself some slack. I don't have to be perfect all the time. And I don't have to hold something of myself back in case others don't like me and I get hurt.

Suddenly, the total abandonment of making love with Robin comes into my mind. The truths we hold dear about ourselves aren't always what we think either. My head's beginning to whirl again, but by focusing my attention on the beans I ground myself. The leaves brushing my fingers, the snap as I break off a pod, that wonderful fresh green smell. I can't resist but open one and pop a bean into my mouth, rolling it around. These little moments of now are priceless.

My meditations are interrupted by my phone. Claire.

"How are you doing, Mum?"

"Fine. Picking broad beans for supper."

"Yum! We're having pizza as it's the first night. With salad of course," she adds. "I've just chopped up about a gazillion tomatoes."

"So what's it like?"

"Raining! But Martha says it will clear up overnight. And Sasha and I have a really neat room with four other girls – I haven't slept in bunks since I was in the Brownies." I tuck my phone between my shoulder and chin and listen to her bubble and bounce while I continue to pick.

Robin appears at the far side of the lawn just as she hangs up. "I thought you'd disappeared down a giant rabbit hole," he laughs.

I wave my phone. "Claire called."

"Great. How is she?"

"I'll tell you while we pod the beans. I just need to ferret around for some courgettes."

"I'll help you. They're quite small still."

Somehow, under a cloak of leaves, our hands brush. His warmth floods through me and once again I am filled with longing, but it is only for a moment because he pulls away, shattering the moment.

I sit back on my haunches. "Did you do that because it isn't what you want anymore?"

He looks at me sideways and brushes the hair from his eyes. "No, because I want it too much."

I nod. I smile. "Me too. But not yet. I'm not ready for it yet."

He squeezes the tips of my fingers then goes back to his task.

Chapter Seventy

"So, I was thinking, we could go to the Mayfly for lunch."

Claire's eyebrows disappear into her fringe. It's a recent habit she's cultivated and it's actually quite sweet. "You're sure?"

"Of course I'm sure. I think... it's what Dad would have wanted, isn't it?"

"To be remembered with a pie and pint." Claire's Irish accent is far broader than anything I ever heard Connor utter and we crease up laughing.

"Except neither of us is going to be hitting the Guinness," I add.

Claire puts her hand over mine on the table. "That's what he would have wanted too. You've done ever so well, Mum. He'd have been proud of you."

It's a year to the day since Connor died. The day when my phone rang at five in the morning. The day when the orchestra pulled every string they could to get us on a flight. The mad dash to Heathrow. All for nothing.

We sit in silence as we both remember him. Her treasured memories will be different to mine. I can still see his face, the moment he first held her, cautiously juggling this most precious bundle, eyes wide with wonder. *Jesus, Isobel O'Briain, did we really make this little beauty?* Before long he was so confident he was throwing her up in the air when he changed her, blowing bubbles up her nose in the bath.

I free my hand and pick up a slice of toast from the rack between us. "So, what do you miss about him the most?"

She screws up her face. "That's hard. There are so many things. The hugs, for sure. I'd kill for a daddy hug right now." Her chin wobbles.

"It's OK, you can cry."

"No. We're celebrating. That's what we said. Celebrating his life."

"We should have bought some fireworks for later. He loved fireworks. He nearly took his eye out with a rocket one year."

"He was a bit of a liability with anything practical, wasn't he?"

"Do you remember when he put petrol in the hire car instead of diesel when we were in the middle of nowhere in Galway?"

Claire giggles. "And when all the hanging baskets fell down one after the other about half an hour after he'd put them up so he just dumped the plants in the middle of the flowerbed all muddled up?"

"That's what I miss the most – the laughs."

"But you were furious with him!"

I look at the table. "I know. And I was like that far too often. I missed out on so much of his fun and that's the saddest thing of all."

"Oh, Mum, don't say that or you'll make me cry. He loved you just the way you are."

"I know. I was exceptionally lucky. Some people never experience love like that in all their lives…"

"And now you have someone else who loves you just as much. I wish some of whatever it is you've got would rub off on me." She rolls her eyes and we laugh until the tears roll down our cheeks.

It doesn't feel right to talk about Robin until we've finished our lunch and dropped our paper boats into the river Test, toasting them with sparkling elderflower as they speed away around the bend and out of sight. Claire senses it too, although perhaps she notices me fiddling with my rings.

"So, are you all set for tomorrow?" she asks.

"Almost. Claire, how would you feel if I moved my wedding ring to my right hand?"

She nods. "It's time. If you and Robin are going to get together again, it feels like the thing to do."

The river glitters below us as I take off my rings and place the plain band on the other hand. It feels alien, as though it has no right to be there, and there is a line of pale skin where it's been for so many years. Once that's done, I fold my engagement ring into Claire's palm and close her fingers around it.

"For you. Wear it for him... for us, really. It's what he would want."

I've thought long and hard about how to makes this special. I looked for a cottage near Kimmeridge but couldn't find one. I even considered another trip to Cornwall but I kept coming back to the same thing: the most precious place in the world to Robin is the fairy tree. It's where we started last time – and in a way, where we ended too. So it's right it's where we should begin again.

I remember the wish I made when we were holding hands all too well: that all the obstacles would just magically melt away so Robin and I could be together. But life isn't like that, is it? Who knew the mountains we'd have to climb before we could properly find each other again?

Although I have every intention of staying overnight, I don't take my holdall. Instead, I tuck my toothbrush, deodorant and some moisturiser into the bottom of my handbag. I want this to be a surprise for Robin, right up until the last moment.

I've promised him a picnic, that's all. Claire was a whirlwind in Marks & Spencer, helping me to pick all sorts of treats we knew he'd love. And tealights to put around the edge of the rug, to flicker and fade as evening draws in. It's a rug I found online, depicting the pagan wheel of the year. He needs to know I'm at peace with his beliefs as well.

I veer between fizzing excitement and the nerves of a

schoolgirl on a first date, but he is visibly moved when I give him the blanket so I know it will be all right.

His voice is husky when he says, "It's beautiful, Izzie."

"I thought so too. And it's a long-overdue apology for what I said at Easter. It was wrong of me to show such little respect."

"Maybe it needed to happen. That was what Jennifer used to say. One action affecting another action, all of them interconnected… Anyway, I won't go on." He grins.

"One day you can explain."

"But not now."

I punch him gently on the arm. "Are you hungry?"

"Ravenous."

"Come on then, let's eat."

There was a time, not so long ago, when I thought a meal incomplete without a drink, but now that I can properly taste every delicious morsel I'm not sure I could ever go back. So we talk about that for a while, and then about his week, and all manner of other inconsequential things in the way close friends do. As dusk falls it's time to make the change.

I stand up, brushing crumbs from my skirt. "Come on, let's go for a walk."

Robin rolls onto his back. "I'm too stuffed."

I reach my hand down to him. "Come on, just into the woods. We might see that tawny owl you've told me about."

He pushes himself off the rug but keeps hold of my fingers and I interlace mine more firmly with his. "That feels good," he murmurs.

"Uh-huh." The desire to kiss him is almost too strong but not here, it can't be here, so I tug his arm and lead him across the lawn and down the slope.

When I stop at the fairy tree he knows. Maybe he did before but decided to wait. He traces the side of my cheek. "It's almost twenty-one years, Izzie. Is the waiting finally over?"

"It is." And before I can say any more his lips are on mine as the branches sigh and the leaves rustle above us.

It's a long time before we stop kissing and I am glad of his arm around my shoulder as we gaze at the tree.

"We ought to make a wish," he says.

I look up at him, his breath warm on my face. "Why would we do that? It seems to me we have everything we need."

Acknowledgments

The Missing Pieces of Us has always been my special child; the book of my heart, if you like. From the moment I saw the fairy tree on the banks of the River Hamble I knew it had stories to tell. And then, one Sunday morning in Winchester, I watched from Caffé Nero as the homeless men gathered at the Buttercross, and I began to understand what one of those stories was.

The book was originally self-published in March 2015 as *The Faerie Tree*. It was edited by the marvellous saga writer Margaret Graham and I am indebted to her for everything I have learnt from her over the years, and for her friendship.

Cut to 2020 and I'd decided to have a fifth anniversary blog tour for the book. The reviews were still fabulous and one blogger, Julie Morris of A Little Book Problem, wrote that the book really resonated in present times and she hoped it would find its way to a large audience. As I tramped my local footpaths and lanes during lockdown her words stayed with me.

Should I submit the book to a publisher? I asked the opinion of a close and trusted writer friend, Polly Heron, and her answer was an unequivocal 'yes, yes, yes!' So I did – just to the one, someone I had wanted to work with for a long time, Charlotte Ledger at One More Chapter. And thankfully she loved the book.

So the last thank you is to Charlotte. The first is to my friend Jason, who took me to the fairy tree all those years ago and without whom the story would never have been written. And my enduring and eternal thanks go to Jim, my husband, without whose patience and understanding I would never have had the opportunity to write.

Eva Glyn, Cornwall, 2021

ONE MORE CHAPTER

One More Chapter is an
award-winning global
division of HarperCollins.

Sign up to our newsletter to get our
latest eBook deals and stay up to date
with our weekly Book Club!
<u>Subscribe here.</u>

Meet the team at
<u>www.onemorechapter.com</u>

Follow us!

 <u>@OneMoreChapter_</u>
 <u>@OneMoreChapter</u>
 <u>@onemorechapterhc</u>

Do you write unputdownable fiction?
We love to hear from new voices.
Find out how to submit your novel at
<u>www.onemorechapter.com/submissions</u>